PICTURE THIS

PICTURE THIS

"Keep your hands where I can see them," Blade Hampton rumbled in a voice like a melted box of chocolates, and stuck something in Ray's back.

Jen paused as that voice twisted inside her chest. Why did he have to sound like that?

"I don't have any money," Ray said, raising his hands. His voice wobbled and rose half an octave.

Jen muffled a snort when she got close enough to see Blade used a roll of Life Savers in lieu of a gun. Another wise guy, huh? Two could play at that game.

The game was even better with three.

"You think I'm stupid?" Blade sneered and reached to pat down Ray's right side.

Jen caught his left ankle with her right foot and jerked hard while pulling on his right elbow. She caught his shoulder as he twisted off his center of balance and slammed him to the floor without endangering a single false nail.

"What you are, is flat," she said, and finished the job by shoving down hard with her heel, grinding his shoulder into the tile floor. The arch of her foot rested on the knob of his collarbone. His five o'clock shadow tickled the tips of her toes. She had the nauseating urge to giggle at the sensation.

He had gorgeous, storm gray eyes. Even more beautiful and mesmerizing than in the photo in Ray's computer files.

Those eyes, right that moment, could see up her skirt...

ALSO BY MICHELLE L. LEVIGNE

The Bainevah Series, Book I: 10,000 Suns
The Bainevah Series, Book II: Fire Priestess

PICTURE THIS

BY

MICHELLE L. LEVIGNE

AMBER QUILL PRESS, LLC
http://www.amberquill.com

PICTURE THIS
AN AMBER QUILL PRESS BOOK

This book is a work of fiction. All names, characters,
locations, and incidents are products of the author's imagination,
or have been used fictitiously. Any resemblance to actual persons
living or dead, locales, or events is entirely coincidental.

Amber Quill Press, LLC
http://www.amberquill.com

Layout and Formatting provided by: ElementalAlchemy.com

PUBLISHED IN THE UNITED STATES OF AMERICA

*Many thanks, kudos and
bows of adoration to the ladies of Solstice Press,
Peggy, Laurie and Carol, purveyors of wonderful fan fiction.
They let me test-drive some characters in several 'zines. Those who
have read "Small Favors" will recognize the alternate identities
of Mark and Gloria Williams and the adventure where
Ray and Jen (under another name) first met.*

*A deep debt of gratitude to
Stephen J. Cannell, Nick Mancuso
and Adrian Paul.*

Author's Note: Gibraltar Island and the Ohio State University maritime research station still exist. As far as I know, there have been no bombs, no smuggling (recently!) and no art thieves on the island. Put-in-Bay, Crystal Cave and its winery, Perry's Cave and Perry's Victory Monument are very real and a fantastic way to spend a summer day.

CHAPTER 1

"Interesting." Jen Holt slowed the scrolling of information on the notebook computer screen in front of her.

She studied the picture of the man included in the latest batch of data sent from Ray's super-secret sources and felt a shiver run up her back. Jen was positive she had seen him before. The question was, where? And if so, would it cause them problems?

Yes, she would be wearing a wig and makeup when they came face to face. She would be in her "Brain by Jell-O, Body by Nautilus" mode, dressed for an island vacation instead of her usual T's and camouflage pants. Suppose she had seen this tall, dark mystery man somewhere before? If she didn't have a clear memory of him, chances were it was so long ago he wouldn't remember her very well, either.

But Jen hadn't survived to the ripe old age of twenty-eight, with blood on her hands and nightmares to match, by relying on chance. She glanced at the tags for the other files pertaining to this man. Interpol had data on him. Big league trouble. She definitely didn't need that in her life.

"I think you'd better look at this." She sat up to look over the top of her screen.

On the other side of the hotel suite living room, Ray grunted a query. He didn't raise his head from studying the three-dimensional mock-up of Worley's castle set up on the dining table. Jen relaxed enough to smile. She'd known Ray for three years now, ever since they ran into each other in a back alley, rescuing kidnapped babies. He was single-minded to the point of obsession, a man of a thousand personas, a former Intelligence operative, and drop-dead gorgeous in a dark, Mafioso kind of way.

He didn't set off a single shiver or spark in her, and that worried Jen sometimes. Something had to be wrong with her, because she liked tall, dark, and mysterious. Like the guy on her computer screen.

Oh. Yuck. The last thing she needed was to get a romantic fixation on an international criminal who would likely complicate their mission to retrieve the senator's stolen painting.

"Remember how you worried we were on a wild goose chase? Because Worley hasn't contacted his usual team of forgers?" Jen waited until Ray looked up, thought a moment, then moved over to stand behind her chair. "Mik Poling." She ran her fingernail down the LCD screen, disturbing the colors in waves. "INS caught him coming through on a fake passport. No reason for him to travel under an assumed name—"

"Unless he's headed for some illegal activity," he finished. "Destination?"

"Cleveland. Just a hop, skip, and a jump from the Lake Erie islands. He's not on that list of Worley's expected guests. Does it make you nervous when Worley begs us to secure his castle, but won't give us complete information?"

"He's not sure if he trusts Mark and Gloria yet." Ray settled down in a semi-squat next to the table and rested an elbow on the edge of it, still staring at the screen. "Which reminds me—no wig this time."

"Hurrah," Jen said on a sigh. She ran her hand through her short, dark curls, grateful for that reprieve.

Why in the world had she made her alter ego Gloria a redhead when she first created the dizzy computer geek? Wearing a wig was the height of discomfort and stupidity. It could be distracting during tricky maneuvers, like running for her life, climbing out a third-story window, or trying to cross a river.

"You'll dye it." He turned just enough for her to see the glimmer of amusement in his big, dark eye.

"Uh huh."

She decided not to fight him on this one, because she had bigger problems waiting ahead. Ray wanted her to expand Gloria's wardrobe. They would be staying at least two weeks on Gibraltar Island as guests of the fat, balding, aging thief whom they had convinced to hire them as security consultants. If someone searched their luggage, they couldn't take a chance on even a whisper of suspicion that Mark and Gloria Williams, computer geniuses and security consultants, weren't exactly who they appeared to be.

Jen hated dressing as Gloria. She preferred oversized clothes, the older the better, and going barefoot—Gloria was a fashion plate. Jen had legs to be proud of, but she hated showing them off and attracting just the kind of attention Ray wanted to use as a distraction. She only dressed up when Ray asked, when their mission required it, because she trusted him to be there if she needed help. There were precious few in the world she did trust. Especially when she let herself look like a woman and act like an airhead.

Jen had learned early to disguise herself as a boy when she had landed on the streets, forced by tragedy to fend for herself and nine other orphans at the age of fourteen. When she couldn't hide her figure, she learned to become invisible. Her adopted sisters hadn't learned that lesson quite as well. Jen had killed a man when she was sixteen, pushing him off a roof when he tried to rape one of her sisters.

"There's something about this guy," she said now, trying to yank her attention off those memories.

"What about him?" Ray didn't look at her, just rested his chin on his arm lying on the table, and studied the screen.

Jen had recognized those eyes before the image had resolved on her screen. Maybe a little more intense, a darker gray when she'd seen them before. Maybe deeper set the first time. Mik Poling's face on the screen was a little too baby soft. It needed a dark haze of stubble. Sharper definition to the cheekbones. A tiny scar near the left corner of his mouth.

Poling's hair needed to be longer. Cleaner. Washed, it wouldn't lie in lank wads but curve back from his high forehead in silky waves. A little dye could get rid of those gray streaks.

Jen wondered if she was finally cracking under the pressure.

She and Ray had spent a week at a resort in New Mexico, "accidentally" meeting and making friends with Danville Worley. When the man learned they were security consultants, using ultra-modern, cutting-edge computer systems, he had begged them to visit his private island on Lake Erie, to examine his situation and recommend a system. Ray then claimed a previous commitment and left, promising to arrive on Gibraltar in a week. He and Jen had settled into a Kentucky hotel to prepare for their mission.

After three days of intense work, Jen needed a change of scenery and something besides hotel food, or she would go crazy.

At the very least, Ray should lighten up and let her go on a junk food binge. That always helped reduce tension and stress when she couldn't get outside or hit a gym and work herself into a sweaty, achy, exhausted lump.

"What about him?" Ray got up and stepped behind her chair, rested his warm hands on her knotted shoulders and started to rub and squeeze.

Once, he had impersonated a masseuse at a ladies only club, to get some delicate information. Ray had entertained Jen with silly stories of overweight, oversexed women old enough to be his grandmothers, trying to slip twenty-dollar tips into his pockets.

"I know I've seen him before. Can't remember where, or connected with what..." Jen moaned as Ray's hands unknotted her aching shoulders.

"Poling's been operating out of the country for the past eighteen years. If you met him while your folks were still alive, you would have been too young for him to recognize you now."

"Hope so." Jen smiled. Leave it to Ray to pick up on exactly what worried her. "Still, I know I've seen this guy. Maybe under an alias? The name doesn't ring a bell at all."

"Another name," Ray mused.

He grew very still, and Jen hated it when Ray turned to ice, his thoughts flying at the speed of sound. He usually came up with an idea that was especially nasty, tricky, and effective. Something that knocked their enemy off balance permanently. Something she hated to follow through on, but did, because she knew it was necessary.

Why did Ray keep coming back to her to work with him, anyway? She knew he hated taking partners, hated letting anyone close, yet he watched over her like a mother hen with one chick. Jen knew better than to flatter herself that Ray was in love with her; the man kept his heart so well shielded under all his masks, she sometimes wondered if he knew where it was hidden.

"Got an idea," he finally said, and gave her shoulders one final, hard squeeze before stepping away. Jen turned to watch him, and saw a crooked little smirk on his face. Ray picked up his notebook computer from under the dining room table and flipped it open. Her heart sank when it beeped and turned on.

Jen wondered if she had time to make a run for it; just abandon her computer and head for the hills. Now was not the time for Ray to find out she had been picking away at the elaborate layers of security he had built into his computer.

It was really his fault, she silently argued, as Ray tapped across the keyboard. He shouldn't have locked her into that storage shed during their last job. She had nothing to do for three hours but worry he was going to get his head blown off. He shouldn't have left his computer with her. She needed to hack to work off nervous energy.

"Uh huh." Ray sat very still for a moment longer, then that brilliant grin lit his face. He crossed the room and set his notebook down in front of her. "Recognize him?"

Mik Poling's younger, better-looking brother gazed out of the screen at her. The stubble, the lack of gray in his longer, cleaner hair—this was the man she had seen before, not Poling.

"Who is he?"

"My former partner, Blade Hampton."

*　　*　　*

For a bunch of crooks using an antiques shop to cover their activities, these guys didn't have the brains to protective their collective backside.

Or else they were too cheap to invest in any security measures stronger than deadbolts.

Or, so arrogant they thought no one would have the guts to steal *back* something they had stolen.

Blade Hampton preferred choices A, B, and C. Choice D was that he had lost his touch, hadn't found any of a dozen different alarms, and the police were already on their way. Getting caught burglarizing the warehouse of an antiques theft ring wouldn't look good on his resume.

Whatever his options, standing still in the basement of the Livingood Brothers Antiques Emporium wasn't smart.

I'm getting too old for this, he thought, not for the first time. That thought alone made him feel old.

Thirty-six wasn't old. Not for someone who had spent nine years in International Intelligence circles. He had left the Agency four years ago just so he could reach his fiftieth birthday without missing organs or bones, or the birthday altogether.

Blade scolded himself to get back to the job at hand. He gave himself twenty minutes, tops, to find Mrs. Weatherby's heirloom silver tea service and get out of the warehouse without leaving a sign that he had been there. Not easy with dust over everything.

The dust did, however, reveal the traffic patterns running through the warehouse basement. Blade played his flashlight across the floor until he found the trails across the bare cement. All that dust meant someone didn't know diddly or didn't care squat about antique preservation. Proof the Livingoods were idiots.

He followed the trail to the shelves laden with at least a dozen silver tea services. Only one had been made by Paul Revere, however. Blade only had to lift up two sugar boats before he found the right stamp.

At least the Livingoods were organized crooks. And it was clever to use their legitimate antique business to bring victims to them. Too bad they had a pattern of stealing from people who brought items in for appraisal, within a week of the visit. Blade mused over the possible statistics of people who were burglarized after appearing on *Antiques Roadshow,* while he slid the silver pieces into the padded cloth bags he had brought. He checked his watch. Six minutes to go. He grinned as his heart picked up the pace a little. Finally, some excitement.

He needed more than excitement. If he wanted to get into more challenging work, he needed a partner. Someone to watch his back so he could take risks larger than breaking into warehouses in the middle of the night.

His cell phone vibrated against his hip as he finished re-setting the lock on the big, old-fashioned sash window that had originally let him into the antiques shop. Blade grinned at the mental image of the brothers' consternation when they discovered the broken lock had fixed itself. Tucking the padded bag of silver pieces under his arm, he stepped into the shadows behind the building. Then he pulled out the cell phone and flipped it open.

"Hampton," he said under his breath.

The trees lining the gravel parking lot shielded him from the light of the full moon—another overlooked security problem.

"Time," Cynthia Osgood chirped.

"He's back?" Blade grinned into the darkness.

"Drunker than a skunk. Do skunks drink?"

"This one does. I'm half an hour away."

"I haven't even called the sheriff yet. Take your time." The woman sighed, all the weariness of lost and regained hopes in her voice. It was for people like Cynthia that Blade kept his Agency-trained reflexes and skills honed.

Cynthia Osgood's organization tracked down kidnapped children. She had a stable of lawyers who helped convict noncustodial parents who snatched their children. Sometimes they didn't arrive in time to save lives or prevent damage, and the lawyers moved Heaven and Earth to ensure at least part of the debt was paid. Blade handled the risky snatch-and-run rescues for Cynthia. It didn't pay well—he retrieved stolen antiques to pay the bills—but the emotional rewards went a long way.

"Ready for a vacation, pretty lady?" he asked as he slid-walked down into the ravine behind the parking lot.

"For a month. See you there."

"With bells on," he muttered as the connection broke. Blade grinned at the trickle of water across mossy pebbles at the bottom of the ravine, and crossed it in one long step.

He wanted a partner for times like this. Someone to celebrate with him when a break came in a tough job. To gripe with. To smack him one when he needed to get his head straightened out.

If he could combine that elusive partner with a warm body, sweet mouth and a passion for stargazing and hiking, he'd be in paradise. But where in the world could he find a lady who enjoyed the kind of life he chose to lead?

The training and skills—and yes, the bodies—were back in the Agency, but the women he had known there were too hard-boiled. Even worse, some were convinced they had to look and act like James Bond bimbos. He had vowed he would never go back there, where he was just a tool and the little people who really needed his skills fell through the cracks. His lonely nights weren't reason enough to risk getting sucked back into the Game.

The kind of woman he wanted in his life would feel the same way about the little people, the hurting souls who had no big bank accounts or highly placed connections. It was more than ironic that with all his skills in hunting, he couldn't find that one, perfect woman in his life.

*   *   *

Ray sighed and knelt next to Jen, his arm along the back of the chair. If she made a run for it, he could grab the collar of her shirt. It was her favorite T-shirt—black with rainbow-streaked unicorns. She wouldn't risk tearing it, and Ray knew it. The skunk.

"You've been poking through my private files again."

"Again? I only did it once!" Jen closed her eyes, waiting for Ray to burst out laughing.

He didn't say or do anything. When she dared open her eyes a few

7

moments later, he stared at the image of his former partner.

Former partner meant Blade Hampton had been an operative of some kind too, back in those misty Agency days that Ray only referred to in snips and scraps. Jen still wasn't sure which Agency, how long, how long ago, or why he had left. There were bits and pieces in his ultra-secret files that made her think he was on a search, a quest of some kind, but she couldn't figure out for what. Or maybe for whom. His files held biographies and what looked like records searches that had become dead ends.

"Funny how Blade stuck in your mind."

Jen waited, but he didn't press the unintentional pun. Bad sign. She could almost hear the circuits in Ray's mind buzzing at high speed. She turned her attention back to the screen. She got an idea and jumped on it, just to distract Ray. She didn't want him asking why Blade Hampton's face stuck in her memory—and she didn't want to think about it.

"Poling does look like Blade, doesn't he?" She shivered when Ray leaned closer to study the screen. That nasty little smile she had come to know and hate crept across Ray's face. "What if Blade took his place?" she suggested, determined to distract him. "Have him go to Worley's, pretend to be Poling, and take the painting when he's asked to forge it."

"Three-way split?" Ray nodded. That smirk vanished. "The more people Worley's people are watching, the less chance they'll see anything that'll get us in trouble." He got up and moved his computer over to the other end of the table. He barely glanced at her before unplugging the high-speed cable from her notebook and attaching it to his.

"What are you doing?" Something was very wrong. Ray never accepted her suggestions so quickly and easily.

"Back door into the Agency computers." Ray grinned as the connection beeped and clicked into place. "It's easier letting them keep track of people for me."

"Are you up to something?"

"Nothing beyond the usual."

"Ray…" She sighed and turned back to studying Mik Poling's file. She would have to help this Blade Hampton support the false identity for however long they spent on Worley's island. Might as well bone up on the facts now, rather than cram them in later.

"Jen…" he echoed. "What's wrong?"

"You never make changes in a plan so easily. Not this early in an operation."

"Maybe I think it's a brilliant idea." He winked at her. "What Jen wants, Jen gets."

"Oh, puh-lease."

"Maybe I'm just curious to see what about Blade stuck in your memory. It's a red-letter day when you show interest in any of my friends."

"Any of your *male* friends?" Jen slouched in the seat and wished she had something to throw at him. How about a tranquilizer gas bomb, so she could get some peace and quiet until it was time to go to Worley's island?

"Got to admit, I was starting to worry."

"I'm not gay, if that's your problem." She snorted and decided to give tit for tat. "Just because I don't fall for your Casanova act doesn't mean I prefer women."

"We sleep in the same bed half the time we work together."

"Be grateful I don't steal the blankets." Her humor failed, and for a few moments she felt a thousand years old. "I guess I just don't let anybody close."

"Because you're always Joan of Arc, protecting everybody else, and you don't think you have the right to fall in love?" Ray suggested, his voice soft.

"Doesn't matter. If Blade Hampton is anything like you, the only thing we'll have in common is sniping at each other before the mission is over."

"Maybe. Maybe not." Ray winked and went back to work.

CHAPTER 2

"Just like old times?" Cynthia murmured when she brought a cup of steaming, tar-like coffee to Blade, waiting at the edge of the woods.

"Exactly like." Blade downed half the cup in one gulp. "The exact same coffee—tastes like they held onto it that long." He winked at Cynthia.

The moonlight was kind to her, turning her white hair to platinum, hiding her wrinkles, the bloodshot eyes, the burn scars from a fire set by her vengeful ex-husband. If Cynthia wasn't twice his age, Blade would have gladly considered her as his partner. She was perfect; dedicated to a cause, wry sense of humor, no-nonsense personality, and tough to the core. Besides, she liked to pick on him. Anyone who wasn't afraid to do that earned all his respect.

"It has to be tonight."

"It will be." Blade paused, reassurances on his tongue, when his cell phone vibrated again.

Mrs. Weatherby wouldn't expect to hear from him until the end of the week, and Cynthia was the only person who had his most recent phone number, so who could it be?

The caller I.D. gave him a number he didn't recognize, in an area code he was pretty sure was Kentucky. He didn't know anybody in Kentucky. Then again, he had deliberately lost contact with a lot of people since putting the Agency behind him. Blade had hoped they would return the favor.

Curiosity made him press the *Go* button, nod an apology to Cynthia, and turn to walk away from her, across the clearing.

"I think you've got the wrong number," he said, speaking as softly as he could without whispering.

Two hundred feet away, on the other side of the woods, lay another clearing, and a cabin where the county's bully, a wannabe crime boss, kept his young son prisoner. Blade knew how well sound carried at night, and refused to risk any warning reaching the man now, after all the hard work that had gone into this mission.

"Is that any way to talk to the man who saved your life?"

"Considering you keep stealing my girlfriends, yeah." Despite himself, Blade grinned. "I don't want to know how you got my number."

"Sure you do," Ray Porter drawled. "Just don't tell Shylock I still have a back door to all his files. Comes in handy."

"I suppose. What do you need?" Blade glanced at the other people in the clearing; sheriff's deputies, the kidnapped boy's frail, frightened mother, a half dozen of Cynthia's people.

"We need a third who can impersonate an international art forger. Two weeks maximum for set-up, infiltration, and retrieval. Island in Lake Erie. Fun and sun. What do you say?"

"Not interested." Blade swallowed a chuckle. He loved saying that to anyone from his old life. True, Ray was his former partner, and he genuinely missed some of their more relaxed times together. Blade preferred saying "not interested" to Chief Anguilano, but he still enjoyed refusing Ray.

"You're serving your country."

"I'm rescuing a little boy from a drunken slime bag father who'd rather kill him than let the kid's mother have him. That's more important. T-minus ten and counting. *Ciao*."

"No hard feelings," Ray muttered, his voice going thin as Blade lowered the cell phone and pushed the *Stop* button.

Just for a moment, Blade felt a flicker of regret. He wouldn't have minded working with Ray again, just for old time's sake. But rescuing an innocent little boy was more important than all the cloak and dagger, international intrigue and adventure he could remember. Sighing, he put his cell phone back in his pocket and turned to face the others.

"Everything's perfect," Mimi Calhoun murmured. She was the Sheriff's liaison with the battered women's shelter. She tightened her arm around little red-haired Betty Ann Harkness and gave her a hearty grin. It would have convinced Blade if he didn't know all the possible pitfalls in tonight's operation. "We're gonna have your Buddy out by breakfast."

She met Blade's gaze. He nodded, then turned back to the semi-camouflaged van holding enough surveillance equipment to equal the year's budget for the entire county.

Maybe everything was too perfect. After a four-day absence, Josh Harkness had returned to his mountain hideaway and followed his usual routine down to the last detail tonight. Poker with the boys until ten, then out at Jimmy John's to drink and dance until they kicked him and his buddies out at three a.m. All the while, keeping his five-year-old son within spitting—and kicking—distance.

According to Betty Ann, the man could down three six-packs within four hours, relaxing him enough to pour him into bed through a funnel. However, the minute something or someone crossed him, he could shake it off and jump in, fists flying. Or pump lead from one of three guns he kept as close as his own skin. Even on his honeymoon and in the bathtub.

The trick was waiting until Josh was in bed. Then it was lights out until nearly noon. Not gunshots or explosions or earthquakes could wake him. It was nearly four a.m. now. When the microphones planted in the cabin transmitted snores, Blade and the two deputies would sneak into the cabin and take little Buddy. They would have him and his mother over the county line within half an hour, then out of the state in two hours. By the time Josh woke up and drank enough coffee to realize Buddy was gone, the trail would be cold.

If a situation looked this perfect, Blade knew it was on the verge of falling to pieces around him.

"Movement in the bathroom," the woman technician in the van murmured. She glanced over her shoulder at Blade and rolled her eyes, giving him a good idea what she heard.

He stepped closer. When was Josh going to start sawing wood? Blade hated operations that required equipment and people to coordinate. He preferred to evaluate the scene, get in, rescue the child or woman or antique, and get out as fast as humanly possible. Nice and simple, with no one to depend on but himself, and no amateurs or innocent bystanders to get hurt. Times like these, he really needed a partner to make sure he didn't miss anything.

Preferably a pretty partner, who wanted to celebrate a successful job and work off all that adrenaline. In private. And then hold him through the dark night hours, when the nightmares of his doubts and could-have-gone-wrongs woke him.

"Movement in the front room," the technician reported. "Sounds like a cupboard—"

"Back door's opening," a deputy reported, his voice crackling through the radio clipped to Blade's belt.

Blade signaled the others to stay put, then dashed through the intervening woods between the two clearings. He would have preferred to have the boy's mother and the getaway vehicle closer, but with the moon full and bright tonight, Josh never would have missed the van. Even drunk, he had a reputation for being able to shoot the eye out of a bird at fifty feet.

Blade came to a stop, pressed up against the lone beech tree at the edge of the twenty-foot-wide cleared space that ringed Josh's cabin. He knew he had lost weight, but he would never be skinny enough to hide behind the tree. Holding his breath to keep his hand steady, he leaned out to look.

The door opened a little more than a foot. Blade drew his gun, slid the safety off and waited.

A pale little face topped by curly red hair peered out into the moonlit clearing. It looked like Buddy had rescued himself.

Blade's brain ran through the options. He could wait until the boy stepped outside. Or try his charm on a child who didn't know him, and coax the boy across the clearing, without making any noise. Or run for Betty Ann and get her to urge the boy to run for it. Or trust his legs to race across twenty feet of moonlit clearing, grab the boy, keep him silent, and race back to cover. All while feeling a target glowing on his back.

Everything depended on one question: How soon until Josh realized the boy was gone?

A bellow like a wounded bear rocked the cabin. Buddy scampered across the clearing. Blade leaped out from behind his slim cover, aimed to intersect the boy's path, so he could just scoop him up and keep moving.

The door slammed open and Josh Harkness crashed into the doorframe. He already had his newest toy drawn, a sleek silver infrared-assisted model. Josh's connection to international arms dealers was why the Sheriff didn't just waltz in, flash custody papers, and take the boy. He and his deputies would be cut down before he got his hand out of his pocket.

Blade pushed those considerations aside in that split second of horror when he realized Josh had that infrared dot planted smack in the middle of the back of his fleeing son's head. Clamping his jaw tight shut against a roar of blind fury that threatened to choke him, Blade changed his trajectory. He wanted to hurl curses to match the ones spilling out of Josh's mouth, but Blade agreed with Miles Naismith Vorkosigan—a war cry simply warned the enemy.

Josh turned, a sneer cracking the black blot of his beard. He started to swing his gun hand to change his aim. A deputy shouted. Josh hesitated. Blade leaped, modifying his tackle so the barrel of his own gun slammed Josh deep in the gut.

His head impacted with the cabin wall. Through the stars filling his vision, Blade saw little Buddy vanish into the darkness beyond the clearing.

*   *   *

"You'll like Blade," Ray said, never lifting his gaze from his computer screen. His fingers flew, filling the too-quiet hotel room with a steady buzz of tapping.

Jen knew better than to remind Ray that his former partner had turned him down. "I think I'll get a few hours of sleep before the crack of dawn hits. How about you?"

"You two are a lot alike. His parents died in a car wreck when he was a kid. Unlike you, he didn't have anybody to fight for, so he got messed up by the system."

"Poor guy," she murmured.

"He got in trouble for a while, so he decided to become a superhero to make up for his crimes." Ray flashed her one of those crooked grins that made her think the real Ray Porter actually peeked through the multiple masks he always wore. "Yeah, old buddy Blade would make a great...addition to the team." He glanced over the top of his notebook screen at her.

Ray studied her until Jen wanted to jump up and run, or start scratching. She held still and met his gaze, knowing that she couldn't run and couldn't hide anywhere. Ray always found her. Most of the time, that was a comforting thought, because that meant he was dependable, and he cared about her enough to look. Outside her nine adopted siblings, Ray was probably the closest friend she had.

What a depressing thought, a silent voice chided in the back of her mind. *That's what you get for thinking every man who smiles at you is either out to scam you or is a murdering rapist psycho. Time to find a knight in shining armor before you get too old to have some fun.*

Yeah, Jen silently agreed. *But where?*

"Did you read Poling's file?" Ray asked, finally lowering his gaze.

"Most of it."

"He's a ladies man." He clicked on the command to print out the information on the screen. "He likes intelligent women. And fortunately for us, married women."

Ray's grin made Jen think that under that sneaky, brilliant, creative mind lay a little boy who never grew up and found great delight in stink bombs and hand buzzers.

"When the husband is an oblivious jerk who loves his work more than his beautiful wife, he deserves it if she fools around on him." Ray resumed his rapid-fire tapping through the Internet. "I hear islands are rather romantic. Hard to resist."

Jen's stomach dropped into her heels. So that was Ray's plan—Gloria was going to have an affair with a foreign art appraiser-forger-thief?

No. Blade Hampton had turned Ray down. She admired him for being able to say no, because she certainly couldn't say no when Ray wanted her help.

To his credit, Ray always seemed to turn up when she needed tricky, delicate help. Sometimes she wondered if he did that just so she couldn't turn him down later.

"Glo is getting bored," Ray murmured. "She wants adventure and excitement. Hooking up with her computer sciences teacher was exciting eight years ago. Not anymore."

"Ray..." Knowing she was going to regret this, Jen took a deep breath and made herself ask. "How intense an affair?"

That nasty smile of Ray's grew by three degrees.

"Blade will never agree to it, even if you do get him to help us."

It occurred to her that Blade's picture must have made a deep, strong impression on her, to remember him after just a glimpse. That meant her hormones were interfering with common sense. And that meant big trouble, if she had to play romantic lead opposite him.

Everybody and her sister knows I suck at romance, Jen wailed silently. Why did Ray have to get it in his head that she was attracted to Blade, just from one glimpse of his picture?

"Oh, ye of little faith," he murmured. His grin widened and he sat back, nodding at his screen. "Bingo."

Inside, Jen went down on her knees, praying.

"Saving a little boy from his psychotic father is certainly more important than stealing back the senator's painting." Jen waited, but Ray just nodded. "Does he do that a lot?"

"Rescue kids? Let me tell you something about old buddy Blade." Ray tapped a few buttons, then clasped his hands behind his head and slouched. "The biggest reason he left the Agency was because of all the little folks who kept falling through the cracks. The ones with emergencies and tragedies that destroyed their whole world, but didn't amount to a speck of dust in the grand scheme of things. He didn't like that. Blade isn't able to stand back and see the whole picture."

"No collateral damage," Jen murmured.

She had heard that too much growing up. Accepting collateral damage had destroyed the network of people who had raised her, leaving her on the streets in charge of younger children. She refused to accept collateral damage—the individual would never be sacrificed for the good of the whole while she had any say in it.

Blade felt the same way. She liked that. The warm feeling growing inside her was rather surprising, since it was directed toward a total stranger.

"Exactly."

"So…" Nothing in the world would make her admit to Ray that she wanted to know more about Blade. However, she could try to trick him into revealing things. Maybe it would take his mind off hoodwinking Blade into joining them. "So, why did you leave the Agency?"

"Shylock."

"Jerk bosses are everywhere. I seriously doubt he was trying to do your thinking for you. That kind of ruins the whole purpose of training you guys to stand on your own."

"Smart lady." Ray winked at her and leaned forward to start tapping commands into his computer again.

Jen sighed and got up to retreat to the bedroom. As she closed the door, she heard the printer start up. She felt sorry for Blade Hampton, wherever he was. Ray didn't know the meaning of the word no. That was probably how he had cheated death and disaster for so long, but it also made him cocky to the extreme.

*   *   *

Blade paused, wincing, in the hospital doorway. The rising sun sat at the perfect angle to slice horizontally into his eyes. It hit the back of his brain and geometrically multiplied the ache where he had hit the cabin. His ribs ached from the single punch Harkness got on him before Blade took him down.

He felt good. Fantastic, in fact. Buddy and his mother were safely out of Josh's reach, even if he managed to break jail. Cynthia's legal beagles had the connections and clout to keep them safe against the slimiest lawyers Harkness might bring in to fight for his alleged fatherly rights.

A few bruises and aches were a small price to pay for the satisfaction that made him want to shout until the mountains surrounding the hospital echoed. If he weren't so tired, so badly in need of a shave, shower, and a four-course breakfast, Blade thought he might have tried dancing.

"Hampton." That silky baritone glued Blade's feet to the asphalt pavement. "What a surprise to run into you here."

Blade bit back a retort as he turned to face the man he least wanted to see. Going into a battle of wits with Chief Anguilano was like facing a nuclear bomb buck-naked.

"Has Porter called you yet?"

"Why would he? Better question—how do you know he will?" Blade headed across the lot to his Jeep.

"He keeps finding back doors to the Agency's files. It's less effort to let him in and monitor his searches. Last night, he only took your phone number." Chief Michael Anguilano—aka Shylock—tilted his dark, sleek head slightly to one side and gave Blade a shallow smile, those perfect teeth brilliant in the morning mountain sunlight.

Blade hated him, just because he moved so smoothly, looked so fresh, energetic, and in control. The night he had just gone through was no excuse for feeling and looking like something that had been run through the swamp and then spread out on the twenty-yard line during the Superbowl. Shylock was at least twenty years older than him, but he could go for weeks at a time without needing food or sleep. Blade wondered yet again if his former supervisor wasn't a robot. He had speculated that people like Anguilano got the supervisory jobs because of how they looked in expensive suits and how many diplomatic functions they could attend without going stark raving bonkers.

From his conservatively cut Brooks Bros navy suit to his glossy boots and maroon tie, Anguilano looked like a successful businessman running a few errands before heading to work in a high-rise building fifty miles away. Only the operatives he supervised ever saw the shark lurking behind those deep-set, dark, almost sleepy eyes; the claws in those manicured, blunt fingers. The man who held the reins on the best operatives the Agency ever trained—and never let go, even when they quit.

"Porter's getting good. We only have the vaguest idea what he's up to now, or even where he is." They came to a stop four feet from the front bumper of the Jeep. He looked Blade up and down, taking in his ponytail and faded jeans. "You're doing good work. We honestly miss your contribution."

"Thanks." That cannon ball sensation of surprise hit Blade's stomach, even after years of telling himself he didn't care about Anguilano's praise or opinion. "I'm curious why you're paying so much attention to Ray and his activities."

"More than to yours?" That smile warmed and widened. "Jealousy isn't you, Hampton, so I'd say it's concern for your old friend."

That flicker of approval lit his eyes, then he turned his head, looking around the half-empty parking lot. Anguilano stepped over to the Cherokee and put one foot up on the bumper, which meant he was here for more than just a pep talk. Blade crossed his arms and leaned back against the front grill. He decided to listen until the painkillers started working. Yes, he was curious. Anguilano wouldn't be here if he didn't have something to say.

"Why do you keep tabs on me?" Blade asked, forestalling Shylock as he opened his mouth to speak.

"We take care of our own. You know that."

"You keep forgetting I quit." He almost laughed.

"For the time being. You'll come back when we have something you need. You and Porter." Anguilano's eyes slid closed a notch, reminding Blade of a sleepy, well-fed cat. The vicious, sly breed content to let the mice play just out of reach, until he needed a snack.

Anguilano took a small black case from his inner coat pocket and put it on the hood of the Jeep. The size of a larger cell phone, it had five tiny lights down one side. The green one flashed gently, paused five seconds, flashed again. A white noise device, Blade suspected. He wondered how much of this was to show off the latest toys and how much was serious paranoia. Who would be close enough to listen, or even try to listen, at this time of the morning?

"Did Porter ever tell you why he left the Agency? I didn't think so," Anguilano said, when Blade shook his head. "He was upset when I confronted him on his secret activities. As if no one in the world had any right to know what truly drives him. Let me tell you a bedtime story, Hampton," he continued quickly, as if he expected to be interrupted by a snide comment.

"Many years ago, among the powerful Fascists in Italy, there was an influential man who had five daughters. He was an astonishingly clear thinker, and an astonishingly moral man. Nationalism took a second place to justice. He didn't like what was happening around him. He knew Italy was doomed, so he sent his daughters away to America, where he correctly guessed the war would never touch.

"Unfortunately, his name was already linked with enemies of the United States. The Secret Police would never let his daughters out of Italy, and the bureaucrats in the U.S. would never let them in. So, he separated his daughters, gave them false identities, and sent them to different parts of the country. Only he knew where they were. The plan was to escape Italy, flee to America, find his daughters, and they would all live happily ever after. However, this is no fairy tale, and this clever, good man died and never rejoined his daughters. Who had no idea where to find their sisters."

"So Ray's trying to find his...what, aunts and cousins?" Blade slid down to rest on the bumper. He bit his lip to keep from wincing when that move revealed more bruises than he recalled. "That's not against Agency policy. Using inside contacts for personal matters is permitted, if it doesn't endanger national security."

"Hmm. No. But those daughters were illegal aliens. It's iffy whether marrying citizens would make them legal, because of how they entered the country. Porter didn't start on his quest until his mother died, leaving him all the documentation she had. She was the youngest. Still a child at the time the entire masquerade started. What sort of information do the older sisters have? There are hints they knew information to use as insurance for their safety. Their father was an idealist, but also a realist." For a moment, those too-bright eyes took on a distant look. Anguilano sighed.

"Porter's searching for the other four sisters and their descendants. We have no idea what time bombs are waiting to explode even now, so long after Mussolini's reign collapsed. He wouldn't listen to my friendly warnings and offers of help."

"He wouldn't take your interference." Blade snorted. "You probably wanted in on the fun."

Anguilano's foot slid off the bumper and hit the pavement with a crack. He stood up straight, losing that lazy, cat-in-the-cream complacency. Blade wondered what he had stumbled on, just before the

19

mask slid into place again.

"Maybe." He picked an imaginary piece of lint off his immaculate shoulder. "Porter isn't the kind of man who leaves just because he's angry, or someone invaded his treasured privacy. I found information he wouldn't have found for ten years. I put it where he could find it and he snatched it up like a starving beggar. When I confronted him, he got angry."

"Even though he walked away from the Agency, you keep bringing him back, blackmailing him into doing jobs for you."

"He's the best at what he does, the man of a thousand faces and voices." A thin smile cracked Anguilano's composure. "Perhaps he is so good at being other people because he has no real past of his own. No roots. Not like you." His smile widened, sending a chill up Blade's back. "And you, Hampton, are very good at what you do. That's why we keep tabs on you too."

"I'm flattered."

Blade kept his voice and expression sour to hide the jolt that ran through him. Why had Anguilano become involved in Ray's search? Why had he told Blade so much? Anguilano was playing a game. The key to staying alive was figuring out the game and running away as fast and as hard as he could.

"You owe Porter your life, a dozen times over."

"Ray owes me too."

"True. Friends guard each other's backs, Hampton. When he calls you—if he hasn't already—consider that." Anguilano nodded, scooped the little black case off the hood of the Jeep, then simply walked away.

Something strange was definitely going on here. Anguilano didn't give warnings unless it profited him or the Agency. Blade had more than a sneaking suspicion his former boss was more than interested in Ray's search. Anguilano preferred to play games and get information without anyone guessing what he wanted. That was why those who worked under him referred to him as Shylock.

Anguilano wanted Blade involved in Ray's latest job. That was good enough reason for Blade to stay completely out of it.

CHAPTER 3

Nice.

Blade let his *Antiquarians Quarterly* drop three inches so he could watch the pale green vision stroll across the marble lobby. Finally, something under the age of eighty in this backwater hotel crammed with faded gentility. Nothing wrong with enjoying himself while he waited to meet Mrs. Weatherby and turn over the silver, was there? He honestly liked antiques, but sometimes a man needed fresh blood.

Fresh *was* the word for the red-haired sylph who paused to study the sprawling flower arrangement on the table between Blade and the front desk. The mahogany table had to be a century old—she couldn't be more than twenty-five. Those legs would make a ballet dancer envious. The way she moved in those one-inch heel pumps made Blade think she would rather be barefoot. He couldn't make out details like eye color or if she had freckles, but her skin was a warm gold that belonged on a country girl, a forest ranger, a horse trainer. What was she doing in that lace-trimmed frock, mincing around the lobby clutching a purse the size of a soda can? Blade imagined her more comfortable in cut-off jeans, a halter-top, barefoot.

What was she doing alone? A smile stretched his lips. Blade ignored the twinge in his tightly wrapped ribs and braced himself to stand, cross the lobby, and introduce himself.

"Hampton?" a dusty voice wheezed behind him.

Blade nearly waved the intruder away. The sooner he got rid of the silver tea service, the sooner he would be free to make dinner plans, right? He looked once more at the girl across the lobby, mentally ordered her not to leave his sight, and turned back to greet his client.

"Mrs. Weatherby." He stood and gestured at the seat opposite him, so he could watch his pretty target without appearing rude. Blade prayed the saggy, gray woman the size of a Brunhilda would finish her business quickly.

In the twenty minutes it took to mop Mrs. Weatherby's tears and listen to her whimper yet again through the history of the silver, the girl in green circled the lobby twice before settling into another seating group. She retrieved a Mickey Mouse lollipop from her tiny purse and looked around the lobby before unwrapping it. Blade grinned, until her dark eyes met his for two electrifying seconds.

He jerked his attention back to Mrs. Weatherby, who had finally put her soggy handkerchief away to write a check. He looked at the girl again, in time to see her take her first tiny lick at the lollipop.

Suddenly, the dusty lobby felt too warm.

Blade tried not to stammer his thanks as he took Mrs. Weatherby's check. He saw that tiny pink tongue flicking at the edge of his vision. Mrs. Weatherby lumbered to her feet and held out her hand to shake his. That put the girl directly over the old woman's bowed shoulder, where Blade couldn't ignore her.

He thought his heart beat in time with her licking.

It hasn't been that long, has it?

Mrs. Weatherby hugged him. Her pillowy arms could strangle a sumo wrestler. Blade distinctly heard someone snicker, but when the old woman released him and tottered out of the lobby, he looked around and saw no one watching him.

He turned back to the girl and took a couple deep breaths to steady himself. He was a private investigator, a former agent for the government; he had a reputation to uphold. Stammering and breaking out in a sweat would not do it.

She bit off one candy ear. The crunch reverberated around the lobby. Blade took one step away from his chair.

"Gloria? Sweetheart, what are you doing?" a chiding male voice called, from directly behind Blade.

He groaned as he realized someone *had* seen his exchange with Mrs. Weatherby. Blade had studied the lobby before he chose his spot; he should have heard someone approaching across the marble floor, aided by the echoes thrown off that domed ceiling. Who could sneak up on him? Who would want to?

Then Blade recognized that voice. A chill moved across his scalp. His chest tightened as a broad-shouldered figure dressed like a rich, color-blind golfer passed him and headed straight across the lobby toward the girl of Blade's dreams.

"No," Blade groaned. "Anybody but her."

From the way the girl flinched, she seemed to feel the same way. Blade grinned when she shoved the lollipop between two pages of a magazine, jammed it down the side of her chair and stood to meet the man.

He turned now, confirming Blade's suspicions. The tinted, silver-rimmed glasses were new and the geeky clothes meant a disguise and a job in the works. Ray Porter's tastes ran more to black leather jackets and jeans. That outfit, and hair so full of gel his curls lay flat, couldn't change a face that belonged to Hollywood's idea of a Mafioso hit man/leading man.

A face Blade knew all too well. He owed his old friend and former partner his life—but *not* the girl of his dreams!

It figured Ray would already have his hands on the only decent female in a ten-mile radius. Blade watched the girl wrinkle her nose when Ray shook his finger in her face. He reached for the magazine where she had hidden the lollipop and she slapped his hand away from it. The move put her hand into a stray beam of late afternoon sunlight coming through a high window and a diamond ring flashed there in clear view.

Ray didn't dress like a geek, and the world would end before he turned in his freedom for marriage. Even for that dream-become-flesh that he caught inside the curve of his arm and led to the registration desk. Ray's code of ethics kept him from fooling around with a married woman, so that left only one option. Ray was on a job, and the girl was working with him.

But that left new questions.

Was she an active participant, or just a cover story? Part of the disguise, or partner?

Knowing how Ray felt about being partners with anyone, Blade doubted that. It made him nauseous to think that Ray used her for distraction. Blade surprised himself by hoping she was as stunning mentally as physically. When had he started to care?

He drifted toward the desk, pretending to look for something to read as he strained his ears to overhear the exchange. Ray signed them in as Mark and Gloria Williams. Blade drifted past. It was hard to keep moving when he couldn't drag his gaze off the perfect curve of Gloria's rear end—and Ray's hand too close to sliding south from her waist.

Ray only involved civilians if he couldn't pull off the job on his own. Sometimes, though, Ray did let Shylock talk him into helping out another agent who had run into trouble. If the girl wasn't just window dressing, did this mean Ray was working for Shylock? Or did Shylock have something on Ray to *force* him to take a partner, despite his standing rules?

That had to be it. Blackmail of some kind.

Ray had been sleeping with one of their Academy instructors when their training team went on an exercise that turned deadly. She died. The investigation had cleared Ray, but Blade suspected he never forgave himself. Ray made it a rule never to sleep with the women he worked with. Those few partners who could keep up with him, whom he trusted to guard his back, Ray stuck to like glue, but when he left the Agency, he went solo.

Which brought Blade right back to the first question. As one of Ray's few partners who had lived to tell the tale, Blade felt a responsibility for this girl. The thought of something going wrong and that graceful body twisted in pain and covered with blood made him break out in a cold sweat.

Then a new question raised its ugly head: What if Ray knew Blade would be here, and had come to talk him into joining the team? Ray *had* found his cell phone number in the Agency's files. Anguilano had been keeping track of him.

Despite himself, Blade knew he had to get some answers. He needed to impress on Ray that when he said no, he meant no.

Or, maybe he should play along for a little while and find out if Gloria needed some rescuing from Ray.

When they headed for their room, Blade followed.

*   *   *

"He's following us," Jen murmured.

She had been checking the reflections in the polished brass and strips of mirror tiles as they traversed the labyrinth of halls in the hotel. It was the man from the lobby.

Blade Hampton. The name suited him.

Jen had wondered why Ray brought them to this hotel, when the one they had been using, thirty miles away, was just fine. She knew something was up when he told her to wander around the lobby for a few minutes before he came inside to register. When they got to their room, she was going to have to sit him down and give him yet another lecture on making his temporary partner work without any relevant information. Especially if he wanted her to play gooey-sweet, adoring little Gloria on this job.

Or maybe she should just avail herself of Ray's computer the next time he left her alone for more then ten minutes, and dig out all the information she wanted, for future blackmail. Maybe she should take the pieces of Ray's quest and solve it for him. Wouldn't he be steamed if she solved the riddle before he did? Jen grinned, just thinking of his frustration. It would serve him right, wouldn't it?

Turnabout was fair play, after all. She knew frustration not long ago when she realized Blade Hampton sat not twenty feet away, watching her, and she didn't dare approach him.

She could have walked over to him, introduced herself, and warned him to run for his life before Ray showed up. Three seconds after recognizing Blade, Jen realized Ray had put her there as bait.

Two more seconds, and she didn't know whether to strangle Ray or hug him, because making her bait meant she was the kind of girl who would indeed catch Blade Hampton's attention.

Then three more seconds to realize that it wasn't her, but *Gloria* that Blade followed through this half-abandoned hotel. Jen hated Gloria.

She considered warning Blade to run, and maybe give him her phone number, to call when the job with Worley ended. They could team up to teach Ray a lesson.

Then the old woman had joined Blade and Ray crept through the shadows of the echoing lobby's perimeter, and it was too late to do anything but play along.

Jen rested her cheek on the Ray's muscular shoulder, despite the scratching of the neon lime and burnt orange sweater, and concentrated on keeping her legs from tangling with his. She loathed playing perky little Gloria. She would rather race against time to decode something vital to national security—with limited RAM and a power outage to make things interesting—rather than pretend to be on a never-ending honeymoon.

Not that Ray wasn't a good partner. He showered every day. When their disguise forced them to share a bed, he never stole the covers. And he never snored. He actually treated her like she had a brain and he trusted her gut instincts. It was like being on a vacation to work with someone who watched out for her, because she usually protected everyone. She really did like Ray, but not when she found herself in one of his games, and no clue which game was being played.

"Spotted," Ray murmured, and turned them right when they should have turned left to get to their suite.

This hotel was a mausoleum, a bee hive done in marble, brocade and subdued lighting. All very lovely, of course, until she got close enough to see the faded patches, the cracks in the flooring, the water stains in the ceiling. She hated the place, despite its echoes of grandeur. It was nothing more than a rabbit warren of hallways and neglected conference rooms, escalators, and mezzanines. Just how many restaurants did one hotel need? The exercise room, indoor pool, and Jacuzzi, she could understand. The boutique, tanning spa, beauty parlor, and coffee shop/bookstore pushed the envelope. It cost money to keep them open, with no customers. Jen was very careful of money, having grown up with so little. She hated waste.

Besides, Jen hated being in places that required a map.

At least it had bathrooms every fifty yards. Bathrooms came in handy when dealing with unwanted shadows.

Yet, was that quite true? She liked knowing she had intrigued Blade Hampton enough to make him follow them.

She liked the sensation of his gaze on her. It sent pleasant shivers up her spine and through her middle. She had seen him grin when Ray caught her with the candy.

If she left the two former partners alone, she would find out soon enough what Blade wanted.

"Hon," she simpered, raising her voice to be heard by their silent companion. "I just gotta make a little stop. Is that okay with you?" Jen fluttered her fingers in the general direction of the ladies' restroom, now coming up on their right.

"Sure." Ray released her shoulders. "The phones are just around the corner. I need to make a call. Meet me there?"

"Perfect."

"Wait a second." His eyes sparkled with that nasty mischief she hated seeing focused on her, then he planted a kiss on her before spinning her around and aiming her at the bathroom door.

Ray continued down the hall in that amble that so perfectly suited the oblivious computer genius he portrayed. Nothing at all like the mystery man who preferred shadows, black leather, and dark glasses.

What was that kiss for? Jen fought to stay in character as she headed for the door. She put a little extra swing in her hips for the benefit of the shadow and fought not to wipe her mouth until the door closed behind her.

Ray had done it for Blade's benefit. Why? And why hadn't he warned her?

"There is something very wrong with me," Jen whispered, after checking to make sure she had the bathroom to herself.

Ray was one of the most gorgeous men she had ever met. Add to that package a wicked funny bone, a sense of honor and decency and a knight errant kind of self-sacrifice. So why didn't it do anything to her pulse when Ray held her? How come her brain didn't short-circuit when he kissed her?

Why did a lopsided grin from a complete stranger across a hotel lobby make her insides go into meltdown?

Jen took a deep breath to brace herself and clear her head, winced at the heavy cherry scent of the air freshener, and turned back to the heavy faux walnut door. She pushed it open just enough for a half-inch crack, and watched their shadow saunter down the hall a good five yards behind Ray.

She certainly did like them tall and lean. Thick, glossy black hair pulled back in a ponytail that just brushed wide shoulders, which were sleekly wrapped in a brown corduroy blazer. His sand-colored hiking boots whispered across the gold-glazed tile floor.

Jen didn't need to see the intensity or color of those deep-set eyes to know this was a predator…and that starts with P which rhymes with T for trouble. She had survived this long by listening to that itch in her scalp and the chill up her back that warned of danger.

Jen clenched her fists, digging her fake nails into her palms, and opened the door to step out into the hall. Too bad she had to watch his backside for this little ambush. All muscle, wrapped in form-fitting faded denim. She had never understood why her friends got such a charge out of studying male posteriors. Now she did. He could be an acrobat or a dancer. Or a Musketeer. She did love swashbucklers and mystery men—Captain Blood, Zorro, and the Green Hornet in particular.

"Down, girl," she whispered.

It escaped her why being partnered with hunk-of-the-decade Ray didn't put a single flutter in her middle. She always got a good night's sleep on her side of the bed and never woke in the night wishing he'd bend the rules to try *something*. Ray was all man, with dreamboat eyes.

His hands could crack safes, soothe a child's tears, and make a woman a brainless pudding. Jen had seen him do it numerous times when their situation demanded it.

Just never to her.

Which was probably why she got hot flashes watching Blade Hampton follow Ray down the hall. Her head knew it was good to be ignored; her hormones were in a snit and raring for trouble.

Jen stepped out of her green leather pumps and crept down the hallway, one with the shadows. The Invisible Man had nothing on her, when she wanted to move unseen.

Ray kept his back to her and Blade, now caught between them. He fumbled through his pockets for change, dropped three quarters on the floor and bent to pick them up. Jen caught his wink from under his bent arm.

The creep was having *fun* with this! She was tempted to turn around and run the other way and let him deal with this problem on his own.

"Keep your hands where I can see them," Blade Hampton rumbled in a voice like a melted box of chocolates, and stuck something in Ray's back.

Jen paused as that voice twisted inside her chest. Why did he have to sound like that?

"I don't have any money," Ray said, raising his hands. His voice wobbled and rose half an octave.

Jen muffled a snort when she got close enough to see Blade used a roll of Life Savers in lieu of a gun. Another wise guy, huh? Two could play at that game.

The game was even better with three.

"You think I'm stupid?" Blade sneered and reached to pat down Ray's right side.

Jen caught his left ankle with her right foot and jerked hard while pulling on his right elbow. She caught his shoulder as he twisted off his center of balance and slammed him to the floor without endangering a single false nail.

"What you are, is flat," she said, and finished the job by shoving down hard with her heel, grinding his shoulder into the tile floor. The arch of her foot rested on the knob of his collarbone. His five o'clock shadow tickled the tips of her toes. She had the nauseating urge to giggle at the sensation.

He had gorgeous, storm gray eyes. Even more beautiful and mesmerizing than in the photo in Ray's computer files.

Those eyes, right that moment, could see up her skirt.

She hated skirts. Especially the short little cutey-girl skirts she wore as Gloria. Even as she wished she wore her usual jeans, Jen heard an echo of Ray in her memory, telling her it was time to change Gloria's image and wardrobe.

She hated it when he was right.

Ray slumped against the opposite wall and laughed hard enough to raise tears. Silent laughter, his face red and his shoulders shaking.

"Don't kill him, Jen," he finally said after several painfully quiet, strained moments. "He's a friend."

"Don't bet on it," Blade grumbled. He swallowed, and the motion of his Adam's apple rubbing against her big toe sent a flutter up her leg. It took all her discipline to keep from jerking backwards and giggling while hopping on one foot. He raised the hand holding the roll of Life Savers. "Wild cherry?"

Jen ignored him—and the stream of filthy comments his offer brought to mind—and took three precautionary steps back. She prayed her face wasn't as red hot as it felt, even as she wondered which color panties she had put on today.

"Blade Hampton, meet Jen Holt." Ray stumbled forward and stretched out a hand to help his former partner get to his feet.

"That answers a couple questions." Blade ignored Ray's hand, which earned Jen's respect, and he grinned at them both as he got to his feet. "She's your partner, not your cover."

"Both." Ray glanced up and down the hallway. "Busy?"

"Would it do him any good if he said yes?" Jen asked. That earned her a scowl from Ray, but a wink and a wider grin from Blade. Her interior temperature rose a good ten degrees.

"I just finished up a job." Blade watched Jen as he spoke. "I'm just curious enough to let you buy me lunch while you tell me the scenario."

CHAPTER 4

"You're not a redhead."

Blade sat up straight and watched Jen emerge, sans wig, from the hotel suite's bedroom. That forlorn note in his voice couldn't be disappointment, could it? No. Just a leftover reaction to the trick Ray had pulled on both of them.

That look in Jen's eyes, he understood deep in his gut, in the soft spots he kept well armored. Confusion. Shame. Disgust. That fractured feeling of realizing he'd been left out of the loop. Jen hadn't liked being used to pull a joke on Blade.

Blade wondered if he could talk her into helping him give Ray the old heave-ho off the room's sixth floor balcony.

"No joke." She raked her fingers through a short mop of tangled hair the color of Dove dark chocolate. Her eyes were like chocolate too. Dark, with a touch of bitter richness.

"We still have to take care of that little detail while we're camped out here," Ray said. "Tonight." He gave her a sideways smirk. She rolled her eyes and sighed.

Blade felt something tense up inside himself in reaction to the intimate little by-play. From the way she shook her head, he suspected Jen felt just as disgusted with Ray's gloating good humor. Like she wanted to wipe that smugness off his face. Preferably with an ice bucket.

She stretched out in the chaise lounge by the window and flicked at the curtains with her bare foot. Then she turned her attention full on

Blade for the first time since they reached the suite and she retreated to the bedroom while the two old friends caught up on things. "I assume you've known this arrogant jerk longer than me?"

"Sounds like you've known him long enough," Blade said with a chuckle. He got up, crossed the living room, and held out his hand. "How about a mutual aid society?"

"You've got a deal." The touch of her hand as they shook sent an electric jolt through him. Small bones, sturdy under the thin, tough layer of muscle. Hands that could do as much damage as her feet. Or maybe give an equal amount of pleasure?

He preferred Jen over Barbie-doll-cute Gloria. She wore faded camouflage pants, three sizes too large, and a fishnet shirt in Day-Glo green over a gray, skin-tight aerobics top.

"So," Blade said, when he'd taken a seat on the arm of the couch midway between Jen and Ray. "You know what I've been up to. What's your scenario?"

"Ever hear of Dordt?" Ray asked.

"Yeah." Blade half-closed his eyes as he mentally flipped through the files of his memory. "College in Iowa."

"He's good," Jen murmured. She winked at him.

"Some painter too," he hurried on, to quell the warm sensation that audacious little wink sent through him. "Dutch?"

"Heinrich Wilhelm Dordtmann." Ray turned his chair to make himself the apex of a loose triangle. "Little-known painter up until eight years ago. Then he became all the rage among the artsy elite in Atlanta."

"La de da," he muttered. That earned a muffled snort from Jen. He winked back at her and she blushed.

"The big draw of Dordt's work is that he left so much unfinished. That, plus a fire in a gallery that held almost eighty percent of his known paintings."

"Instant rarity," Jen offered.

"And that's where you come in." Blade leaned forward, resting his elbows on his knees. "Someone stole a painting and you're retrieving it before the insurance company pays up."

"Not exactly." Ray glanced at Jen, effectively giving her control of the briefing.

That surprised Blade. Ray usually insisted on taking the reins, so all the pressure and responsibility rested on him. Blade understood. They both slept better when they weren't relying on an unknown to keep

31

their heads on their bodies.

The question suddenly uppermost in Blade's mind was what other rules Ray would decide to bend or break now. And what exactly did Jen mean to him, that he would change the rules?

Would Ray keep his hands off Jen for the duration of the job? They weren't lovers. Jen would have taken a seat next to Ray, close enough to touch, if they were. Neither watched the other with that combination predatory/possessive look Blade had seen shared by Ray and his string of lovers. Judging by the irritation in Jen's voice, there was no infatuation to smooth over the rough spots in this relationship.

Blade didn't want to consider why that realization made him feel like he'd just inhaled nitrous oxide. As one survivor among Ray's ex-partners, and an ex-Marine, he had a duty to make sure Jen got out of this job alive. Untouched. By *every* definition.

"Enter Senator Melinda Carlisle of Iowa." Jen sat up and crossed her legs. "She inherited 'Unfinished Number Ten,' also known as 'Kitchen in Blue.' Art critics have no imagination," she added, momentarily taking on an affected, Boston-snob accent. She grinned, and Blade saw her as a mischievous child.

For a second there, he mentally flashed to her slim, elegant legs and those pale green panties, just before she stepped back and took her foot off his windpipe.

"There was a whatchacallit—a codicil in her grandfather's will. She isn't allowed to sell it for ten years. If she tries, the painting goes to the Guggenheim. Unfortunately, the senator's husband ran into some financial problems. They secretly sold the painting."

"A forgery has been hanging in its place ever since," Ray added. "The new owners agreed to keep the purchase secret until the full ten years elapse."

"But someone stole the painting," Blade guessed.

"Worse." Jen grimaced. "The forgery. We have to get it back before Worley finds out what he's got, or the senator's career is trashed. Three times Worley has stolen something of immense value, then forged documents to prove he's the rightful owner. Then, when someone catches him with the stolen valuables and tries to throw him in jail, he turns around and sues the victims and the people who were helping them. It's taken some fancy maneuvering to keep innocent people out of jail, and Worley has never served a day of punishment."

"So you two are going in to steal the painting, instead of bringing in the authorities to haul the guy away," Blade mused, thinking aloud.

"You can't let him discover the painting's a forgery and you can't arrest him, because either way the senator's reputation is trashed and the painting goes to the museum. Sounds like a fun job."

"What do you know of Danville Worley?" Ray asked after only a moment's pause.

"Flamboyant, arrogant, but nothing dangerous. He bought the Cooke mansion and Stone Lab, that Ohio State University research station out on Gibraltar Island in Lake Erie. There was a big ruckus about misuse of funds. Maybe he fixed things to buy it illegally?" Blade frowned as his brain shifted gears.

Downsizing his career from international skullduggery to civilian catastrophes kept him out of the loop. He still checked in with his information sources, just to avoid surprises, but not as often as he would have liked. Staying informed was the only way to stay alive. International nastiness had a way of filtering down to the little people he enjoyed helping.

"If we can get that proof while we're making the retrieval, it's icing on the cake. He bypassed historical preservation regulations and turned it all into a gaudy castle. Allegedly, he closed up the old caves and tunnels used by the Indians and the Underground Railroad," Ray said. "My guess is those tunnels have been put to other uses. We're ninety-five percent sure he's responsible for the Dordt theft. Fortunately, he ran into Williams Cyber-Tech and Security Systems and discovered he needed to upgrade the entire island's security."

"That's you two?" Blade glanced at Jen. She shrugged. "That's a lot of prep for a fast, in and out operation."

"We've used it three times before. Never saw any need to dismantle it. Jen's an artist when it comes to creating fake people. Sometimes even I believe Mark and Gloria exist."

"You?" He grinned at Jen, delighted when she shrugged again and a crooked smile caught one corner of her mouth.

"I'm very good at lying." She uncrossed her legs. "I'm up for tea. Any takers?" She headed for the kitchenette tucked between the living room and the door of the suite.

"What do you have besides that stuff that smells like rotten mulch?" Ray winked at Blade.

"It's very good for your digestion, Mr. Williams."

Blade hated that cozy little exchange. They sounded like a married couple who had gotten past the moonlight and roses into the friendly bickering stage that would last them for the next eighty years, if they were lucky.

"This, from the woman who single-handedly keeps Hershey's in business," Ray muttered. "From all the sugar you eat, you should be the size of this hotel."

"Everyone needs at least one vice." Jen gave them an innocent little smile Blade didn't believe for one moment.

"Ray could loan you a few," Blade offered.

"No thanks." She wrinkled up her nose. "I never borrow earrings, boyfriends, or bad habits." She vanished into the kitchenette.

Blade wondered what she'd think about him "borrowing" his ex-partner's "wife." And immediately slapped that thought down. After all, wife was a four-letter word, along with "baby" and dozens of others that created an allergic reaction in him.

"She's that good?" Blade asked, as Jen ran water.

"Best little pickpocket, sneak thief, and hacker I've ever worked with." Ray got up and went into the bedroom, to return with his notebook computer. He tossed the modem cable to Blade, who bent to plug it into the phone on the antique coffee table.

"Where'd you get her? Jail?"

"In a dark alley. Kidnapping babies." Ray didn't glance up from the screen as his fingers danced over the keyboard.

"You're kidding."

"Her best friend was dating an escapee from a doomsday cult and got pregnant. Daddy got nabbed by the cult leaders just after she told him the good news. When they found out about baby, they decided the kid was their property. Jen was already trying to find Daddy, so when baby disappeared, she had enough to find him and steal him back. I was after another baby."

"Lovely world we live in," Blade murmured. He stepped around the coffee table so he could watch over Ray's shoulder.

"We decided we were on the same side and needed a frontal assault. Jen whipped up Mark and Gloria as cover. Seems the cult needed new Web designers. The greedy slimes didn't even know what hit them before we had the kids and were out of there. Since it gives us carte blanche to poke our noses into sensitive areas, we decided to leave the identity and business standing."

"And whenever you need a wife for an operation—"

"Jen's about the best partner I've ever had."

"You hate having partners," Blade said.

"True. Here we go." He turned the computer so the screen was at the right angle for Blade to see clearly.

It showed a diagram of Gibraltar Island and Worley's castle, with topographical markings to show height and foliage, and lines in the bedrock of the island where tunnels and caves were supposed to be.

"How much did you pay for that?"

"Worley gave it to us, along with a three-dimensional mock-up. We're planning on getting there Friday. Three more days to prepare." He leaned back in the chair. "Want to play?"

If he turned his head a few degrees, Blade could see Jen working in the kitchen. He heard the pinging of the microwave. Did he want in, just to be near Jen?

Had Ray brought Jen along, knowing Blade would be attracted to her? Maybe even feel protective of her? Was Ray resorting to emotional blackmail to force Blade to his will?

He had only known Jen for half an hour. True, he felt responsible to keep her from getting hurt by either Ray or the mission, but *why* did he feel that way? If Ray accepted her as a partner, she was more than able to take care of herself.

Why *did* Ray invite Blade to join them? He wouldn't have taken the job in the first place if he thought he and Jen couldn't handle it. Something had changed during preparation. Ray had mentioned something about an International forger. A new player had been added to the mix. Blade wondered if he should be flattered or worried that Ray had immediately thought of him to balance out the change in the equation.

Something sticky was in the offing. If not Ray's nasty sense of humor, then there was an ulterior motive in all this.

"You're not trying to talk me into going back to working for Shylock, are you? With the senator involved, is this an Agency job? Are you recruiting?"

"Me?" Ray widened his eyes in wounded innocence. "I'm the last to talk anybody into working for that bloodsucker."

Blade crossed his arms and slouched in the chair. He met Ray's gaze, unblinking, until the other man sighed and shrugged.

"A simple job. In and out. With a vacation on the Lake Erie islands thrown into the package. Worley's trying to get a little house party going for the entire summer. We'll be among the first guests to arrive, because he wants that security system set up. We're arriving ahead of schedule, just to throw him off balance. It'll be easier to do the job with no witnesses. If your man really is there to make a forgery of the painting, you can hand off the—" Ray snorted "—original forgery to us. We're gone before the dust settles."

"Sounds simple enough," Blade allowed. It was simple, compared to other jobs he had worked with Ray.

His imagination conjured up images of Jen in a bathing suit, stretched out on the deck of a sailboat, and him kneeling over her to rub on suntan oil. Lots of oil. A string bikini.

For a chance to spend time with Jen and protect her from the Casanova of the Inner Circle, he *should* consider the job.

Ray's smile twisted into that mischief-filled smirk that always spelled disaster for those on the wrong side of his schemes. Blade wondered which side he was on, as he bent his head over the computer schematics and he and Ray settled down to theorize and plot.

*   *   *

Halfway through Poling's dossier over a room service lunch, Blade knew he could pull off the identity switch. No problem. He was up-to-date on the latest forgery techniques. Whether Worley asked him to authenticate or forge the Dordt, he would immediately take the stolen fake and vanish. It would shorten the time Jen could be in danger, but it would also shorten the time he could spend in her company.

Problem: Did he do this for old time's sake or to work with Jen? Did visions of impressing her with his sleuthing talent, razor sharp instincts, and killer reflexes dance before his eyes? Did he follow a mirage out into a desert of frustration?

Heck, he was hot enough already to fry an egg.

If he had the wrong reasons, better to pull out while they could still find someone else to impersonate Poling.

The wrong motivation could get all of them hurt or killed. Blade didn't want Jen's blood on his hands.

He wanted *all* of her *in* his hands.

Back off and think with your brain, not your—

"What do you think?" Jen handed Blade a travel-worn passport and other paperwork. A soft, lemony scent surrounded her. Blade wondered if she tasted as fresh and clean as she smelled.

"It's you," Ray said. "Work of art, like always, Mrs. Williams." Something inside Blade snarled. "Remember what I told you about keeping your talents hidden."

"Beware recruiters who come on to me with the for-the-good-of-the-country spiel," Jen said with a chuckle. She flopped down on the couch and reached for the junk food buffet on the coffee table.

Watching her tuck away their lunch and then dive into snacking only an hour later made Blade grin and shake his head in admiration. How did Jen stay so limber and athletically slim, if she ate like that all the time?

His grin faded as his imagination pulled up images of Ray helping Jen work off all those extra calories. Blade mentally patted himself on the back for agreeing to camp out on the couch here in the suite, instead of getting his own room. Ray knew better than to try the horizontal mambo while Blade was within hearing distance.

Didn't he?

"The more you warn me," Jen continued, "the more curious you make me. I might agree to an interview, just to meet Shylock."

"You told her about Shylock?" Blade felt like he'd been kicked in the gut.

Their former Agency boss was not a person he would inflict on anyone. His worst enemies, granted, but not Jen. After that encounter with Chief Anguilano in the hospital parking lot, Blade was glad for every bit of warning Jen got.

"Not much to do when you're tied up, waiting for a building to blow, except talk." Ray smirked. "Just one thing lacking for you to play Poling."

"If working for Shylock is so great, how come both of us are flying solo?" Blade continued, turning to Jen. "Did you ever think of that?"

"We're working solo," Ray said, "because I'm a loner and you're a super-hero searching for a disguise and Jen..." He sighed and visibly searched for words.

"No sexist remarks from you, Mr. Williams," Jen said after hastily swallowing a mouthful of barbecue chips.

Blade groaned silently, watching her lick her fingers clean.

"I was just about to say, you're the ultimate team player, who knows how to motivate your partners to perform beyond the call of duty, pulling off miracles even I find hard to believe." Ray held out a hand. Jen tossed a can of iced tea to him. It smacked smoothly into his palm, with the ease of long years of practice.

Partnership practice. Blade shook his head, trying to shake away the images that filled his mind—Ray and Jen together, a lot closer than they were right that moment.

"He means I always make people feel like I'm a pathetic little thing." Jen reached for the chips and dug her hand in without rustling the bag. Blade admired that kind of manual dexterity. What could she do when she was off-duty, facing a totally different kind of physical hunger?

"She turns everyone around her into a knight in shining armor," Ray elaborated.

"Shining armor takes too much effort keeping it shiny. Give me the Black Knight any day."

"So you can break his face and use his armor for flower pots."

That earned a chuckle from Jen, which covered up the groan Blade couldn't muffle. Jen didn't *need* him. It sounded like she didn't need anyone.

"What was that last detail?" Blade asked, to detour away from that depressing thought.

Ray smirked and reached over to yank on his ponytail.

"We'll need to touch it up with gray too," Jen added, while Blade digested that requirement. "It'll look...distinguished."

Was there a caress in her voice when she said that? The throb that worked down to Blade's groin said yes. He suspected he'd shave himself bald if Jen asked.

All right, so Jen was his sole reason for joining this little retrieval mission. One of these days, Ray was going to realize the time he'd wasted and start making moves on Jen. Blade had to be there to protect her. Even if she didn't need a knight in partially-shined armor.

CHAPTER 5

"I have to warn you, I didn't study cosmetology." Jen took a deep breath and wished her hands would steady. She didn't need to drip silver dye all over Blade.

Not that he wouldn't look good in silver. Dull platinum armor, instead of that clunky, gleaming monstrosity King Arthur wore in "Excalibur." Blade didn't need to gleam blinding bright. One smoldering look from those eyes—

She squeezed the cup of silver hair dye a little tighter and got to work before either man wondered what was wrong.

"I trust you completely," Blade said, oblivious to the turmoil in her head. And chest. And nestled between her hipbones.

"Jen's an artist," Ray muttered without lifting his head from the fax that just came through.

"Trouble?" she asked.

"They're going to release Poling unless we can give them a reason for delaying him."

"The truth always works." Blade winked at Jen. "Tell them there's an imposter running around, and since his reputation isn't that spotless to begin with…"

Jen chuckled, appreciating his fast thinking. It also steadied her hands. She got to work streaking Blade's hair, one hair at a time.

She'd almost cried when he let them cut his gorgeous, thick hair without a whimper.

"You're going to need to use a gel to get it to clump like Poling's," she murmured.

"As long as I don't smell like a perfume factory, fine." Blade started to shrug. "Sorry."

"That's okay." She resisted the urge to smooth her hand over his shoulder. He hadn't really changed position.

Blade, smell like a perfume factory? Never. She'd never met a man who smelled so good. Most men she had worked with or fought against smelled of dirty, salty, metallic sweat. Blade smelled clean. Like cedar wood or sea breeze early in the morning.

He smelled safe. That was a crazy parallel to make, but Jen suspected her brain wasn't wired right. It kept her alive, so why fiddle with what worked?

Ray had a quiet sense of being wounded and wise that let Jen relax around him. He smelled warm, familiar, from the moment they met in that alley. Blade smelled like apple wood fires and baking bread, clean sweat and wool shirts. She knew she would get the same comforting, warm message from his hands. His smiles were full of humor, when not touched with that wistfulness that stole her breath. He'd been hurt. Maybe he was lonely.

What did she really know of men, except that ninety percent had hurt her friends? Then again, her friends had suffered, but they'd taken risks and eventually found Prince Charming. She, who had kept herself busy rescuing her friends and free of all entanglements, would likely never find anyone.

Was there such a thing as *too* cautious?

Jen stepped around to Blade's right to do that side of his head. The touch of silver gave more definition to his sculpted face. Like accent marks or italics on a page, it brought to light the alert, intelligent man she had observed so far.

How much private time would they have on Worley's island, away from the roles they played? Blade impressed her as being bedrock dependable, and she didn't want to get close enough to destroy that impression. She didn't want her first real white knight to fall.

Jen looked at Blade as she stepped back to review her handiwork. Really looked at him. Did she honestly want a white knight? He would look silly in armor plate. He was more the chain mail and leather type, with his hair hanging free, battle light in his eyes, face fierce, and covered in sweat.

Jen dropped the dye cup.

"That bad, huh?" Blade slid to his knees and dabbed at the dye on the carpet with the towel slung around his bare, muscled, scar-laced shoulders.

"Long day." She repressed a gasp when their hands touched.

His hand felt hot, lean with muscle and hard. It trembled, just before he yanked it away.

Jen bit her lip against a totally ridiculous smile and bowed her head so she wouldn't have to look at him. Her heart hammered in her chest and her imagination tore free.

Blade thundered across a torn battlefield, mounted on a black horse. He knocked the sword from her hand and swung her up into the saddle before him, making her pitiful resistance useless.

Black knight, yes, but a knight all the same.

*   *   *

"Old buddy, old pal," Ray drawled when Blade came back from studying his new look in the bathroom. "Do me a favor?"

"Depends." Blade knew better than to trust that smirk.

"Jen has to do a little shopping, and I just got bombed with some old business that has to be cleared up *now*."

"Ray," Jen groaned.

"We have to make it believable that Poling will fall for Gloria. He's too sophisticated for the current look."

"I really hate it when you're right." Jen rolled her eyes and tried to smile at Blade. "Hazardous duty, trying to turn me into a fashion plate. Are you up to it?"

"Shopping? What could be so hard about that?" Blade winked at her and his heart sped up when Jen actually seemed to blush. What had he done? "Can I borrow the 'Vette?" Ray hesitated. "Come on, Pops, hand over the keys."

*   *   *

"He's not driving the 'Vette," Blade muttered for the fifth time as he settled behind the wheel of his Cherokee.

"It doesn't fit Mark Williams's image. Fuddy, emphasis on duddy." Jen sighed. "I miss the 'Vette, too. A lot more comfortable than my motorcycle."

"Whatever." He jammed the key into the ignition. Then he glanced at her and a slow grin creased his face.

"Will you cut that out?" She ran shaky hands through her freshly-dyed auburn hair. It still felt wet. Or were her hands sweaty?

41

"You look good," he said as they left the parking lot.

"I feel like an idiot."

"Even idiots are allowed to look cute." He put the Jeep into gear and pulled out of the parking spot.

"Oh. Thanks ever so much." She kept her tone dry but inside, something turned cartwheels. Blade thought she was cute!

Stop it. Stop it right now. Get your mind back on track.

"Okay, Ray thinks you need help picking out a new wardrobe." Blade tapped on the steering wheel, waiting for the red light to turn green so he could pull out onto the street. "What you wore this morning was fine, if you're working the distraction angle. There's a lot to be said for wholesome. Sometimes it's a lot more sexy than see-through and ultra-short."

What she wouldn't give to distract *him* a little.

"We need a complete wardrobe, in case our luggage is searched. Sometimes I could just strangle him."

"Yeah, a dozen people have tried," Blade said. "Ray's got a neck made of lead pipe."

"Matches his head," she grumbled, earning a chuckle from him. "He thinks you know more about women's underwear than I do."

"Oh."

Long silence filled the Jeep as they drove through three more intersections. Jen finally got up the courage to look at him. Was his face a little redder?

*   *   *

They started with shoes at the mall. Blade wondered if he was suicidal, and braced himself to endure hours of studying Jen's legs.

Jen thought her one-inch pumps were too high. She flat-out refused to touch the strappy, spiked sandals Blade gave her.

"Look at it this way," he said, fighting not to burst out laughing. He wondered what the clerk at the front of the store thought about their whispered argument. "It's a weapon."

That caught Jen's interest. She took the sandal and studied the spike heel from all angles, probably considering the damage it would do to flesh and bone. Blade considered the distraction angle, and how watching her sway around on those stilts would set any man's blood boiling until his brain short-circuited.

They came away from that store with four pairs of deadly, glamorous shoes and headed for the next store, full of scarves, costume jewelry, and perfume. Jen opted out on the first dozen things he suggested; they made too much noise. Blade enjoyed changing her perspective about things from the inconvenience they caused her to how she could use them against other people.

Next stop—a cookie shop. Blade's teeth ached at the mere thought of triple-chocolate cookies. Jen inhaled two and saved the third for later. Studying her trim form and graceful movements, he admitted she worked it off fast enough. Blade remembered what Ray had said about Jen's sweet tooth.

"So, what exactly were you going to do on Worley's island before Poling entered the mix?" he said when he called a halt to get some coffee. They settled down in the mall's food court. Jen bought a peach smoothie.

"Our usual cover of gooey lovebirds. We'll have full access to the island to set up security. Now Gloria and Mik play tourist while Ray does the spying." She shrugged and stirred her straw through the pink, icy slush.

"Sounds like a lot of time sailing and sun-bathing."

"Getting skin cancer." Her eyes twinkled as she said it and Blade grinned back.

His smile faded as he slipped into a daydream of spending time sun-bathing with Jen. This was a definite step up, for him. How come his jobs usually involved dusty warehouses or sitting in dark, filthy alleys in the rain, while Ray got the glamour posts and beautiful, intelligent, witty partners? Blade needed to change his line of work.

Or bump off Ray at the first opportunity.

Jen sucked down a third of her smoothie in seconds. Blade shook his head and couldn't help a few chuckles.

"What?" she demanded.

"What's with you and sweet stuff? It doesn't stick to you longer than five seconds, but..." He shrugged. He wondered why he noticed everything she did, said, ate; the slightest shift in her attention or mood.

She put down the smoothie and really looked at it, dipping the straw in and out a few times. "We never had treats when I was a kid. I guess I'm making up for it. For all of us," she added in a softer voice.

Blade sensed this was one of those personal areas he would be smart to avoid, until Jen offered to explain.

*   *   *

"What do you think?" Jen held a lacy white ensemble to her

shoulders and turned to face Blade.

The gown hung to her ankles and had no side seams, just held together with dozens of bow-tied ribbons. The matching robe was sheer gauze trimmed in lace. It flowed like a snowy Christmas scene over her gentle, athletic curves. Blade imagined mistletoe hanging in the canopy of a bed. He envied the lucky dog who got to unwrap that Christmas present.

"Hot. But *not* something an old married couple would buy."

"How long have *you* been married?" She slid the hanger back into the lingerie rack. "Since you speak from experience."

"Never happen."

"Burned once too often?"

"Me?" He put back a red and black lace number, ready to proudly proclaim that no one had ever walked out on him.

Something in Jen's eyes clogged the words at the back of his throat. She was the last person he wanted to perceive him as a use 'em and lose 'em kind of guy.

"I don't get to stick around anywhere for very long," he said, in what he hoped was a reasonable tone of voice.

"I know the feeling. Sometimes I get jealous of Mark and Gloria. They have each other."

As they moved through the store, Jen put a few more outfits to her shoulders, oblivious to how all that lace and silk made Blade choke. He finally talked her into a silky jade pajama outfit—long sleeves, long pants, and a square neckline. The mental image of her wearing it around Ray made Blade's pulse and respiration do the cha-cha in panic.

"What do you wear to bed now?" he had to ask.

"Scrubs. If it's cold out, good old standard gray sweats."

"Oh. Okay." He bit his lip against a sigh of relief.

This was not happening. He was not feeling the territorial impulse after less than a day of knowing this girl.

This capable, brilliant, dry-humored, graceful, down-to-earth girl who didn't seem to need anyone's help. Except to learn how to be a sexy, dizzy young bride.

"You know, I'm the only guy in here. If I stick around too long, people are going to think I'm...warped." Blade grinned when Jen smothered laughter. He gestured at the benches out in the mall, two stores to the right. "Meet me there?"

"Sure."

Blade skimmed through the store, fleeing suffocation. He glanced back to see Jen head for the X-rated section. If she bought that black and red number...

*   *   *

When they returned to the hotel, Ray had set up the castle model, so they could brainstorm strategy. The plans Worley sent them didn't match the official architectural diagrams on file with Ottawa County. Worley had made a few additions to his castle to protect his treasures. He invited Mark and Gloria Williams to the island to protect those treasures. Jen just hoped Worley hadn't left out important details like hidden passages, sound-proof chambers, and dungeons where unwary guests would end up for the rest of their drastically-shortened lives.

More information came in from Ray's contacts. Jen sat down to study it while Ray and Blade worked on the castle diagrams and strategies. Before she stopped listening to them, they started discussing how to get down into the natural caves and tunnels under the castle, in case they needed an alternative escape route or hiding place.

By early evening, Jen had a sugar hangover that made her seriously consider learning to drink beer. Even her usual drowning-in-sweat workout in the hotel's exercise room wouldn't take away the bloated, brain-in-neutral feeling. It was Ray's fault. He might have teased her about all the junk food she consumed, but he had bought enough to feed an army. He put it all within easy access while they played dueling computers.

Blade made her nervous. For the first time in her life, a nice guy made her nervous. She liked the tiny buzz of energy that traveled up and down her spine and crackled in her fingertips every time she caught him watching her. Still, that couldn't keep her from cramming something into her mouth every time her fingers weren't busy. What was wrong with her? Jen knew her passion for junk food was some twisted psychological problem, a compensation factor to make up for all those days—weeks, really—when there wasn't enough food in the hideout to feed a single rat, much less ten hungry, frightened, angry children. Jen knew the reasons and reactions, so why couldn't she control herself?

Ray started making noises about taking a break for dinner. Jen didn't want to eat again for the rest of her life, or tomorrow morning, whichever came first. Then information filled her computer screen that made her forget her aching head.

"Trouble," she said, and scrolled down the screen to read all the information.

"What kind?" Ray stood and stepped around the table to lean over her shoulder, his hands braced on the back of her chair.

"One of Worley's guests just arrived. Two weeks ahead of schedule. I thought we were the only ones allowed to do that." Jen stopped on the photo and groaned.

"Magda Torrene?" He nudged her hand off the mouse and clicked the control to enlarge the photo.

The woman had high cheekbones and blacker-than-black hair framing her face in a cloud of curls that couldn't possibly be natural. Mascara enlarged and elongated her eyes like an Egyptian. Scarlet lipstick clashed with her rusty red V-neck plunge sweater.

"How do you know her?"

"I don't, really," Ray muttered. "You know her?"

"I wouldn't let you meet her in a dark alley."

"Uh huh." Ray grinned and sauntered back to his chair to sit down. He closed his computer case, glanced at Blade on the couch, and crossed his arms on the table. "Spill."

"Magda Torrene writes the Anastasia Peach novels." Jen waited for a reaction, but he didn't even blink. She glanced at Blade, and he didn't react either. "You know, that PI who carries padded handcuffs, and thinks she's having a bad day if she isn't groped by noon." She wanted to kick Ray under the table when he chuckled. "She should have died halfway through her first book from carelessness. Or a dozen STDs."

"So why is having the author on Worley's island a problem?"

"Magda Torrene claims to have been a police detective in real life. We don't want her getting curious, do we?"

"I think we can handle her."

"Better bring lots of penicillin."

"If she's the only other guest, we'd better change our plan of attack," Ray said after a moment of silence. "I'll handle Magda and keep Worley distracted and you two search. Think you can handle that?"

"I think I'll have fun and Magda can handle both of you."

"Something makes me think you've read more than a few of her books." He flashed her that innocent grin she didn't believe for a minute. "Jealous?"

She settled for giving him a "you wish" sneer and slouched until she couldn't see him over her screen. That little voice inside—the little girl who still believed in fairy tales and handsome knights—responded,

"Only if she goes after Blade."

"So, how do *you* know the name?" Blade said.

He wore that crooked little smile he had worn when they showed him Poling's picture and he realized he would have to cut and dye his hair. Something in his smile promised paybacks. Jen's headache began to dissipate. Blade was on her side.

"If you're suggesting I read those books...Well, one. Just to see what the fuss was about." Ray closed his computer with a snap. "The main thing to remember, folks, is that Magda Torrene is an innocent bystander. No matter what kind of books she writes. With her present, it's imperative we get the job done and out as quickly as possible."

"Borrow a 'copter from the Coast Guard, drop some C-4 at night, snatch the painting during the panic, and get out of there." Blade turned his head just enough to wink at Jen, so Ray couldn't see.

CHAPTER 6

Blade jolted upright and awake when the first moan filtered through the closed bedroom door. He swung his legs off the side of the couch, then stopped. Was it any of his business what Ray and Jen did during down time?

The clenching in his chest and his desire to feed Ray a knuckle sandwich told him their extracurricular activities already meant a whole lot more to him than was wise.

Another moan. Blade gritted his teeth and fumbled for the pillow, to pull it over his head. The moan became a whimper.

That wasn't pleasure. That was fear.

A sob broke from Jen's throat and Blade slammed through the bedroom door, with a vague memory of leaping over the couch. The light between the two queen-size beds came on.

The snap-shot, frozen moment stayed in his mind for years afterward. Ray, his hand on the lamp, sliding out of the right-hand bed, dressed in running shorts. Jen, huddled against the headboard of the left-hand bed, dressed in scrubs.

Sweat plastered her clothes to her limbs. Her eyes were wide open and glazed. Incoherent words spilled from her mouth, volume rising with every syllable. Tears spilled down her face.

Ray leaped, grabbed Jen, slapped a hand over her mouth and rolled her into a tight embrace.

"It's over," he whispered, and shook her a little. "Jen, it's over. You're safe. It's okay." He raised his head and seemed to see Blade for the first time. "Water."

Blade stumbled into the bathroom. What he really wanted was to hold Jen while she whimpered and struggled her way out of her nightmare. He ran the tap until the water was clear and cold. He nearly dropped the glass when it occurred to him that Ray had too much practice with Jen's nightmares.

Jen sat up on her own, arms wrapped around herself, when Blade stepped out of the bathroom. Ray plumped the pillows and made her sit back against the headboard and reached for the glass of water. Blade ignored him and sat down on Jen's other side. He put the glass to her lips and held it for her while she gulped and spluttered, until her trembling hands steadied enough to hold it for herself.

"Better?" Ray moved back to his own bed and sat on the edge of the mattress, just watching her.

Blade didn't like that warm, concerned expression Ray wore. It was nothing like the masks he used to control and manipulate people to get his job done.

"Embarrassed, but I'll survive." Jen's voice sounded rough, as if she had screamed for hours.

"Which one was it?"

Blade decided he had heard enough. He started to slide off the mattress, but found his hand captured between Jen's hands and the glass. She flicked a glance at him, then away. Something inside him warmed when he realized she wanted him to stay.

"The oldest one. I should have known working on that mockup of Worley's castle would bring it on." Her voice cracked as if sand filled her throat.

Blade guided the glass back to her lips. His thumb brushed against her sweaty chin as she swallowed the last mouthful.

"Thanks." She managed a thin smile. "When I was little, we lived in this big old house that I thought was a castle."

"Makes sense." It didn't, but Blade knew the important thing was to let Jen talk it out until she felt better.

"Why not tell Blade?" Ray said. "If you hold it inside, it'll just keep festering."

"It's not festering!" Jen's hands closed around Blade's, almost to the point of pain. She glared at Ray, which cheered Blade more than he liked to admit.

Jen and Ray had a friendship relaxed enough to tease each other, some affection, but nothing physical. Blade sat close enough to take Jen into his arms and hold her if she started crying again. He was happy, and that meant he was a sick man.

"My folks...there were a lot of us. A lot of grownups. It was like a commune, I guess. A big family. My parents were the leaders. Information brokers." She shrugged.

Blade's mouth went dry, getting a close-up view of movement underneath those damp cotton scrubs.

"They could get information on anyone and anything. They had connections all over the world. Like a huge spider's web. They got the wrong people angry with them. I was almost fourteen when...everything went wrong."

"You don't have to tell me," Blade whispered.

"No." Jen shot him a sideways glance. A tentative smile. "Ray's right. I need to talk about it. The others don't like to talk about it, but I need to."

She took a deep breath and let go of the glass—and Blade's hand—to rake sweaty hair out of her face. When he put the glass down on the bed, she reached for him again. From the corner of his eye, Blade could have sworn he saw Ray smile, just for a second. No way in the world was he going to explore *that* territory right now.

"Our parents sent all us kids—ten of us—to a place in the country, where we could be safe. But their enemies were just as good at digging up information as my folks. They bombed the house before we even got there. We ran back home...and it was in flames. We had to protect the nest egg, and I was the oldest, so I had to protect everybody."

Nest egg? Blade mouthed, turning to Ray. The other man just shook his head, meaning he should leave that question for later.

"When I dream of my folks, I always dream that I get there just as the house explodes." Jen's voice shuddered. "I'm so close, I just know I can get in and save them."

"They were dead long before you got there," Ray said in a soothing voice. "There was nothing you could have done."

"I know." She closed her eyes and sagged against the headboard. "Sometimes I think I shouldn't have gone into hiding. We could have played dumb. Convinced people we didn't know what was going on, that we were just scared kids. Nobody would have come looking for us. We would have been taken care of."

"You don't know that."

"No." Jen opened her eyes and caught Blade staring at her. A crooked grin caught one side of her mouth. "You're wondering what the heck we're talking about, right?" She sighed and stretched. The way her damp cotton scrubs clung to her lean shape turned up the heat in the room. "My folks had information going back more than a century. Where skeletons and treasures are buried, all over the world. They knew it was still dangerous, even after so long, so they kept it hidden in encrypted files, any kind of media, multiple storage, hidden all over. They left the key and the treasure map with us kids, so we'd have bargaining chips to protect ourselves against the self-righteous, slimy—" Her mouth twisted and a stream of foreign words spilled from her lips.

Blade nearly laughed, impressed, as he caught a few words and realized Jen used half a dozen languages, all mixed together in an angry stew of invective.

She stopped short, likely halted by whatever expression he wore. Jen stared into his eyes for a few seconds, then she blushed and a ragged chuckle escaped her.

"You don't happen to have a psychology degree, do you?"

"Nope." Blade reached for the glass, when what he wanted to do was tell her he had a ready, dry shoulder if she needed it. "More water?"

"I need something stronger." She raked sweaty hair out of her face again. "Chocolate syrup, straight from the bottle."

"What you need is sleep. Want some help?" Ray stood and crossed the room to the dresser and his closed suitcase.

"Dr. Porter's snake-oil. No thanks." Jen pretended to shudder. "Do you trust any of his magic powders?"

"He's saved my life a time or two," Blade admitted. "Amazing how much of a mad scientist's laboratory he carries in that little black bag of his, huh?"

"You need your sleep." Ray changed course and yanked a T-shirt off the chair at the end of his bed. He pulled it over his head and gestured at the door. "I need some coffee. Join me?" He gave Blade a meaningful nod and went out into the living room.

What Blade really wanted to do was join Jen. He liked the idea of holding her until she slept, then staying to keep the nightmares away. "Sleep tight," he muttered, and hurried to follow Ray. What was he thinking, caring so much, getting so protective of someone he had just met?

"Might as well get some more work done," Ray said, and turned the light on over the dining table.

"Does she have nightmares like that a lot?"

"We don't share a bedroom often enough for me to know."

Blade didn't want to pursue that line of thought. He stomped into the kitchenette and snatched up the coffee carafe.

*   *   *

Blade lay on his side on the couch when Jen slipped out of the bedroom at six the next morning. She bent to yank the blanket off the floor and tuck it back around him, then paused. An old friend of Ray's, from his Agency days, was likely to break her neck before he completely woke.

Shaking her head, Jen crossed to the kitchen to see if there was anything to eat before she went to the exercise room. She didn't want to face Blade after that nightmare last night. Especially not when she had lain there in the dark, listening to the low rumble of voices and wishing Blade would come back and hold her hand.

Even worse, she wished she had been wearing that white lacy confection she had bought. Would he have done more than hold her hand? The problem with that was that Ray would have seen her in it. Jen most definitely didn't want Ray seeing her in it.

She blamed Ray for her brain and hormones being all out of whack. He kept more secrets from her than usual. Maybe she was still upset over the game he had played, using her as bait to lure Blade in. Especially since he had won.

There was something going on. Even taking into account Mik Poling's arrival and Magda Torrene coming to the island early, she and Ray could have handled the job just fine without any extra help. This was a minor league operation, so why had Ray worked so hard to get Blade's interest? Ray never did anything without several layers of hidden agendas. The same gut instinct that had kept her alive at age fourteen said Blade Hampton was more important to this operation than Ray let on. But why?

Not that she wouldn't like having Blade Hampton around. Jen smiled ruefully as she finished inspecting the echoing refrigerator and reached for a cupboard door. She liked his sharp sense of humor, his different way of looking at the scenario—and even the way her breath stopped short every time he skewered her with those gray eyes.

Who knew a cupboard door could creak like a gunshot?

Blade leaped from the couch and was halfway to the kitchen before the creak ended. For a moment he stared at Jen, his chest bare and heaving, creating interesting patterns in the coarse, blue-black curls that emphasized every muscle.

"Up late playing *Doom*?" Jen forced herself to turn and hunt for something to eat—anything, no matter how bizarre. Otherwise she would stare at that chest and follow the arrow pointer of hair down to the unbuttoned waistband of those jeans.

Not good. Hormones were most definitely not allowed out to play until the job was over.

"Playing what?" Blade asked.

"How late did you stay up, working?"

"Long enough I don't want to know." Blade scrubbed his eyes with his fists. "I'm getting too old for this kind of crap."

"You'll never earn your *Man from U.N.C.L.E.* decoder ring with that attitude." His bark of laughter sent warm shivers through her. "Seems the locusts hit last night after I went to bed. I'm hitting the coffee shop next to the exercise room. What do you want me to bring back?"

"Whatever you're getting Ray." He headed back to the couch and reached for his boots.

"Him? He's been awake and out for nearly half an hour."

"I hate him. He's six years older than me, and he acts like he's indestructible." Blade yanked hard on one rawhide lace.

"He has coffee for blood, and if he didn't love extra garlic on his spaghetti, I'd sleep with a wooden stake in..." Jen forgot what she was about to say, as her gaze met Blade's.

So, that was what people meant when they said they fell into someone's eyes. She couldn't get a good grip on her train of thought—which had left the station without her, long ago.

"Face it. He's Superman."

"Nope. I've seen him in his underwear. White. No cape or red boots." Her face burned as she wondered if Blade preferred boxers or briefs, and what color. Or maybe none at all?

Straighten out, girl!

"So..." She swallowed hard, trying to kick-start her brain. "Is Blade your real name?"

"Munroe." His crooked grin emphasized the tiny scar next to his mouth.

"Oh." Jen nodded. "Blade suits you better."

"Glad you approve." He stood up from tying his boots. "I think maybe I better join you. Us decrepit old folks need all the exercise we can get."

*   *   *

Ray caught up with them in line at the coffee shop, debating the merits of oat bran apple muffins over the old standby fry cake dripping in chocolate syrup. Blade looked up and saw Ray in the window of the coffee shop, watching them. Just watching. Blade hated that calculating look, the tiny sparkle of mischief and satisfaction. What was his former partner up to now?

Ray nodded to him and gave a tiny salute; two fingers tipped off his eyebrow. Then he yanked the door open and came into the shop. Blade almost laughed when Jen gave a tiny groan. She also had experience with Ray at his scheming worst, and knew what that smirk and the jaunty angle of his head meant.

He and Jen definitely had more in common than he thought.

"Coffee break's over, children," Ray murmured as he slid his arm around Jen and drew her out of the line. "It's about time you dragged yourself out of bed, sweetheart," he said, louder, with that rich, fake laugh Blade wanted to yank out of his throat. It made him think of politicians who kissed babies while plotting to poison the environment.

Ray kissed Jen's cheek as they left the coffee shop.

Jen didn't even blink. Didn't miss a step. Was she so used to playing Gloria Williams, getting kissed by Ray meant nothing to her? Blade stopped short in the doorway, stunned by sudden euphoria. Jen *didn't* react to Ray's kiss. Other women would be red from hairline to painted toenails after a single, meaningless kiss. Jen just kept walking.

No, not walking. Ray and Jen turned and waited for him while Blade stood in the doorway, feeling like he had discovered a pimple the day before the prom.

"Flight arrangements all set," Ray said, when Blade rejoined them. "This afternoon you're heading out on a courier plane to make connections and appear to come in on a trans-Atlantic flight. You'll hit Cleveland tomorrow morning." He reached into his blazer and pulled out a manila business envelope, crammed to bursting with papers.

"Still keeping up the old connections, I see," Blade said as he took the envelope.

The three kept walking as he jammed the envelope into his back pocket. Blade didn't look at Jen. He didn't want to know her reaction to his imminent departure. The plan was that he would arrive at Worley's island, complaining about international flights, and get to know the layout before Mark and Gloria Williams showed up.

The smoother the job went, the sooner Jen could safely leave the island. It might mean an abrupt end to their make-believe love affair, but her life was more important than his pleasure. Wasn't it?

CHAPTER 7

"Jen. Blade."

The too-quiet tone of Ray's voice sent a shiver up Jen's back. She glanced over at Blade, who read one more time through the file on Mik Poling before leaving to catch his flight.

"Come look at this." Ray never raised his gaze from his computer screen, and held out a hand to beckon.

She stepped around the table and leaned against the back of his chair, looking over his right shoulder. Blade stood where he could lean against the wall and look over Ray's left shoulder.

Jen's first impression of the man on Ray's screen was of elegance. Cold. Thick, wavy brown hair spilled over a wide, high brow. Deep-set, vibrant blue eyes, wide cheekbones, narrow nose. She sensed an arrogant touch to him—a fleshier version of Peter Cushing but with none of the warmth he displayed in *Star Wars*.

"Guy Sarpantine. The story is that he has his hands in nearly everything that can possibly be illegal. If he isn't directly involved, he has influence over those who are."

"He's one of Worley's guests?"

"Scheduled for later this summer. Shortly after we're supposed to finish setting up the security system. My contacts are worried because he's broken all his known patterns, and that means he's up to something. At this time of the year, he's usually on the Riviera." Ray leaned back in his chair and rested his chin on one hand as he studied the screen. His unblinking gaze made Jen itchy. "If I thought there was the slightest chance he'd show up while we were there…" He glanced at her, and his smile was paper thin. "First thing I'd do is burn all those sexy clothes Blade made you get. Then I'd lock you in your room and try to give you a couple infectious diseases."

"Isn't that overkill?" She tried to smile, but that hardness in Ray's eyes told her a different story.

"Overkill is Sarpantine's specialty," Blade said. The coldness in his voice seemed warm and comforting compared to the ice in his eyes as he stared at the man on the screen.

"We'll be long gone before he shows up, Jen. And if you ever see this man anywhere, run." Ray gripped her hand, giving emphasis to his words. "In a lot of ways, you're still innocent. And you're pretty. That combination can be deadly if Sarpantine sees you. He doesn't like to waste time when a woman catches his eye. Date rape drugs are just the tip of the iceberg."

"So, I won't eat or drink anything he might have touched." She shrugged.

"You'll run to the next country, if he shows up." The steel in Ray's voice and the fire in his eyes shriveled her comical retort before it reached her lips.

"If he shows up while we're in the middle of the job, we can't exactly pack up and leave," Blade said.

"So, you hold him down and I'll stomp his head into the ground."

"You get all the fun jobs." He rolled his eyes in mock exasperation, but his attempt at reassurance and humor didn't work. "Don't worry, Jen. He's not coming anywhere near the island while we're there."

"And if he does?" she had to ask.

"Let's hope Magda Torrene decides to run interference."

"If he even drools in Magda or Jen's direction," Ray said in a dangerously calm voice, "he's a dead man."

Why, Jen wondered, was Ray so protective of Magda Torrene? He didn't know her. That didn't mean he would abandon her to Sarpantine's slimy clutches, but why the white knight vehemence all of a sudden?

She caught her breath as suspicion slammed through her gut. Was Magda on that list of people Ray planned to investigate; the list she had barely started to read when she had hacked into his files? She definitely had to get some time alone with Ray's computer, and do a far deeper investigation. And soon.

*   *   *

Blade watched the ground recede beneath him as the first of his three connecting flights lifted into the air. He had already contacted Danville Worley to let him know Mik Poling was arriving ahead of schedule. The aging thief sounded genuinely delighted at the news, and Blade had it on good authority the fat man couldn't act his way out of a wet paper bag.

If Worley had the slightest suspicion something was wrong, Blade would have heard it in his voice. The man would have hesitated, stammered, or stumbled over his words. Worley was relaxed. He didn't mention his early guest, Magda Torrene, and Blade didn't know what to make of that.

He smiled as he remembered Jen's voice and expression when she described Magda's books. If her reaction to the woman stayed just as strong, just as negative, it would certainly add to the distraction factor provided by their fake love affair.

Blade's stomach dropped at the thought of Magda chasing him. He hoped Jen put on a good performance, so no one would wonder why notorious Mik Poling chose sweet little Gloria over available, experienced, sensual Magda. Maybe the angle he should use going in, was that men always wanted a challenge. Someone who was too easy to obtain was no fun. It might even work in their favor that Magda Torrene had showed up early. He could give her the brush-off from the beginning, using that attitude.

The only real problem Blade could foresee was remembering that it was only a game, a role he played, and he wasn't falling in love with Jen.

*   *   *

Funny, how someone could so quickly become a part of the scenario in little more than a day. Especially when she hadn't even known he was alive a week ago.

Jen slouched a little further in the extra-wide couch and stifled a sigh. She tried to tell herself she missed bantering with Blade, not his gorgeous face and the warm, clean scent of him. Certainly not the way his eyes went wide and burned when she modeled some of the outfits he recommended.

She smiled, and knew it was a nasty smirk. She did love getting him flustered. It didn't take long to realize the skimpy, fragile outfits that bothered her the most, which Blade said would do the best distraction work, were the very ones that tied his tongue into knots. Sometimes, she could have sworn steam escaped his ears. Jen knew she won half her wardrobe battles with Blade because, though he might advocate those clothes on principle, he didn't want *her* to wear them.

Jen hoped that was because Blade liked what he saw and didn't want other men to see her looking that way.

That brought on another sigh. She could run around this suite in her underwear and Ray wouldn't notice. Not that she wanted him to. That was like trying to cuddle up and get smoochy with her foster-brothers or her alleged cousin, Tyler Jackson. She felt comfortable with Ray, like he was her long-lost blood-kin. Ray took care of her like she was his little sister.

Emphasis on *little*.

Sometimes she could strangle him.

Especially when, the more she thought about it, she knew Ray had something else up his sleeve. Why had he sent Blade shopping with her? Ray could have called some friends, told them her size and the kind of clothes he wanted, and the wardrobe would have been delivered without any fuss or the need for her to put on shoes.

Shopping with Blade had been fun, and Jen had never liked shopping. That meant Blade was the reason.

Another sigh.

"Bored?" Ray asked without glancing up from his computer.

"Fried brain. I need a break or I'll be useless tomorrow." She slid a little lower in the couch. Even the old stand-by of ordering one of every dessert in the hotel, just to irritate Ray and satisfy her growling sweet tooth, didn't hold much appeal.

"Enjoy the rest while you can. Starting tomorrow, you're Gloria, twenty-four/seven."

*   *   *

Blade flinched as he caught a glimpse of himself in the bathroom mirror. Either he got used to his shorter hair and the streaks of silver, or he stopped looking in mirrors until this job was over.

So, here he was in his room on Worley's island. The trip to Sandusky, Ohio had been uneventful. He spent it boning up on Mik Poling's vital statistics. When he reached the marina in Sandusky where he was to cross the lake to the island, he put all the papers in an outdoor grill at a state park by the docks, doused them with lighter fluid and waited until every scrap was black and crumbling into dust. The temptation to hold onto his reference material was a trap that could get his throat slit.

Worley's groundskeeper, Hanson, met him at the marina less than half an hour later and took him to the island by private launch. At the docks that faced north to Canada, they were met by the other groundskeeper, Heinrich. Neither man was much for small talk, and seemed to resent Blade's innocent questions about the staff, which guests had arrived already, and what Worley planned to do for the next few weeks.

Hanson and Heinrich could have been brothers—lumpy body and face, receding hairline, protruding brow, gray-blond hair, perpetual scowl, and hulking shoulders. Blade didn't know whether to laugh or run for his life when Hanson walked him to the front door, carrying his duffle and overnight bag, and a woman who surely had to be his sister opened the door. She was Martha, the housekeeper. Another woman, Greta, was the cook. Blade wanted someone to wager him that Greta looked enough like the other three to be their sister.

Either that, or he had walked onto a movie set for another tiresome movie about Nazis and cloning experiments.

Martha and Hanson escorted him to the tower, which held all the guest rooms. Neither one offered any explanations, other than to tell Blade to make himself comfortable and their employer would be back from the big island in another hour to greet him.

The circular staircase wound up through the tower four stories. Blade's room was on the third floor. One other door opened off the landing. He had to assume, since no one was forthcoming with details, there was another suite sharing that level with his. He could only pray Jen and Ray were assigned to the same floor, to make communication and secret meetings a little easier.

Miss Torrene, Martha muttered before she and Hanson left Blade alone, had a room on the first floor.

Blade said a quick prayer of thanks for that good fortune. Not that climbing two flights of stairs would do much to discourage her, but he would at least have some time to throw himself off the balcony. Women like Magda Torrene didn't scare him so much as they made him feel like snakes crawled up his back while he hung above a tank of moray eels.

Blade didn't consider himself a sexist or a cave man, but there were just some basic rules he felt the world should follow. Men did the hunting in a relationship, and the women ran until they felt like catching the man. Women were to be the backbone of the home and society, setting the rules for what was good, pure, and true. Men divided into two camps—those who tried to hurt and corrupt women, and those like Blade who beat those same men to a bloody pulp. They were the good guys, who got to ride off into the sunset with a pretty lady like Jen.

"Tomorrow isn't coming any too soon," Blade whispered. He crossed his bedroom and tugged aside the floor-to-ceiling pale blue curtains that hid the sliding balcony door.

It offered him a good view of the main harbor of Put-in-Bay. That meant the other balcony looked toward Canada.

Before he turned back into the room, Blade noticed one of the many boats tooling around the harbor headed straight for Gibraltar Island. He waited, watching, staying still in the shadows cast across the balcony that ringed the entire tower. He could walk from his balcony door to the door of the other suite. Something to keep in mind if Ray and Jen ended up there.

There were only two people in the boat. A heavyset man in a gaudy red and blue Hawaiian print matching shorts and shirt. And a woman with long black hair, dressed in red that even from that distance clashed with the red the man wore. Blade would have gladly wagered that was Magda Torrene. *Didn't the woman know any other colors than red and black?* He remembered Jen's distaste for the woman's books, and wondered if he would have gained a good idea of how her mind worked if he had read one. Or two. Judging from the snide remarks Jen made, he knew it would irritate her if he did read one. Especially if he liked it.

He rather liked the idea of making Jen jealous. That wasn't part of the battle plan, though. Blade watched the boat come around the tip of the island. He circled the balcony, keeping the boat in sight and studying its passengers until it was nearly to the dock directly underneath him. Then he turned and went back into his room.

He had just finished putting away his clothes, debating if a little uninvited exploration fit Mik Poling's profile, when there was a knock on the door. He waited a few seconds before going to the door to look out.

"Mik Poling." Danville Worley held out a sweating, meaty hand.

Up close, his brilliantly colored clothes did nothing to tone down the red of his complexion. Judging from the rolls of fat and the glistening sweat beading on his face, neck, and arms, both high blood pressure and his weight affected him. His tiny brown eyes were lost in his cheeks and Blade was positive that thick matt of hair was actually a wig or a badly-done weave.

"I'm delighted to finally meet you," Worley continued, shaking his hand and releasing it. "Welcome to Gibraltar Island."

"Glad to be here." His voice settled into the lazy, burring drawl he had picked off tapes of the real Mik Poling's conversations. "So, what's the scoop?"

"We're not talking business for a while yet. You and Magda are the first of my guests. There will be eight of us soon, and we're going to enjoy ourselves, first. What's the good of all this money if I can't have some fun, eh?" He chuckled, jiggling far more realistically than any department store Santa Claus.

"Yeah, great," he said with a totally genuine smile. "I could use a vacation."

Blade smiled because he knew there would only be the five of them. The other three guests expected this week were being detained by different government agencies. Ray had notified the agencies currently most eager to put those three into custody. Blade enjoyed a feeling of warm satisfaction to know that this little expedition to save a senator's reputation would benefit many others.

"Come meet Magda. We dine informally tonight," Worley continued, as he headed for the stairs. He paused at the top, and Blade realized his host expected him to follow. "When the others get here, then..." He chuckled and gestured expansively. "I enjoy playing lord of the castle."

Yeah, and the castle is about to come toppling down around your ears. Blade followed him down the circular stairs. If he hadn't read the dossier on Worley's activities, he might have pitied the man.

"My friend, as a favor to me..." Worley paused on the landing just before stepping down into the marble-paved entrance hall. For a moment, Blade thought the man flushed a slightly darker red than sunburn and high blood pressure could be blamed for. "I know your reputation. As a master of creating and detecting forgeries, as well as your skill with the ladies."

"Don't worry. I have no plans to create a forgery and leave it with you while I make off with the original."

That, at least, was far more truth than Worley would want to hear.

"Oh, no, not that." Worley shook his head, and his flabby jowls waggled. He nearly smiled. "I am bringing in two geniuses in security, to protect my new treasure. I'm not going to take it from its safe place until they have finished their work. I want them to be happy while they work. So I must ask a great favor of you. They are husband and wife, and the lady is sweet and innocent. I ask you, as the man of honor you are, don't play games with her heart."

"You think her big bad security chief husband will beat my face in?" Blade said with a grin.

"Hardly. The man is a fool and wouldn't know how to make a fist, let alone use it." Worley snorted contempt. "No, I want you to leave lovely little Gloria alone so she won't be distracted while she's doing her work. Please? The sooner they are done, the sooner you can do your job and perhaps earn a bonus for...speed." He offered a hollow little laugh.

"Yeah. Sure. Whatever." Blade shrugged as if the idea of seducing a computer geek's wife bored him.

Inside, he felt like he had been handed a map to a mine field. Worley himself already suspected what would happen and was trying to head off lover-boy Poling before he got his engines revved. He played directly into Ray's plan—which meant he was distracted, thinking more about his guests' activities than the safety of his precious stolen painting.

Blade wished he looked forward to playing a hot-blooded lover in pursuit of an innocent, unsuspecting lady.

The problem, he knew from the start, was that he wouldn't be acting. Every hungry look and sigh, every sweet word he lavished on Jen would be based on a very real and growing desire for her. Painful as all get out.

"Magda," Worley called as he led Blade through the dining room. They exited through French doors onto a patio overlooking the vast expanse of lake. "Magda, darling, I'd like you to meet Mik Poling, another guest for the next few weeks."

On the other side of the buffet table set up on the silver-white flagstones, a slim figure in red and black lounged against the raw stone wall. That particular spot offered a less-than-spectacular view of the docks, on top of a short cliff. Blade had laughed when he first saw the setting, and wondered how Worley had let his designer cheat him so badly in that area.

Then the woman turned and Blade forgot about the view as his instincts went into battle-ready survival mode. A goblet of wine in one hand, she put her back to the disappointing view and looked Blade up and down twice before responding. Her scarlet lips parted in a slow smile, and she licked them slowly.

"Mr. Poling, how delightful to meet you. Our darling host has told me practically nothing about you."

She oozed off the wall and sauntered over to join Blade and Worley. If he hadn't seen her six-inch black glittery sandals lift up and set down again, Blade would have thought she moved on wheels. Or maybe floated. Maybe slithered.

All of Jen's worst fears about Magda Torrene came true before his eyes. That cold finger down Blade's spine told him the hungry fire in her painted eyes was all for him.

He cursed Mik Poling's reputation, which required him to respond to the woman like a kid in a candy store. It was definitely time for Mik to become bored with easy targets. Blade was glad he had made those battle plans before he arrived. If he hadn't been prepared, his blood might be at the boiling point already, with no place for the steam to go.

He remembered thinking about his rules for men and women. Blade suspected he would bend those soon, and pray for Jen to rescue him from this walking, breathing lamia.

CHAPTER 8

"Thanks," Ray said into his cell phone. He tapped Jen on the shoulder as she picked up her computer case to walk down to the dock. She turned and he gestured for her to wait.

Now what had happened? The boat from Worley's island pulled in below them. The whistling of the wind off the lake made good interference if anyone tried to listen to them talk, but now was not the time for a last-minute conference or change of plans.

"The owners of the real painting know," Ray said under his breath. He looked past Jen, down the wooden steps, and waved to the pilot of the fifty-foot launch. The wide-shouldered man raised a hand, but otherwise didn't pause in tying up the boat.

"How did they find out?" Jen refrained from asking what they were going to do. Ray already had a plan in mind, she knew. That's what she loved and hated about him.

"That doesn't matter. They know what's at stake, so it's not like they're going to blab it to the press." He picked up his computer case and slung it over his shoulder, then wrapped his other arm around her waist. "Smile, Mrs. Williams. This is the most glamorous vacation you've taken since your honeymoon."

"Where did we go on our honeymoon again, Marky-poo?" Jen stifled a squeak when Ray dug his fingers into her ribs in rebuke. "Why is it bad news that the other owners know?"

"They've hired their own PI to help out."

Ray guided her down the steps. Slowly. They could take their time, since the pilot had only now climbed out to load their luggage from the dock into the back of the boat.

"Work faster, get out sooner?"

"We don't need any rookie players joining the game at the last minute," he agreed. "Tell Blade as soon as you can."

"What's the PI look like, so we can be ready?"

"No idea. Be grateful they warned the senator, or we could have been blindsided at the worst possible time. Hey there!" he called, raising his voice and using the clipped tones he had created just for Mark Williams. The pilot of the launch paused with the last piece of flower tapestry-covered luggage in his hands. "Your boss sure knows how to live. How much does a boat like this cost?"

Jen sighed. There were times when Mark Williams, computer geek and social klutz, was amusing. Now was definitely not one of them. She climbed on board, pretending to need Ray's help, and settled down on the nearest padded bench. Jen let Ray keep the pilot busy with inane questions while she rolled the latest bit of news through her mind.

A new, unidentified player in the game was not good news. Did this PI know there was already a team working to retrieve the forged painting? If so, why had he agreed to join the hunt? Did he think they were incompetent, after spending four weeks on preparation? Or was he an arrogant jerk who would rush in, try to yank the painting from their grasp and claim all the glory?

At the very least it would take some effort for this PI to get onto Worley's island. Jen considered the timetable for this job. With only a little adjusting, they could get it compressed down to a week. If Mik and Gloria jumped into their alleged love affair this very night, it would be more than understandable if Mark got jealous, rushed the security work and beat it off the island. No one would be suspicious at all.

Jen closed her eyes as the launch pulled away from the docks and the lake breeze slapped at her face. Her best jobs were the ones that required a quick insertion, obtaining the object with minimal fuss, and just as hasty retreat. So why did the revised plan suddenly make her feel tired and depressed?

*   *   *

"I wonder if Gloria gets seasick."

"We're on a lake, and it's a little late to think of that." Ray slid an arm around Jen's shoulders and gestured at the docks of Gibraltar Island, just ahead of them.

"Duh." Jen managed a thin smile and let herself be mesmerized a few seconds longer by the splash of the waves against the bow of the launch. "I've been here before." She gestured to their left, past Perry's Monument overlooking the wasp waist of South Bass Island. "The most relaxed summer of my life. Tyler likes to come here just to get away from the pressures of his business. He rented four cottages for us and we just sat in the sun and ate and relaxed."

"I want to meet this cousin of yours one of these days. How exactly are you related, anyway?"

"Dunno." Jen turned her gaze from the monument and back to Gibraltar. "His folks were always aunt and uncle, that's all. When you don't have anybody in the world, you don't question the few relations you think you do have. Know what I mean?"

"I know exactly what you mean," Ray muttered, just softly enough his words were nearly drowned in the roar of the launch's motor, the rumble of the wind, and the splash of the waves.

"Someday, I'd like to retire to the islands."

"You'd hate it, isolated all winter."

"I'd love that part."

She tried not to twitch her shoulders under the weight of Ray's arm. Physical closeness with him had never bothered her until Blade showed up.

In the two days since Blade left to take up Poling's identity, she had found it hard to concentrate on anything but him. That became a problem when Ray drilled her on the layout of Worley's castle and all the possible hiding places for the missing painting. If Ray hadn't volunteered gobs of information about Blade's career in the Marines and the Agency, she might have broken down and begged for it. Why *had* Ray become so talkative?

Maybe he was worried about Blade?

If Poling got away, Ray's pals in INS and Interpol would let him know. But what if a friend of Poling's waited at Worley's castle and tripped up Blade? How would they know they were walking into a trap if Blade couldn't warn them?

You're getting paranoid, she scolded herself. Any more of this worrying and she'd throw herself into Blade's arms and burst into tears the first time she saw him.

Bad idea.

Bad for their cover story and fake identities and any hope of respect from Blade. She sensed he respected people who could stand on their own two feet. Tears would turn him off faster than drilling him about his sex life on their first date.

"And there he is," Ray murmured, and gave Jen's shoulder a squeeze before stepping away from her side. "Center stage and looking bored out of his skull."

Bored. She had to play Gloria as bored too. Jen raised her gaze and looked everywhere but at the lean figure walking down to the dock with paunchy, sweating Worley to meet the boat.

Amazing how much detail she could pick up without looking. Wide shoulders, draped in a muted blue silk shirt, that the lake breezes molded to his chest with such perfection. Black pants that emphasized his long legs. A black-haired woman with lips as the red as the dress painted on her hung on his arm.

Blade could give lessons in bored. It radiated off the rocky shore of Gibraltar Island and Worley's castle. It screamed he was so bored, he couldn't be bothered to remove the bimbo leach at his side.

Ray whistled softly as he returned to her side. "Will you look at that? Wonder who worked fastest."

"It's a wonder she can work at all, standing upright."

"Meow." He chuckled. "I read one of her books, remember. Stacy Peach makes James Bond look like a tired old man who needs Viagra. I'd say you've got a fight on your hands, except…"

"Except what?" Jen flinched at the desperate note that tried to creep into her voice.

"Except Blade looks miserable. He's going to be mighty glad to start chasing you, I think." Ray winked and stepped away, toward the prow of the boat.

Jen blinked hard, straining her eyes. She hoped Ray was right. How was sweet little ditzoid Gloria going to compete with that slinky monochrome model glued to Blade's side?

How was she, Jen, going to rescue Blade from that woman?

*   *   *

"Hello, neighbors." Blade leaned back against the balcony railing so he could look through the open sliding door into Ray and Jen's suite. "You don't travel light, do you?" He nodded at the notebook computers and wheeled crates full of equipment for setting up the security systems.

"Sorry—lousy with names." Ray offered that goofy Mark Williams grin Jen was coming to loathe.

68

"Mik. Poling," Blade added after a few seconds, during which he scanned the room.

His gaze came to rest on Jen with all the weight of a safe, and a hot tingle of electricity. She didn't have to pretend to be stunned for the benefit of Worley's man, Heinrich, who had brought their luggage upstairs.

It had arrived after a rather long delay, meaning their equipment had been searched. Worley had taken them on a quick tour of his castle that took nearly an hour, yet they beat their luggage upstairs. Still, the delay wasn't long enough for the inspectors to find anything really dangerous, so why waste the time at all?

Worley, she decided now, was paranoid, but *stupid* paranoid, and not nearly thorough enough. He certainly deserved to be cleaned out and spun around a few dozen times, just like they planned.

"What's all that gear for?" Blade crossed the five feet of balcony to the doorway.

He lounged against the frame, still watching Jen instead of the gear. Heinrich flicked a glance at him, then at Jen. She saw the tiny scowl the man gave Blade and wondered why. The last thing they needed was to get the help irritated with them.

Or maybe that was Blade's plan. Get everybody irritated so they all watched him make a play for another man's wife. It would leave the landscape neglected, ripe for Ray to pluck.

It just wasn't fair that she would have to spend so much time playing sweethearts with Blade and none of it would be real—with an audience, to boot. Jen could almost wish Ray's plan called for Mark Williams to make an idiot of himself with Magda Torrene and leave *her* to hunt for the painting.

"Oh, we just carry that with us everywhere." Ray dropped into one of the antique French Provincial chairs. He shrugged, raked his fingers through his hair, and pushed the bridge of his glasses up higher with his thumb. "We do lots of consulting-type work, and it pays to be prepared. Even when we're on vacation. Right, baby doll?"

"Right." Jen settled on the edge of the bed to watch Heinrich unload the last piece of equipment into the six-foot-deep walk-in closet. "Where are you staying, Mr. Poling?"

"Mik. Please call me Mik." Blade stepped through the doorway, keeping one hand on the frame as he looked around the room. "We're all here to play. No formality. And, as luck would have it, I'm right across the landing from you two lovebirds."

"That's good," Ray muttered, closing his eyes. He crossed his hands over his stomach and slouched a little.

"Really?" Blade waggled his eyebrows at Jen. "Why would you say that?"

"Don't like being alone in a place like this."

"And what do think about this, Gloria?"

"Fine with me." She toyed with the lacy edge of her sundress and wished she could get into her sweats and go for a good run to get rid of the tension that made her want to break something. Or grab the nearest candy machine and shake it empty.

"All done," Heinrich grunted. He stepped back, closed the closet door and wiped his hands on his drab green work pants. "You need me to do anything for you, Mr. Poling?" he added, as he stepped for the door.

"Nope. Everything's hunky-dory. Thanks, Hank," Blade said. He nodded and gave Heinrich a fake, too-wide smile as the man finally left.

Silence. Jen counted her heartbeats. She listened to Heinrich's footsteps on the hardwood floor of the landing, and then going down the steps.

At twenty-five, Ray opened his eyes, reached into his jacket pocket and brought out the security scanner delivered to the hotel just yesterday. He looked at the LCD screen no bigger than his thumbnail as he flicked the green beam of light around the room in a slow, overlapping pattern.

"Idiot," he finally said, and turned off the device.

"All clear?" Blade asked in his own voice, not the drawl he used for Mik Poling. When Ray nodded, he let out a huge sigh and slumped down into another of the French Provincial chairs by the door. "This place is a fancy loony bin, but still a loony bin."

"Magda giving you trouble?" Jen didn't care how nastily sweet her voice sounded.

"Can you loan me some garlic and a silver cross?" He shuddered, but his grin made her feel better.

"Has Worley heard about his delayed guests?" Ray asked.

"Whimpering and complaining about how unreliable they are. He doesn't suspect a thing. Yet."

"Good. What's the word on the painting?"

"*Nada.* Worley likes to show off his toys, and he's determined to play and have a good time before anybody gets down to work," Blade said.

"Is that the impression you got?" Ray turned to Jen.

"He's more interested in playing lord of the castle than Jack Benny and his vault." She shrugged. "With the security we've seen so far, I don't know what he needs us for."

"There is no honor among thieves. Worley stole it, so he expects someone to steal it from him."

"Who else knows he even has it?"

"Yeah," Blade pointed out, "but a guy like him likes to boast. And speaking of honor among thieves..." The Mik Poling lecherous look had vanished, but the intensity that replaced it still made Jen shiver. Pleasantly. "Worley's already convinced Mik is going to make a play for Gloria and distract her and Mark from their job."

"Perfect," Ray whispered. "Dinner's in an hour. We'd better start getting dressed. Ready to be swept off your feet, Mrs. Williams?"

Jen nodded. Something thick caught in her throat, so she was afraid to speak. She looked away from Blade. She didn't want to see the Mik Poling mask slide back into place.

*   *   *

Blade sauntered across the inlaid wood floor, pretending to study the haphazard pattern of walnut, golden oak, and cherry shades under his feet. Worley had told him all about the trouble he had obtaining it. Like most things Worley owned, the original owners had been reluctant to part with it. The man didn't seem to value anything unless acquiring it caused someone distress.

People like Worley should never be allowed to breed, Blade had always believed. They should be punished drastically, to discourage anyone who thought that kind of life was glamorous. But then, Blade would have nothing to do, without the scum of the Earth to battle and trick and frustrate.

Worley's voice echoed off the vaulted, gilded plaster ceiling and the windows. He was especially proud of the antique windows, stolen from a French chateau. So proud, he didn't use curtains to soften the acoustics.

Even Worley's accent was fake—rolling and rich with a little whiny sneer, like King Tut in the old *Batman* TV series. Blade suspected Worley wore theater makeup. After all, he constantly performed for his lady guests.

Blade gritted his teeth and told himself Jen only played a role. That glimmer in her eyes came from boredom. She had confided to him that Worley's ostentation made her nauseous. She walked through his vast, gilded house and could only think of all the orphans and foster children who could be fed by the money this house required just in maintenance. This castle would make an excellent orphanage for at least one hundred children. Blade admired her for hating so much wastefulness.

Still, she acted too much like Magda. Twittering with glee at being the focus of Worley's attention. Ooing and aahing over the riches scattered around them—excessive to the point of being vulgar, if anyone asked Blade's opinion.

No one had asked his opinion yet, which worried him. He was supposed to be here to verify the stolen Dordt was genuine. Worley refused to talk about the painting. Blade had kept busy identifying the few genuine articles among Worley's treasures and evading Magda's red-painted talons. The first time she tried to attach herself to him, at hips and lips, his main concern had been whether he was up-to-date on all his shots. She had to be a walking incubator for a dozen deadly diseases, at least. For all he knew, she was on a liquid diet—blood and wine.

Maybe he could ask Jen to get into a cat-fight with her? Push her off Worley's artfully engineered Lover's Leap?

"Fascinating place," Ray commented as he wandered around the perimeter of the room.

Ray looked like a prosperous geek. Silver-rimmed glasses just a shade too large for style, the lenses tinted pale blue. His thick black hair combed back from his forehead to make his face look square. Hunched shoulders under a cardigan a little too bright green, clashing vaguely with his sage green pants. It took skill to mishmash colors so they seemed to work together and yet subconsciously screamed like fingernails on a chalkboard. Blade was grateful Ray hadn't chosen plaid.

Jen belonged on a magazine cover. She wore a sundress in pale blue with a border of strawberries and leaves along the bottom. Sandals in pale golden leather with low heels. Tiny earrings and necklace in matching strawberry motif. Blade knew she would smell of strawberries. That pale pink lip gloss probably tasted of strawberries. He wanted to walk over there and steal a kiss in front of everybody. It made him ache, like he wore a parachute harness too tight in all the wrong places. Every part of Jen's outfit accented her innocent elegance and made Ray look more goofy by contrast.

"How much do you think everything here cost?" Ray played Mark Williams, super-nerd, to the hilt. His voice was just loud enough to be heard by their host.

Worley's smile widened, but he didn't even glance over at him. Blade had already decided Worley lived for envy.

"Oh, almost as much as the originals," Blade said after a momentary pause.

"Originals?" Ray-Mark rocked back on his expensive heels—leaving a black scuff mark on the glossy floor. "What are you talking about?"

"Good forgeries cost." Blade shrugged and turned away, pretending to be bored with everything and everyone.

"Glo thinks it's great." He tagged after Blade. "I wasn't too hot about taking this job, not quite in our line of work assembling security systems for private residences but..." He shrugged. "Glo wanted a vacation, and she wanted to see a real castle and my Glo gets whatever she wants. Isn't she a beauty? Can't believe she's all mine."

Blade took his partner's words for the cue they were and concentrated all his attention on Jen-Gloria. Anyone else listening to a rich geek would take those words as a challenge. Anyone else would try to romance the moron's wife out from under his nose, just to teach him a lesson.

The problem was, Blade wanted Jen *before* this scheme had ever come together. If he spent every waking moment pretending an affair with her, when would he ever get to know her? He would kiss her and hold her in his arms when the scenario demanded it, and none of it would be real.

He was in big trouble, if he felt this way about a woman only a few days after meeting her. Correction...a few days after she knocked him on his back and stepped on his throat. Blade smiled, conjuring that image of Jen's lean, graceful leg, topped by a glimpse of pale green panties.

Get your mind back on business, boy, or all three of you are dead in the water.

"Yeah, you're a lucky man," Blade said, after a pause. "Take good care of your pretty little lady, Mark."

Ray-Mark chuckled and babbled about how he had met Gloria in a college computer class he taught. Blade played at being bored Mik Poling and gladly walked away halfway through the monologue. Ray-Mark didn't even notice.

Across the room, Magda's eyes glimmered with malicious laughter. Blade hoped she would give up assaulting his bored façade and choose another target. Which meant Ray. He almost looked forward to watching Ray tie Magda into mental knots, when she tried to set her claws into him.

*   *   *

"Where is Magda?" Worley asked the next morning. He paused in the middle of his spiel about the wonderful day they would have on South Bass Island, investigating its quaint treasures.

Ray, Jen, and Blade stood with him at the docks, about to board the smallest of Worley's three boats to cross the bay to the community of Put-in-Bay. The morning sun shone blinding bright on the water and the breeze blew strong and cool. Jen felt glad to be alive.

It also helped to be wearing shorts and sneakers instead of her ridiculous high heels and skirts. For some reason, she always felt half-naked when she wore skirts, vulnerable. Not that she would be stepping on someone's chest or throat any time in the next week or so, but the next time she did it, she didn't want him looking up her skirt.

Unless he were Blade.

Jen's face felt unaccountably warm, despite the chill in the breeze off the water.

"Thought she was right behind me," Blade said in his most bored, Mik voice.

Jen imagined Magda would be just behind Blade. Ogling the view and yielding to the temptation to touch. She remembered his references to the woman being an Anne Rice reject, and wished she could solve the problem with a stake through Magda's heart.

"Excuse me," Worley muttered, and strode away from the docks. He puffed up the stairs to the long patio and vanished around the corner. A moment later, the French doors off the ballroom clicked open and closed.

"You don't suppose she fell off her stilts and broke her neck?" Blade said.

"We couldn't get that lucky." Jen settled down on the edge of a wooden planter box full of petunias.

"Nope, not lucky at all." Ray nodded, directing their gaze up the stairs. Magda scurried down the steps with Hanson.

She wore navy blue today. Short shorts that would have made Daisy Duke blush, and a halter top that seemed all strings—more

74

appropriately, a spider's web—in back.

"Silly me." Magda flounced along the wooden walkway and jumped into the boat ahead of them. "I made a wrong turn. I have no idea how I ended up where I did, but Mr. Hanson was kind enough to help me get out without breaking something." She turned to the man and wrinkled up her nose and made a kissing gesture toward him. Hanson scowled and turned back to the house.

Maybe Magda was silly, but Jen felt a shiver along her scalp that told her otherwise. Gut instinct said those smears of dusty grit and grime on Magda's hip, calf, and the side of one hand came from the tunnels that existed before Ohio State University set up their research station.

During the grand tour of the castle yesterday, Worley had mentioned the tunnels, but said they had been blocked off. The few that remained accessible were too dangerous for his guests to even look at, much less visit. He had shown them the barred and padlocked door outside the castle, leading down into the tunnels, and then took their tour indoors again. Jen knew what the underground caves and tunnels were like from exploring on South Bass Island. From the looks of things, Magda had done more than wander through the off-limits area. Looking for something?

Worley sweated and puffed down the steps to rejoin them. Magda apologized profusely, walking her fingers up and down his arm and giggling. Jen wondered if the woman had no pride at all, even as Worley accepted her apology and smiled again.

She glanced over at Ray and found him studying the gray-brown smears on Magda's leg too. He looked at her and winked. Then he clumped across the deck and deliberately stumbled, ending up in a heap on the floor with Magda.

The woman squealed, but she didn't sound offended. Jen could have sworn Ray's hands were in five places at once, all seemingly accidental. Magda blushed, but she kept laughing.

"That man should get a purple heart," Blade whispered in Jen's ear. His breath brushed the side of her face and her neck, sending her insides into meltdown.

Fortunately, the engine roared into life and the boat pulled away from the docks, and Jen didn't have to answer. She shivered a little when Blade took her hand to help her into a seat. Would his touch always send those electric pinpricks up and down her spine, or would she get used to it?

She prayed that never happened.

CHAPTER 9

All that warm, drowsy day, Jen had to remind herself this was only a role, a game, and she played a computer twit being swept off her feet. Otherwise, she would have fallen into the dream that it was just her and Blade, exploring the island and getting to know each other.

Magda let them know she was an expert on speed boats and sailboats. She loaded them with more information than any of them could want to know, just in the time it took to cross the stretch of water between Gibraltar and Put-in-Bay. When they reached the docks at the town center, she demonstrated her knowledge of the types of golf carts the day-trippers rented to tool around Put-in-Bay. The island offered historical sites, museums, shops, restaurants, and beaches to visit. South Bass Island provided a bus service or bikes or carts to rent. Jen wished they were all on bikes, but Worley would have had a heart attack within a mile. It would only be harder to retrieve the painting if their portly host died on them.

Worley drove them around, playing tour guide and acting as if he owned the entire island. Jen almost burst out laughing when he donned a navy blue captain's cap and took up the entire front seat of the eight-seater cart.

First stop was Perry's Cave, where Admiral Perry allegedly set up headquarters during the Battle of Lake Erie. Blade put his arm around Jen to steady her down the narrow concrete steps descending into the cave. His touch made her wobbly.

In some ways, the cave reminded her of the basement where she and her adopted siblings hid during those first few months after their parents died. The damp in the air, the smell of wet stone, sitting water and slimy things growing in the dark clung to her bare arms and made the ground feel unsteady under the treads of her too-new sneakers.

Blade insisted on holding her hand. That made it hard to hear the guide's stories about the cave. Jen tried to concentrate on their companions, to hold off the sensation she would turn into just another puddle on the gritty floor.

Magda squeaked when the guide talked about bats living in the cave, and took the opportunity to grab hold of Ray's arm and hang on. Ray must have seen it coming, because Jen saw him take a side-step that let Magda stumble across him instead of into him. She hit Worley and her face went as red as her clothes usually were, as she struggled back to her feet.

Jen exchanged tiny grins with Ray as the guide went on to point out the old, mineral-crusted pipe running through the cave below the waterline that pumped water across the island.

Blade got the guide talking about the caves under the island and prodded him into speculating on caves that might exist under Gibraltar Island. Jen couldn't decide if he simply matched Magda's know-it-all maneuvers, or he searched for information.

Blade seemed to know all the history of the Lake Erie islands, and all about wine, and none of it seemed false. He proved that when they crossed the street and visited the winery attached to Crystal Cave. Jen knew nothing about wine, but Blade waxed so eloquent about island wine, she wanted to learn.

"No, honey." Ray shook his head and pushed his glasses higher on his nose. "I don't think that'd be smart, do you?"

Jen glanced at Magda, saw her smirk and wanted to punch the slinky vamp.

"What harm could it do to just take a couple sips?" Jen forced a Gloria giggle.

"Remember our wedding?"

"How could I forget?" She batted her eyelashes at him.

"Well, you forgot how you almost fell off your high heels and broke your ankle after just one glass of champagne." Ray grabbed hold of her arm and squeezed twice. Definitely a signal, but of what? "Go look at all the pretty stones over there." He gripped her shoulders and turned her to face the gift shop.

Jen's protest died in her throat when she saw the man standing by the opposite wall, looking at a display of geodes. Ray squeezed her shoulders, gave her a meaningful look, and sauntered back into the bar area to rejoin the others.

Tyler Jackson. What in the world was her pseudo-cousin doing here on South Bass Island?

Jen's face burned. She had been getting gooey over Blade, when she should have been on the alert to avoid complications. Complications such as her childhood partner-in-crime seeing her, calling her by name, and blowing her cover story to atomic dust.

Ty looked good. A self-made millionaire at twenty-seven, he could go anywhere and do anything he wanted, but like her, he chose to devote his resources to helping the "family." He had been born with the Midas touch and had honed it in those aching years when fear, anger, and the hunger for revenge had welded the ten of them into a synchronized whole.

Mari had been the master of disguises, able to make them all look far older than their years, to shield them from perverts and Child Welfare workers. Jen had been their data coordinator, weaving new identities together from stolen glimpses into files and the fragments they had salvaged from their destroyed home. The Sanders twins were their thieves, keeping them fed and clothed. Lila, Amber, and Devon were better scouts and point guards than Green Berets, keeping them one step ahead of danger. Tyler learned early to turn a handful of change into enough money to feed them for a week. With his fake identification, he set up bank accounts and played the stock market. He gave them the insulation of money to obtain a home, then computers to rebuild the network their parents had ruled.

No one of the group grudged Tyler his wealth, because he plowed more than two-thirds of it back into their efforts to help abandoned and abused children. If Ty wanted to spend the summer goofing off, Jen didn't grudge him the down time. But why in the world had he chosen to do it now, and here, during a job that could blow up in her face?

"Hey, cuz," she murmured as she stepped up beside him.

"Thought that was you." Tyler didn't turn from studying the display behind the glass. Their eyes met in the reflection.

More than any of the others in the family, Tyler truly could be a blood relative. The two of them had the same big, dark eyes and glossy dark, soft curls with just a hint of red in the summer sun. He stood a head taller than her and his hands were wider, fingers longer, but there was a striking similarity in the general shape of their faces and hands.

They even had a tendency to put all their weight on their left hips and cock their right knees out to the side.

Jen noticed that posture now, twins reflecting in the glass. She corrected her stance, putting both hands behind herself and rested on her heels equally.

"Fun and games?" Tyler murmured.

"Can't talk about it."

"Can't or won't?"

"No time."

"Might need your help." He moved over to the next display case, making it easier to see into the next room and keep an eye on the other four.

Worley gestured at the menu on the wall, probably waxing eloquent about the wines available here. Ray wore his patented golly-gee look of geeky awe. Magda looked slightly nauseated. Blade looked bored. Then he glanced over at Jen and their gazes met just for a moment.

"Help with what?" Jen moved over to the display case of amber jewelry for sale, next to the cash register.

Tyler followed and rested his elbows on the metal frame of the glass case. He toyed with a few key rings made of crystals.

"I think somebody's after Rufus. He'll barely admit he's been sticking his cyber nose where it doesn't belong. I swept him out of town to avoid some leg-breakers. I figure, he's in trouble because of data I asked him to hack for me."

"You could have asked me." Then Jen wondered if that was technically true. "Can I help?"

"I know you have connections you don't talk about." Tyler squatted to look into a display case from the front. "Maybe ask if somebody Federal can take a look our way."

"Wow."

"Somebody's sneaking around at the B&B where we're staying. If Rufus gets hurt, it's my fault. I asked him to check things. I gave him the equipment to do it."

"You're just a nice guy who likes to help geeks follow their passions without fear of starvation." Jen smiled.

"If you weren't my cousin, I'd marry you. You know that, don't you?" Tyler pressed his hand over his heart for a moment.

"Heart-breaker."

"Family reunion?" Blade stepped between them.

Tyler slowly rose to stand upright. Jen felt the protective tension radiating from him. None of her foster brothers had ever needed to defend her, but she had always known they'd risk broken bones for her sake. Jen felt a flash of gratitude for Tyler, quickly replaced by fear for him. Ray had given her a thumbnail sketch of the self-defense training Blade had taken in the Marines. She didn't need to exercise her imagination to know Blade could take anything in this room and turn it into a weapon if he had to.

"I don't know what you're talking about, Mik." Jen forced out her silly Gloria giggle.

"Tyler Jackson." Tyler held out his hand. Blade looked him over before gripping his hand. "I was just asking the lady what she'd recommend. There's this young lady living next door. I'd sure like to make friends, but I don't want to scare her off with something too big and expensive right at the start. Know what I mean?"

"Flowers," Blade said, just a little too quickly. "Unless she's allergic, you can't miss with flowers."

Jen felt a dropping sensation inside. Blade would probably never give her flowers. Or would he soon, as part of Mik seducing Gloria? The flowers wouldn't be anything but a stage prop. Jen found that the saddest thing she had contemplated in a long time.

Oh, straighten up, you nit!

After a few more empty comments, Blade wandered over to the other side of the gift shop. Jen didn't doubt he strained his ears to spy on her. Didn't he trust her to protect their cover?

"I'll let you know what's up when it's all over," she murmured, and stepped around Tyler to look into another gift case. "How long will you be around? And where?"

Tyler glanced up at the sound of a footstep. Jen bit back a snarl as the long-absent clerk shuffled over to the register.

"What's available across the street?" he asked, turning away from the counter. She didn't have to glance past Tyler to know someone watched them.

"Lots of rocks and dirt. There's some pretty stuff. What do you think of this?" She gestured at the bins of polished bits of semi-precious stone sitting by the open doorway.

"Did you drop this?" Tyler bent down. A piece of paper appeared at his fingertips and he stood and handed it to Jen. She nodded her thanks and glanced at it once as she put it in her pocket. An address and phone number were written on it, and "all summer." She could get hold of Tyler if she needed help.

Would she need help? It took an effort of will not to glance over at the next room, where the other four were probably tasting wine. Jen had no idea if she could handle a glass of wine or not, because she'd never tried it. A sense of injustice rose up and choked her. There were so many things she didn't know about, just because she'd always played it safe. She had responsibilities, people to protect.

Well, maybe it was time to relax and have some fun. Ray watched over her like she was his only child, and that irked her too, now that she thought about it. But if she had someone watching out for her, why couldn't she relax and let someone else be the guard dog at the gates for a change?

"I'd better run." Tyler stepped toward the door. He winked. "Who's the geek and who's the spy?"

"They're both ex-spies. One's my husband and the other is trying to have an affair with me." Jen rolled her eyes and found her sense of humor returning when Tyler snorted. "The fat guy with the bad rug is our target."

"What about Elvira?"

"Pass the garlic. But about your pet computer geek, Ty...be careful. He isn't as harmless as he seems. I don't trust him."

"You don't trust your own shadow, cuz." He winked and put one foot through the open door.

"I trust you."

Surprise widened Tyler's big eyes for a moment. He seemed about to say something, then shrugged, nodded to her, and vanished outside.

A shiver crawled up Jen's back. Didn't Tyler believe she trusted him? He was as close to family as she'd ever had. Why wouldn't she trust him?

That brought her back to her thoughts about relaxing and letting someone else run security for a while. Jen wondered if that was half her problem. She had a hard time letting go and trusting someone long enough to have fun.

If she didn't learn to do that, she suspected the only love affairs she would ever have would be fake ones, performances played out with an ulterior motive.

*   *   *

"What's with the 'cousin' thing back there?" Blade asked. The roaring of the wind, Magda's renewed lecture on wine, and the grumbling of the golf cart going down the road covered his voice.

Jen and Blade sat in the back seat. Ray and Magda sat in front of them, with Magda clutching Ray's arm as if she couldn't sit up straight on her own. Blade figured she was trying to make him jealous. Worley had the front seat all to himself, simply because he took up most of it.

"We grew up together." Jen leaned close enough to talk, but not close enough to suit Blade. "Our folks were murdered, and all us kids stuck together for safety."

"What about the girl he wanted to give something? Trying to get you jealous?"

"Me? Why?"

"Maybe he's a kissing cousin."

"Ty? I don't think so. If he says there's a girl he's interested in, it's true." She smiled, glancing up at him. Blade felt a light, warm sensation move through his chest. Then she gasped as the cart whipped around the corner.

Blade gladly wrapped his arm around her shoulders and tipped her upright. Not that she had fallen, but that was something Mik Poling would do. He was supposed to seduce the innocent little computer technician, wasn't he? Sometimes Blade felt disgusted by the roles he played, but today wasn't one of those days. Jen blushed faintly and wouldn't look at him, but she didn't move out of the circle of his arm. Blade liked that.

He hoped she didn't consider it a performance, because right now, it was very real for him.

*   *   *

Jen wanted to kick Ray. She wanted to kick Blade, when she caught the glances the two men shared whenever Magda and Worley were distracted by sightseeing. They looked smugly satisfied with their plan so far.

Every time Magda dug in to enforce her alleged claim on Blade, Jen wanted to yank on her hair, positive it was a wig. She prayed Magda's bust was all foam padding. How could someone so skinny *not* pad her bra? Every time Jen got the urge to inflict physical damage, she had to remind herself that Gloria was an oblivious little idiot, getting swept off her feet, and she wouldn't know another woman was horning in on her territory. Knowing that it was all a game for the three of them didn't help because it *wasn't* a game for Magda.

As the conflict escalated, Ray-Mark stepped further back into the shadows where he thrived and watched everyone. Soon, Jen knew, he could vanish for hours at a time and no one would ever realize he was missing. He could explore and hunt for the painting while Gloria and Mik kept the others entertained.

Jen should have felt satisfaction, but only had a headache. She wanted Blade to keep playing Sir Gallant, helping her in and out of the golf cart as they visited the island's maritime and sea life museums.

How could Blade put so much hunger into his voice, and make his eyes burn like that when he actually felt nothing?

She'd probably faint the first time he kissed her—or maybe throw up. Or would she be so frustrated by then, ready to explode, that she would forget her role and punch him?

Every time she daydreamed of wrapping herself around Blade, Ray reminded them of his presence and their mission.

Ray wanted to go see the longest continuous bar in the world. He whined when Worley and Blade voted against it. When they went down the street to get ice cream, he asked for a flavor they didn't have, then grumbled and stomped out of the store.

"Peaches and cream, huh?" Blade took up what seemed to be his favorite position: leaning over Jen's shoulder.

She could have understood if she wore a sundress, because it fit Mik Poling's reputation to try to look down her front. Jen was frazzled enough to admit she wouldn't mind Blade trying to look for himself. The warmth of Blade's breath on her neck made her shiver.

"She's just a down-home little gal," Magda said with a simper and a fake Southern accent.

"Pure and sweet and wholesome, more like," Blade responded. "That looks really good. Mind if I take a taste?"

"Taste?" In any other situation, Jen would have thought of twenty different responses, but her mind refused to cooperate now. Today. With Magda sneering at them. That glimmer of purely sexual hunger and teasing in Blade's eyes froze her brain.

"Just to see if I should get some of my own." He waggled his eyebrows at her and stepped closer.

A tingle raced up her arm when he took hold of her hand and guided the ice cream to his lips. Jen went hollow inside when he stuck out his tongue, ever so slowly, and took a tiny, leisurely lick at the side of her ice cream. All the while, he watched her, but she couldn't seem to take her gaze off his tongue.

This is stupid! a part of her roared, deep in her mind. Jen had a brief mental image of her common sense and survival instincts, bound and gagged in a dark corner infested with spiders and dust, while some hormone-driven, weak-kneed mute held the driver's seat of her body.

"Try this," Magda offered, stepping over with her cone. The ice cream was so deep dark chocolate it looked black, glistening with oozing syrup and chunks of fudge.

Triple chocolate sin. Jen had wanted that flavor, but Magda beat her to it.

"I don't think so." Blade released Jen's hand.

"Too sophisticated? I'd think you'd have a very…mature palate." Magda took a long, leisurely lick of her ice cream.

Blade winced. He looked at Jen, one corner of his mouth quirking up in that smile she wished was meant for her—Jen—not for ditzoid Gloria.

"Overkill," he said, and stepped to the counter to order peanut butter chocolate. "Simple is best."

"Too simple is boring," Magda nearly growled.

"Maybe." Blade paid for his ice cream. "But not this time. Want to share?" he asked Jen as he stepped back over to her and put his cone within two inches of her mouth.

Magda snarled and stomped out of the ice cream shop as Jen smiled and nodded and opened her mouth.

She watched Blade, looking deep into his eyes just as he had done to her, and stuck out just the tip of her tongue to taste his ice cream. Blade's lips parted as she took the little lick. Instinct clamored, and Jen took a second, larger taste. Blade swallowed hard and his hand trembled.

"Glo?" Ray stomped back into the ice cream parlor. "Babycakes, what's taking you so long? Sorry, Mik. Gloria's a genius when it comes to finding one rotten code in two gig of files. Ask her to choose something simple like ice cream…" He held out his hand. "Come on. I want to go check out the airport. Maybe we should buy a plane."

"She was helping me choose what I wanted." Blade hooked his arm through Jen's and neatly tugged her out of Ray's reach.

Jen opened her mouth to tell them to stop the jealous cave man act. Then she looked past them and found Magda and Worley watching through the screened doorway.

When *wouldn't* they have an audience?

She stumbled when Blade turned the cone and dragged his tongue over the little dent she had left. Magda made a choking sound and slammed her way down the wooden boardwalk. Worley scurried after her.

"That should keep her claws out of my back for a while," Blade whispered. His voice cracked with suppressed laughter.

Jen wanted to shove his ice cream cone up his nose.

"That wasn't what we wanted," Ray muttered back. "The more ruckus you three cause, the less people will be watching me."

"You're just scared she'll go after you next," Jen retorted. It was either tease Ray or tie her insides into knots. "Are you up to date on your shots?"

"Watch your mouth, Mrs. Williams." He winked at her.

"I'd rather do that, thanks," Blade said. He released Jen's arm, caught her hand, and pressed a kiss against the palm.

Jen couldn't seem to get her brain back online during the rest of the tour of the island. The problem here was that her emotions had engaged, along with her hormones. The stories Ray had told her about Blade, rising above life on the streets, becoming a Marine Corps hero and getting recruited by the Agency, only added to her interest. She admired him. She couldn't step back and treat this like a play on stage because Blade was a real person to her, not a target, not a prop, not a co-player.

If only Blade's attentions were real.

CHAPTER 10

Heinrich met up with the tour party at the bottom of Perry's Victory Monument, ostensibly to discuss dinner with Worley. The staff couldn't call to consult with him because he had left his cell phone at the castle. Several items hadn't arrived on time and the menu had to be changed. Supposedly.

Blade didn't trust Heinrich. What else was written on the sheet of paper he gave his employer to look over? He glanced over at Ray, who had been griping about a headache the entire time they had been at the top of the monument with its 360-degree view of the island and Lake Erie. Ray nodded, then tipped his head toward Worley's handyman. Blade had no idea what Ray was about to do, only that he had a plan. Well, they had always succeeded when Ray led and Blade played along, back in the days when their lives and the country were on the line. He could still play along. He just prayed it didn't involve leaving him alone with Magda.

"Hey, this is great timing," Ray said, when Heinrich turned to go. "I have got this killer headache. Mind if I hitch a ride back to the island? Wouldn't want to ruin it for the rest of you, making you go home early." He shuffled over to follow Heinrich.

"Sir?" The handyman turned to Worley.

"Yes, of course. By all means." Worley widened his eyes at Heinrich and nodded vigorously. His smile looked forced.

Blade wondered if Heinrich wasn't so much a servant as a co-conspirator. Worley couldn't have succeeded so long if he was the idiot he seemed. That meant his henchmen were brilliant and willing to let him pretend to be the boss, while they did all the thinking. Or he was boss in name only, and too arrogant and silly to realize it.

That might change their plans. He had to get alone with Ray and mention that suspicion before evening. Ray had the first snoop shift tonight. Insomnia from a headache would be a good excuse for wandering around where he wasn't expected, but would Worley's henchmen accept that excuse if they caught him?

Ray climbed into Heinrich's golf cart to ride back to the docks with him. Blade caught a glimpse of movement from the corner of his eye and saw Magda about to pounce on him.

"Gloria." Blade made his voice oily. "Pretty lady, what are you going to do now that Mark's abandoned you?" He slid an arm around Jen's shoulders.

"Oh." Jen's eyes went wide. "Well, I guess I should go with him, shouldn't I?"

"Not on your life," Blade growled under his breath. He walked her down the steps to the road, where their golf cart waited. "Leave me to Magda's clutches and I'll haunt you for the rest of your life."

Jen snorted, smothering laughter. She glanced back over their shoulders and frowned.

Magda shrieked. Blade turned and leaped, prompted by instinct. He didn't reach the steps in time. Magda went down, one leg crumpled under herself. She hit the bottom step and rolled.

"Oh. Oh. Oooh!" Magda pulled herself upright before Worley could huff down the steps or Blade could kneel next to her. "My ankle. I really did a number on it." She wrapped her hands around her left ankle and whimpered.

"Gee," Jen said. "Guess we all have to go back to the island now, don't we?"

Something in her voice made a chill race up Blade's back. As if he could read Jen's mind, he knew what she suspected. Had Magda fallen on purpose?

*   *   *

"Like she doesn't want any of us alone on the island," Ray said an hour later, when Jen reported on what had happened.

"Maybe she's working with Worley?" Blade said. "Since you were going to show up before everyone else, she decided to show up early too, to keep you out of trouble?"

Jen wondered why it didn't make her feel better to know there was more dirt to Magda than showed on the surface.

The three sat on the patio overlooking the docks. Ray lay sprawled on a wheeled chaise lounge with a wet cloth across his forehead, pretending to suffer a headache. Jen wanted to smack him. He always seemed to gain such enjoyment from playing his roles and irritating people.

"Could be," Ray said slowly.

"She probably gets a lot of her Stacy Peach stories from real-life criminal activities, then," Jen offered.

"Half right." He waited. Jen wasn't about to oblige by asking for more information.

"You know something about her we don't?" Blade asked.

"Magda Torrene is just a pen name."

"Excuse me." Jen put one foot up on the end of the lounge, tempted to give it a shove and send Ray rolling across the flagstone patio. "I read the page with the copyright information. It's registered under Magda Torrene."

"An alias. Second identity. Magda Torrene, Inc." Ray slid the wet cloth off his forehead and flashed that Mafioso-arrogant grin that reminded her of her long-vanished Uncle Giovanni. "Her real name is Mary Margaret Tortelli, and in real life she's an insurance investigator."

"Insurance." Blade whistled softly. "She's here to help with the forgery. Mik makes fake documents, proving Worley is the real owner, then Magda writes up a report on the painting being stolen from him, and helps him press charges against the senator. He steals three ways."

"I hope not. For Magda's sake," Ray muttered.

Jen didn't like that frown that flashed across his face for two long heartbeats. It was a real frown, from the real Ray inside and not the persona he played.

"He's up to something," she whispered, when Ray left them alone to go pester Helga for more ice for his headache.

"When isn't he?" Blade leaned back against the wall again.

"Doesn't it strike you odd that he knows so much more about Magda than he's willing to let us know? Ray likes his games, but he never withholds information when it could affect a job."

"You're right." His grin returned. "Mrs. Williams, you're a genius. And I'll bet you anything, there's still a whole lot more information he hasn't told us."

"Want to help me find out what it is?"

*　　　*　　　*

As Jen waited for Ray's computer to boot up, she wondered if she had stepped into a trap. Ray never made the same mistake twice, and leaving her alone with his computer and enough time to hack into it was a mistake he had already made. Maybe he thought she wouldn't dare try again?

Maybe she would drive herself crazy trying to figure out his reasoning.

It was likely he had changed his password since the last time she had tried to rifle his files. Maybe he counted on her thinking that. Then again, it was nearly a year since they had last worked together and he had locked her in that storage shed to protect her until he could get reinforcements. She certainly couldn't run with that bullet hole in her leg.

"Stop wasting time," she whispered. Jen flinched as her voice seemed to echo through the guest room.

Blade stood sentinel on the curving stairs, halfway between the second and third floor. When he saw Ray coming, he was to hurry up the stairs, come through her open door and out the balcony door, to retreat to his own room. No slamming doors, and hopefully nothing to tip Ray off that someone had been scouting through his territory while he was spying elsewhere.

"Eenie, meenie..." Jen grinned and started typing. Logic said Ray's passwords would deal with things he never discussed. Among that list was anything having to do with family.

Her heart skipped a beat and a sweat broke out on her forehead when her sixth choice—cousins—let her through Ray's security. She supposed she had been lucky. Ray could have used his mother's name, and then where would she be? She could ask Blade to have old friends back at the Agency look into Ray's files, but that would take too long.

"Okay, let's see what we have on Magda-Mary-Margaret-Torrene-Tortelli," Jen whispered, and accessed the index.

Taking a chance that Ray would have accessed her file when they learned Magda was going to be on the island, Jen checked the dates attached to the files. She knew better than to trust the names themselves. Ray used a filing code she hadn't cracked yet, or a language she had never heard of. Just because she had grown up hearing French, German, Italian, and Russian spoken in her parents' organization, she understood them. That didn't make her a language genius by any means.

Her third try netted her the prize. Jen read through the disappointingly short file four times, trying to memorize as much as she could. She wondered what good it would do her—Magda's date of birth, place, parents' names, education, the four insurance agencies she had worked for, stats on her book sales, last three known addresses. The garbled words at the bottom of the screen made no sense.

Correction. One word did make some kind of warped sense, if she took the slash in the middle to be a division, and they were two shortened words smashed together. The second was Mary-Margaret-Magda's name. Then a flash of insight struck and a hunch she didn't quite want to even make concrete in her thoughts. Jen's hand trembled as she worked the track ball and returned to the main screen.

Leol/Anton.

Leola had been her mother's name. Antonia had been her own name, before trouble forced her family to fake their own deaths and create new identities. Jen barely remembered those serene, sunshine-filled days when she had been Antonia.

The screen blurred and she was surprised to feel hot wet in her eyes. Did she cry from anger, or from those memories she had tried to keep buried so they wouldn't tear open scars and bleed her dry? It infuriated her to know she had seen these file names a year ago when she had hacked into Ray's computer. If he knew information about her lost family and shattered past and he had refused to tell her...Jen didn't know what she would do or say.

"So help me, Ray..." Jen blinked hard, swallowed harder, and pressed the button to open the file.

"Red alert." Blade pushed the door closed, then sprinted in his bare feet across the room.

Jen had the computer shutting down before his backside vanished through the sliding door. She shoved Ray's computer back into its case and under his side of the bed while it was still humming. She continued the motion to sprawl across the bed, grab her own computer, and flip it open. It beeped as it came out of standby and she turned it to block her face. She rubbed a few angry tears from her eyes as Ray slipped through the door.

"Anything?" he asked.

Jen bit her tongue to keep from snapping at him. It would be just like him to know exactly what she had been doing, despite Blade's help as lookout. And just like him to ask if she had gotten very far. She shook her head.

"Nothing we don't already know."

Well, it wasn't a complete lie, was it?

She wondered if she could get away with pretending to be sick, so she could have a couple uninterrupted hours to ransack his files, maybe even copy everything over to her own computer for leisurely perusal.

Maybe she should just arrange for Gloria to become a widow, and run off with Mik Poling.

"What's so funny?" Ray asked. He paused in the bathroom door, his black shirt off over his head already.

"Just trying to think of what to do next to make Magda totally furious. Like, let her find me and Blade in a clinch."

"Mik Poling is a lady-killer. Don't torture Blade, making him live down to that reputation."

"Is that supposed to be—Forget it." Jen logged out. Her face felt hot and her temples throbbed. She felt queasy as the fantasy of Blade kissing her senseless shredded.

Did Ray mean Blade wouldn't want to touch her? Or that Mik Poling was a disgusting lecher?

Funny, how easily the thought of ditching Ray and running away with Blade had turned into something that made her melt inside. Yes, it would be fun to frustrate Magda until she ripped out her hair by the roots. If that was her own hair. Yes, it would be satisfying to pay Ray back for all his secrecy and the headaches he gave her, let alone wiping that smug expression off his face permanently. But the thought of sinking into Blade's arms made her petty thoughts of revenge evaporate.

Too bad Blade never seemed to touch her unless he had to.

"Blade's a gentleman," Ray said. He startled Jen by settling down on the side of the bed. "I've seen the way he looks at you."

"So have I. He's looking at Gloria."

"He's having a hard time separating Gloria from Jen, and I bet he'd love to get you into a dark corner for an hour or two. But he won't try anything until he knows it's safe."

"Great. He's not only a Marine, he's a Boy Scout." Jen wanted to punch Ray when he chuckled. She settled for stowing her computer away under her side of the bed and stretching out on top of the covers. "What's up for tomorrow?"

"Cedar Point."

"Why won't Worley let us get to work? The sooner we get the layout and get the painting, the sooner we're all out of here."

The sooner I can see if Blade's interested.

Jen shivered, feeling something foreign stir inside her. She had never wanted a man's interest, until Blade came along.

"I have the feeling he's waiting for something. Or maybe he just likes playing lord of the manor and showing off."

"He doesn't own Put-in-Bay or Cedar Point." Jen sighed. "Ever been to an amusement park?"

"Dozens of times." Ray got up and headed for the bathroom again. He paused on the threshold. "You never went before?"

"Never safe, or we never had the money, and then when we had the money, there wasn't time." Jen fluffed her pillow and scooted up to pull the blanket down so she could crawl under it.

"If I can help make up for your deprived childhood, then my life is well spent." Ray bowed extravagantly, winked at her, and ducked into the bathroom.

Jen snorted laughter as the door clicked shut. She really did like Ray, even when she wanted to pound him senseless.

She closed her eyes and wondered if roller coasters were as terrifyingly fun as people said, and if Blade would hold her hand on that first big drop.

*   *   *

Magda claimed her ankle hurt too much to go to Cedar Point with the others. She settled down on a chaise lounge with a notebook and urged the other four to run along and enjoy their day while she worked on her next book. Jen didn't doubt Magda would be on her feet the moment their boat got out of sight of the island. Was Magda keeping watch over the painting for Worley? Or was she on the island for reasons of her own?

Nothing in Magda's files said anything about skills as a locksmith or computer hacker. Jen had taken the precaution of locking away her and Ray's computers inside special-made cases that would take a drill to break into and combination locks that re-set themselves if the right combination wasn't used. Even if Magda got into the cases, she would need several hours to break into either or both of their computers. Jen wasn't worried.

As a precaution, though, she had booby-trapped the cases, so anyone prying where they weren't welcome would come away doused with perfume, and their path littered with tiny jawbreakers that just happened to spill from conveniently broken bags. Jen had specialized in booby-traps when she was a child and couldn't afford C-4.

*   *   *

The Magnum was huge. Jen didn't even want to consider the Millennium Force. She settled for the Gemini as the first roller coaster to try.

"No way." Ray gave her his goofy Mark grin. "Sorry, baby doll, but there's no way you're getting me on that thing. Let's try something a little less suicidal."

"Like the carousel?" Blade-Mik muttered.

Jen was thoroughly disgusted with both of them. Thoroughly disgusted with the entire morning. The ride across the lake had been rough, the waves choppy and the sky full of ominous, dark streaks. She knew a storm was on its way. Worley waved away her concerns as if he could control the weather, and wouldn't let it interfere with showing his guests a good time.

The crowds here at the amusement park made her skin crawl. There were just too many people, too much noise, too many bright lights, too much distraction. Jen knew she lived on the edge of paranoia, but always watching her back and trusting few had kept her alive. The expense of getting into the park for the day irritated her. Her feet hurt from the ridiculous strappy sandals that went with her Gloria disguise. Ray and Blade had sniped at each other from the moment they met at breakfast on the patio. Mark's and Mik's dislike of each other added to the distraction element and made it more believable that Mik would try to steal Mark's wife, but Jen hated it.

Now, on top of everything else, she couldn't try one roller coaster? Her first amusement park visit wasn't going to be complete if she didn't get to scream and get sick. Jen wondered if she hadn't let her Gloria role invade her personality. Or maybe it was just too close to that time of the month?

"I'll just ride alone, then," she said, and wrinkled up her nose at Ray.

"Can't let that happen." Blade looped his arm through Jen's and tugged her toward the line to get on the Gemini.

"But—" Ray raised his hands as if to stop them, but Blade just grinned and whisked her through the oncoming traffic.

Looking back, Jen saw Worley shrug and scowl and lower his

incredible bulk onto a nearby bench. Ray tipped his head toward her in a faint nod and Jen wondered what sort of message he expected her to get. She was too far away to read his face.

"That was too easy." Blade slid his hand down her arm, giving her goosebumps, and twined his fingers through hers. "Alone at last, Mrs. Williams. What should we do?"

"Ride?" Jen hid behind her Gloria persona and batted her eyelashes at him.

What was it about holding Blade's hand that made her insides turn to hot fudge and her brain go into freeze mode?

"What did you find out last night? Or did boss-man come back too soon?"

"Oh. Yeah." She mentally kicked herself for forgetting their little conspiracy. Jen took a few moments to ransack her thoughts while Blade led her past the sign saying there was a half-hour wait to ride the Gemini.

She told Blade everything she could remember from Magda's files. That took longer than she anticipated, simply because they had to talk in snatches, with their voices lowered, so the people standing in line with them didn't overhear. There was always the chance that Worley was indeed smarter than he looked, and he had spies to watch them. The delay in putting Mark and Gloria to work on Worley's security system could mean Worley didn't trust them. Ray scanned their rooms for listening bugs and cameras before they had strategy meetings. He hadn't found anything, but that didn't mean Worley wouldn't install them.

Blade was silent, frowning in concentration, for a good ten minutes after Jen gave him the last bit of information. She had told him everything except the codes at the bottom of Magda's files. They were definitely cross-reference notations. Jen had no idea what could link her with Magda, yet there was a file with information about her, with her birth name and her mother's name on it. That was all Jen had been able to glimpse in two seconds.

"That's way too much information to get in just a day or two," Blade finally said. "Ray couldn't have gotten that kind of information pulled together just in the time since we found out Magda was coming here. He already had that file. He's already been investigating her."

"He did seem to recognize her name when I got the data," Jen hated to admit. "But if she's working with creeps like Worley, wouldn't she have a file already put together, and he just accessed it?"

"No mention of criminal activity, suspected or substantiated. No, Ray's up to something else. But why Magda? What's the connection?" Blade glanced ahead of them. "What kind of race can you have with just two coasters?"

Jen opened her mouth to respond, then turned enough to see they were almost to the loading platform for the Gemini. She had been able to ignore the rumbling of the coaster, the screams of the riders, the instructions given over the loudspeakers, while concentrating on Blade.

"Here we go." Blade slid his arm around her shoulders again to guide her across the platform.

"Ray's searching for something, and I think it has to do with people. The code word I used to get into his computer was cousins. Does that mean anything to you? You knew him a lot longer than I have."

"Cousins?" Blade's arm tightened around her. "Oh, does it ever." He gritted his teeth and looked over her head, beyond her, beyond even the support system for the roller coaster.

Blade stayed silent, thinking, until their car arrived and they climbed in. He gripped her hand as they pulled away from the loading platform.

"Shylock came to see me, right after the first time Ray called to ask my help. He told me why Ray left the Agency. He's looking for his family. Seems his mother was one of five sisters who came over from Italy during World War II. They changed their identities and scattered across the country, because they came in illegally. Ray's looking for his cousins. Mary Margaret Tortelli sure sounds Italian to me."

"Poor Magda," Jen muttered. She gasped as their car seemed to tip backwards as it climbed the first hill of the ride.

"What?" Blade chuckled. "Oh, yeah, poor Magda. How'd you like to have Ray for a big brother, always looking over your shoulder? *If* that's why he's investigating her. Might just be a coincidence."

"Yeah, just a coincidence." Jen nodded and braced herself as they reached the top of the hill and the cars ahead of them started to plunge downward.

Jen barely paid attention as the racing coasters jolted and dropped and swung upward again and gravity tried to yank her out of her seat. Inside, she seethed.

I'll kill him, she swore. *If he knows information about my family— our family—and he can't be bothered to tell me, I'll kill him. I'll make him so sorry he ever found me. That lying, sneaking, conniving...*

Tears filled her eyes and the force of the wind in her face tore them away. Jen stared at nothing as the enormity of what Blade had told her raced through her mind.

That explained a lot, didn't it? Ray's heavy-handed protectiveness. His propensity for showing up at regular intervals. The questions he asked about her family. The way nothing ever sparked between them, no matter how much time they spent together. It wasn't that Ray didn't see her as a woman. He wouldn't let anything happen because she was his cousin.

So, what was wrong with her, that he wouldn't tell her they were blood relatives?

CHAPTER 11

The gloomy clouds got blacker and closer to the ground as the morning wore on. Just past lunchtime, spatters of rain and chill gusts of wind swirled through the amusement park. Worley protested loudly, as if it were an insult to him that rain had cut their day short. He offered dozens of alternatives for their amusement, as they scurried back to the marina.

They were drenched and chilled to the bone when they arrived back at Gibraltar Island. Worley sent them up to their rooms to dry off, warm up and change, and promised them an evening of entertainment that would take their minds off their truncated afternoon.

"I'd like it a lot better if we could just get to work," Jen muttered as the threesome reached the landing on the third floor. "What or who is he waiting for?"

"I think it's your turn to snoop tonight, Mrs. Williams," Ray said, and reached around her to open the door to their suite. "I'll keep Worley busy, complaining about how we're wasting time and you want to go to Paris to shop."

"That's Worley, but what about Magda?" Jen bit her lip to keep from correcting herself with "Cousin Magda." She wanted, just once in her life, to knock Ray off balance.

She knew better than to tip her hand too soon, though. She would save her pilfered information for a time when she needed some real ammunition.

"Mik can make a lot of noise about how poor Gloria isn't feeling well, and she's in bed early and he's bored and abandoned. He can play on poor Magda's sympathies until—"

"Until I'm worried about rabies," Blade broke in. "How about Gloria and Magda get into a cat fight while I snoop?"

The sound of a door opening two floors below them made all three flinch. Ray looked over the railing. He grimaced and glanced at the other two, then shook his head.

"Later," he whispered, and opened the door to let Jen go in ahead of him.

*   *   *

Magda still suffered a painful ankle and exiled herself to her room immediately after dinner that evening. Jen pretended to be chilled and exhausted and retired early as well. Blade and Ray kept Worley and the staff busy by playing poker and rummy until nearly midnight.

Jen got as far as the steps leading from the kitchen door down into the cellar, then had to stop when she heard footsteps somewhere below her. The cellar was off-limits because of the dirt and unstable rock, or so Worley had told them. Before retreating to her room, she reconnoitered outside, looking for other entrances into the caves and tunnels that might have been accessed when the university operated its research station here. When she reported to Ray and Blade before breakfast, Blade agreed to make the cellar his target the next night.

He discovered activity at two a.m., evidenced by a flashlight sweeping through the dusty piles of crates and sheet-swathed furniture far below in the blackness, and also had to retreat to avoid discovery. When the three compared notes the next morning, they agreed they had to find some way to get down to the cellar during the daytime, with a good excuse.

Jen prayed for rain. Boredom and restlessness might just prompt Worley to let them get to work on his security system.

*   *   *

"None of this is real?" Jen reached out as if to pick up the Delft blue vase on a pedestal in Worley's reception hall.

Her arms still seemed to glow from a near-overdose of sunshine. Yesterday, they had spent the entire day on the lake, sailing. Worley delighted in showing off his skill with his sailboat and gladly gave them all impromptu sailing lessons. Jen had actually liked sailing. She especially liked it when Magda retreated to the shelter of the pit in the

98

center of the boat, hiding her pale skin under hat and shirt and gobs of white, gooey sunscreen. Jen had stayed out in the sun, thanking the unknown Mediterranean ancestors who bequeathed her a complexion that never burned. Well, almost never. Maybe spending years indoors, studying computers, had reduced her immunity?

She glowed now, a rainy day later. Or was that extra heat from Blade's proximity? She had wandered out of the game room, desperate to move before her muscles locked. No one had followed her right away and she had been delighted, finally able to breathe without worrying someone would see through her disguise. Then Blade joined her. For once, Magda or Worley didn't toddle out after them. She knew the privacy wouldn't last long enough to make any difference. Not the difference she wanted.

"King of counterfeiters," Blade said, just as quietly. "The guy is actually proud of all the forgeries. Seems to think it's class to own fifty reproductions, rather than one original."

"He thinks he owns an original now."

"True." That tiny, one-sided grin flicked across his face.

It sent her stomach plummeting into her expensive sandals as she flashed back to last night's dream. *Blade, following her out into the mist that rolled in from the lake and covered the island. Blade, wrapping his arms around her while the world vanished into mist.*

The foghorn from Worley's half-size lighthouse had awakened her before the dream could go any further. Jen wondered if anyone had told him that a lighthouse that faced another island was a waste of time.

"I suppose if it makes him happy, what does it matter if it's fake or not? Sentimental value makes trash into something irreplaceable," she mused.

"True."

"Ray says this whole place reminds him of a Marx Brothers movie, with the paintings getting switched."

"He's the expert."

"Which makes absolutely no sense at all. He's such a serious, intense guy, and then he's so into that..." She made the mistake of looking directly into Blade's eyes. Why couldn't she have finished that dream last night? "Inspired insanity," she finished with a sigh as she looked away.

"Who says either of us is sane?" That near-dimple returned.

She gave a noncommittal shrug. Blade was one of the most solid, sane people she had ever met. Jen knew that, even though they'd spent more time together playing roles than they had as themselves. He was solid. Real. She had sensed that, even when he crept down the hallway to pretend to hold up Ray with a roll of Life Savers.

The idea of pretending to have a fling with Blade made her feel like the pseudo parquet floor they now stood on was a hologram over quicksand.

Blade was real, so she wanted every sweet word and smoldering look and touch to be real. She would probably never see him after this job, so why tie herself into knots over it?

The rain had slowed until it was barely a mist that made everything glisten in the spill of light from indoors. The world beyond the island had vanished. It had been raining most of the day, forcing Worley to entertain his guests with video tapes and endless games of canasta, bridge, and poker. If anyone had told Jen the drippy gray skies and moaning wind would shroud the island for months, she would believe it.

Still, she was indoors, with Blade, in semi-privacy. That had to be something to be glad about. Even if they couldn't carry on an extended conversation without the fear of being overheard and their deception uncovered, that counted for something, right?

"Looks awful outside," Jen offered, gesturing at the massive picture window framing the watery lights of Put-in-Bay. "But I don't feel like playing billiards or poker, and pinball machines never thrilled me."

Should she compliment Blade on how delicious he looked? Or was Gloria supposed to be only aware of herself at this point in the masquerade?

Blade *was* gorgeous. Tailored black pants, a silky-gray shirt that emphasized his eyes, and black boots that left rebellious scuffs on the floor. Heart-stopping perfect. But would Gloria notice so early in the game? Why hadn't Ray given her any directions beyond "provide a distraction by having an affair with Blade?"

"There's a maze outside." Blade tipped his head just slightly toward the door behind them, meaning someone was coming. He held out his arm. She hesitated, then gingerly rested her hand on his sleeve-covered biceps.

Did he realize what his physical presence did to her?

"Rhododendron maze," he continued as he led her to the ballroom's French doors. "Ever seen one? Rhododendron," he prompted, when she gave him a blank look.

"I can't even spell it. Is that the big, poofy flower with all the tiny petals that attracts ants?"

"Peony, not rhododendron."

"Ah, well, can't stand messy flowers anyway. With my luck, Mark would be allergic to that too."

"Sounds like he's allergic to anything fun. Why'd you marry him, anyway?" Blade asked.

"He's the first one who asked me." She flinched as they stepped outside and the misty air wrapped them in a spray as light as cotton candy. Like walking through a cloud.

"I find that hard to believe."

"What, that Mark had the gumption to ask, or that anyone asked at all?" Jen started to Gloria-giggle. Then she met Blade's gaze and the sound caught in her throat.

Had she forgotten to breathe? Her head felt as if it would lift from her shoulders. His body radiated heat that nearly scorched with his proximity, yet Jen shivered.

"I find it hard to believe no one caught you long ago."

His voice rumbled over her like gravel coated in that cinnamon-scented and flavored oil her friend Halli got for a bridal shower gift. That was definitely the wrong direction for her thoughts, Jen decided, as her face started to burn.

"Well, when you spend your life in the library or staring at a computer screen, no one knows you're around. Is that the maze?" She scampered down the gravel path to the high, glistening green wall of leaves ahead of them.

"I know you're around," Blade whispered.

Amazing, the carrying qualities of damp lake air.

Of course, that meant that even out here, they couldn't have a private, real conversation. Emphasis on real.

"I heard you two are here to put together a new security system," he continued as he led the way through the arched, wrought iron gate leading into the maze.

"Consulting. Advisors, really. We analyze the layout and vulnerable spots and then design a program to coordinate all the pieces of equipment. It's fun. Like putting together a puzzle."

"I like challenges."

She stumbled, her knees turned into jelly by the husky tone in his voice. Jen could only imagine the look in his eyes.

"So, why aren't you hard at work?"

"Danville wants us to relax and get the feel of his island, first. Are you staying for the big party at the end of July?"

"No, unfortunately. I'm working too, but our host sees fit to make me wait to…earn my keep, shall we say?"

"Gee, maybe the poor guy is just lonely and wants to keep lots of people around."

That earned a bark of laughter from her companion that cut through the damp-thickened shadows. His eyes sparkled and his shoulders seemed to shake as he led her a dozen quick steps further into the maze.

"My dear, sweet Gloria. I wish we could be somewhere completely alone. Far away, where your husband or other unfriendly parties couldn't come upon us undetected."

"Why would we want to be alone?"

She nearly laughed when he broke character to glare at her. Didn't he know by now Gloria was a total incompetent outside her specialties of computers and clothes?

"We are alone, though. No one can see us." Blade looked around and nodded, and the perpetual sneer, the stiffness of his Mik Poling mask fell from his face. "Jen," he whispered, and brushed a few damp strands from her forehead.

Blade smiled, and it was really him looking at her, not Mik lusting after Gloria. Every inch of her bare skin tingled as he rested his hands on her shoulders and just looked into her eyes.

"I really hate all this game playing," he continued, his voice so quiet she thought someone standing next to them wouldn't have heard. Just they two.

She could only smile in answer, but from the widening of his smile, the sparkle in his eyes, Blade understood. He took one hand off her shoulder and cupped her jaw, lightly stroking her bottom lip with his thumb. A whimper escaped Jen, echoed by a groan from him.

Please, please, please, she cried silently through the thundering of her pulse in her ears.

Gravel crunched on the path on the other side of the rhododendron wall.

Blade went perfectly still. Jen sensed the ice moving through his veins. The heat in his eyes turned to chill iron as he shifted into super spy mode. She had seen Ray do the same thing a dozen times. The only problem was, he had been romancing *other* women and she knew it was only a game for him, a necessary ploy to get what they needed. It stung like salt in a wound to see Blade react the same way, with her.

As if playing her feelings, even in this semi-privacy, had been just another role for him.

Still, when Blade released his grip on her shoulders and caught hold of her hand, she was ready, alert, waiting for instructions. He led her back down the path to the maze gate.

"I think it's going to rain harder, Gloria. Your husband will have my head if I let you catch pneumonia." Blade let loose that sneering Mik laugh Jen already hated. "We'll have to find our privacy some other time. Some place more comfortable, I think. With a door to lock."

"Why would we want to do that?"

Through the whispering hiss of the mist, Jen could just make out footsteps out of synch with hers and Blade's. Someone else walked the gravel path, keeping pace with them.

Blade pointed down at the path and dragged one foot, making a scraping noise. Jen let out a squeal, guessing what he wanted. He winked at her.

"Gloria? Are you all right? Did you hurt yourself?"

Jen heard the footsteps moving again, faster. Whoever it was hoped to reach the gate out of the maze ahead of them.

"I'm okay, I think. I twisted my ankle. Darn these shoes." She muffled a snort of laughter as inspiration hit. "They were my favorites, and now they're broken!" She slipped her foot out of her detested, backless, high-heel sandals, bent and picked it up. It only took one good pull to yank the heel off the sole. Blade glared at her.

"Let me help you inside." He wrapped an arm around her waist and they reached the entrance of the maze in time to see a dark, draped shape hurry around the side of the house, toward the kitchen entrance.

"Spies," Jen muttered. The kitchen entrance meant four possibilities for who had followed them.

She could have sworn she saw a flicker of red as the figure went around the corner. Like maybe a cloak or an oversized raincoat covered the spy. And hadn't Magda worn a brilliant red caftan today?

*   *   *

Going into the maze with Jen had been a smart move, Blade knew, but he still kicked himself. They had discovered someone spied on them, meaning Worley didn't trust his guests. More important, in those few seconds when they had dropped their masks, he had seen the welcome shine in her eyes.

Which didn't do him one bit of good, did it? How could he pursue Jen's interest in him when they had to keep playing Gloria and Mik?

Why couldn't their unseen shadow have delayed another five minutes, just so he could take her into his arms and find out if her mouth tasted like the ice cream they had shared? Or maybe not cool, sweet ice cream, but spicy warm and welcoming.

They weren't going to get a chance to try anything until they were off the island.

On top of all that frustration, he'd been thoroughly soaked when drizzle turned into an icy downpour when they were ten feet from the door. They couldn't run because Jen pretended an injured ankle. Blade still felt coated in ice now, despite the slow-burning core of fury deep inside.

Jen, of course, looked like nothing had happened when she came down to dinner two hours later. She now sat near the head of the reproduction Versailles banquet table, charming their host, without a sniffle or sneeze or chill. Jen could charm the poison out of a rattler, Blade suspected. She didn't even have to say anything, just flutter those long eyelashes, widen those big, dark eyes, make noises of appreciation, and giggle every time their host said something remotely amusing.

What sounds would she make if he took her into his arms? Would she resist, or melt into him? Blade suspected Jen didn't like to be ambushed, but how could he ever learn the feel of her skin, the taste of her mouth, unless he ambushed her? He suspected he would have to seize a chance moment and drag her into a dark hallway.

He knew he'd better pray she was as hungry for him as he felt for her, or he could end up on his broken back with an equally broken face. Or with other parts of his anatomy seriously disabled.

Still, would she whimper or laugh or moan when he kissed her? Blade knew it would be a deep, hard kiss, cramming hours of sweet exploration into a few precious seconds.

The resulting heat of his imagination drove away the last of his chills. Blade sighed and settled back a little more in his throne-like dining room chair.

Next to him sat Magda, in her signature black and red velvet dress that she almost wore. Blade wondered if she looked and acted the same when she was Mary Margaret Tortelli, insurance investigator. He wondered if her books were any good. He supposed he could ask her, but Magda still eyed him like prime rib, even though she no longer tried to ambush him.

Tonight, Magda tried to set her hooks into Ray. Was it possible she could see through the geeky computer genius image to the Casanova underneath? If he had an ounce of compassion for the woman, Blade would have warned her away. Ray was born to break hearts and never take his own out of storage.

Then again, if the information Jen had snooped meant anything, Ray and Magda were cousins of some degree. That meant every time Magda went into her imitation of Barbarella combined with Elvira, Ray had to be feeling pretty uncomfortable. What was it like to have a blood relative make a pass at him? The thought of Ray not welcoming a woman's advances cheered Blade enormously. Someday, Ray was going to find a woman he wanted desperately and she was going to run from him like he had three eyes and warts. Blade wanted to be there when that happened.

Dinner seemed to take forever. Blade couldn't have told anyone what he had eaten, five seconds after Martha took away the plates. Not good. His powers of observation and memory were what had saved his skin a dozen times over.

"I think in light of our restricted afternoon, we should open up the ballroom. Shall we skip the cigars and brandy?" Worley asked as he stood. He held out a hand to help Jen stand. His rusty chuckle grated on Blade's nerves. "I'm not sure I trust you two ladies alone, even for a few minutes. You're likely to plot some nefarious scheme against us poor, defenseless men."

More like a cat fight, Blade suspected. Magda would probably jump Jen the moment the door closed behind them, but Jen would tear her to pieces without breaking a plastic nail or displacing a dyed hair. The image helped Blade's digestion.

"Oh, dancing. Definitely dancing," Magda cooed, and hooked her arm through Ray's. "Please, Mark? Dance with me? I've been cooped up with nothing to do because of the rain and if I don't move...I could just burst," she added in a low, throbbing voice.

Blade didn't feel sorry for Ray. He could chew Magda up for dessert, and the woman would never know it.

"Ah...sure. Glad to help." Ray swallowed loudly, adjusted his glasses and let Magda half-drag him through the arched doorway into the ballroom. The other three followed.

The room resembled a conservatory, the walls lined with curving staircase plant stands, potted trees and hanging baskets full of trailing vines. One entire wall and half the curving roof was glass. It let the watery light of the half moon spill down on the oak floor and revealed the rain had finally stopped. From this vantage point, facing Canada across the dark water, with only a few points of light visible through the rain, it seemed they were the only people on the entire planet.

Magda flung open the simulated Louis XIV armoire. It held a massive sound system more complicated than a space shuttle. She squealed like a child on a sugar high as she ransacked Worley's CDs and old-fashioned LPs for dancing music.

Magda turned to hot oil the minute the pulsing, sensuous, slow dancing music started. She oozed across the floor and Ray pretended to be dazzled. He tripped over his feet a few times. Blade wondered how hard it was for him to uncoordinate himself. He had seen Ray go through complicated martial arts moves blindfolded, and never miss a step or lose his balance.

"Thank you," Jen said, with that little giggle that set Blade's teeth on edge. "I'd love to, but I just can't."

He turned to see Worley lean a little too close to Jen. Heck, he was practically falling into her chair.

"Why not, my dear?"

Blade wanted to slap the man across the face with one of his lace-trimmed napkins and tell him to stop drooling.

"Well, my ankle feels much better, but I can't dance."

"I can't believe someone so much like a flower could not know how to dance." He clasped Jen's hand against his over-dressed chest. "It would be like the wind not knowing how to blow."

Talk about blowing, you're the expert on hot air. Blade knew Worley wanted Jen to dance just so Gloria wouldn't be alone for too long with Mik. Still, it irritated him.

"Honestly," Jen protested. She squealed when Worley yanked her to her feet. "You're going to regret this."

Blade vowed Worley wouldn't live long enough to regret it. He stayed in his chair, trying not to be blinded by ferns, and watched. The minute Worley's hands went anywhere they didn't belong...

Jen stepped squarely on Worley's polished toes with her spiked heel. When Blade said they could be weapons, he had meant the effect her legs would have on men, not the pain she caused Worley. But what the heck—any port in a storm.

Worley gasped and flinched away, but never loosened his grip on Jen's hand or waist.

Jen tripped two steps later and managed to kick his shins. Worley's florid complexion flashed white. He smiled when Jen gasped an apology. He also moved her out to arm's length, though it didn't suit the music. Blade would have felt sorry for him, but he fought too hard to keep from laughing.

When Hanson appeared in the doorway and beckoned for Worley's attention, Blade could have sworn he saw relief on the big man's sweating face. Worley nearly fled the room.

"Saved by the bell," Jen whispered, as she walked past Blade to take a seat on the other side of the plant staircase.

"Gracefully done." Blade winked at her. Something warmed and writhed inside when she blushed.

"Hard to manage when you actually don't know how to dance."

"You're kidding." Blade moved to the next seat, within arm's reach of her. "Why not?"

"It wasn't a survival skill, where I grew up." She shrugged.

"Where did you grow up?"

Okay, so it was a set-up line, but he really did want to know about her. All about her. Silly things like did she like horror movies or talk in her sleep? He imagined Jen curled up beside him in the loft bedroom of his cabin, watching the stars through the skylight that filled half the roof. Did she like to stargaze? Did she believe in long engagements, or would she like to take one of Worley's boats and cross the lake to Canada and find a justice of the peace tonight?

Whoa, boy. Slow down! Wait until the first kiss!

"Ray will tell you I was raised by wolves." Jen's eyes sparkled. "Actually, that's pretty close. We were…the people my parents worked with specialized in getting information, any way possible. They'd been hurt by very powerful people, and information brokering was the only way to survive. Only it didn't quite protect them."

Blade mentally kicked himself for bringing up the subject. How could he have forgotten that nightmare she had?

"When us kids grew up," Jen continued with a lopsided grin, "we decided to take it a step further and help people. Like you and Ray." Her smile grew so warm, Blade thought he would melt.

She admired him and what he did.

Blade feared he glowed brightly enough to light the room. To control himself, he concentrated on what else she had said.

"I get the feeling, even before the attack, you didn't have a normal childhood."

"Define normal." She winked, but the saucy look faded too soon. "Probably not." Jen turned to watch Ray and Magda stumble and slither across the floor. "We were safe, we were happy, we had fun—we had no idea what we were missing."

Blade ached for her, envisioning Jen as a precocious little whirlwind of energy and wit. Playing dress-up and tea parties. Playing on swing sets and climbing trees. It was a pretty picture, but it shredded in favor of a grimmer image of Jen, pale and quiet, sitting in shadowy corners of libraries looking up information, or learning at her mother's knee how to perform wire taps and disguise her appearance.

"*My* kids will grow up in the sunshine and not be afraid of anything," she whispered, so softly her voice was barely a breath; so intently, it vibrated through Blade's bones.

His chest vanished into a hollow, empty aching. *Her kids?*

"You have kids?"

"Not yet." She still wouldn't look at him. Her lips curled up just faintly. Blade suspected she smiled to keep from crying.

He suspected he knew exactly the hunger that put such force into her words. It ate through him as he envisioned his arms around Jen, and her arms around a baby. Their baby.

Either that, or Worley had drugged their dinners.

Maybe Worley had, because Blade had always believed himself allergic to marriage, babies, and pregnant women, just like Ray.

"Oh, great. Look who's arrived." Jen gestured with her chin at the doorway.

Worley and the newcomer watched Ray and Magda revolve across the floor as the music ended. The man stood a good head taller than Worley, making him at least six feet. Wide shoulders stayed straight and erect under a dark gray-blue sports jacket with the dull gleam of raw silk. The black shirt underneath was likely silk too. The stranger turned and focused his flame-blue eyes on Jen like a starving man confronted with roast swan.

Blade recognized the man and ice roared through his veins. Every instinct sharpened through pain, danger, and Agency training leaped to the alert. All their careful plans and the information they had gathered had failed them. The unexpected and unwanted had arrived.

"My dear guests." Worley raised his wobbling voice.

Ray turned to frown at their host and Blade fought to stay slouched in his chair and not reveal he felt as tight as a violin string. Worley was nervous. More nervous than could be caused by Mik's pursuit of Gloria.

"I'm delighted to have you meet my dear friend, Guy Sarpantine."

Worley looked up at the man towering over him, like a beaten child seeking approval. "He wasn't expected until later this summer, but he delayed several commitments to come now."

Blade chanced a glance at Ray. His former partner nodded once as he escorted Magda off the floor. From that brief flicker of steel in Ray's eyes, he shared Blade's gut certainty that Sarpantine had arrived ahead of schedule to retrieve the Dordt.

Worley led Sarpantine across the ballroom floor to meet them. Ray led Magda to the seating group where Blade and Jen waited. He deposited Magda onto a white wrought iron bench, then took up a position behind Jen with both hands on her shoulders.

Knowing what he did about Sarpantine, Blade didn't blame Ray at all. Sarpantine's eyes gleamed brighter, as if Ray's protective move only made Jen more interesting. Blade fought the urge to wrap an arm around her himself.

Worley introduced Mark and Gloria Williams, emphasizing their roles as computer security consultants.

"Please tell me you're his sister, not his wife." Sarpantine's baritone dropped to a sulky rumble as he addressed Jen. She giggled when Sarpantine fixed her with a scorching gaze. Like a butterfly caught on a pin.

"Nope, married eight years now," she said and tipped her head back to wrinkle up her nose at Ray and fix him with an adoring look. "And just as deliriously happy now as we were the day we ran off to Reno together. Aren't we, sugar bear?"

"Delirious," Ray said with a strained little chuckle, and squeezed Jen's shoulders.

"Why am I always too late when it comes to utterly charming ladies?" Sarpantine caught up Jen's hand and pressed a kiss across her knuckles.

When he turned away, Jen scrubbed her hand on her skirt.

Magda simpered and nearly offered Sarpantine a map to her room when Worley introduced her. The newcomer smiled faintly and nodded to her—then asked to be shown to his room.

The moment Sarpantine vanished through the door, Magda stomped out of the room, wobbling on her five-inch stiletto heels. Her steps sent sharp echoes bouncing off the glass wall and wood floor.

"Whatever you do, don't eat or drink anything he offers you," Ray said, so only Jen and Blade could hear.

Jen said nothing. She didn't move. Her expression didn't change.

She also didn't breathe. Blade sensed her withdrawing, like a fragile sea creature retreating into its shell.

"Depending on the drug, you either remember nothing, you think it's nirvana and want more of him...or you have nightmares for the rest of your life, and no way of proving he did it. It all depends on whether he likes you or not."

"Everybody likes a challenge," Jen murmured, "but let's try for some moderation, shall we?"

Ray's bark of laughter was little more than a growl. He squeezed Jen's shoulder and leaned down close enough his lips brushed her hair. Blade nearly hated *him* for a moment.

"Don't worry, Mrs. Williams. I always take very good care of my wives." Ray slid his hands down her arms and grasped her elbows to lift her to her feet. "I think a strategic retreat is in order. Let them think Magda's attempt at a rumba got me—" Mischief flickered behind the geek glasses. "—romantic."

Blade bit his tongue and kept his clenched fists in his lap. Ray had been about to say horny, hadn't he?

CHAPTER 12

"Cold?" Ray nodded at the sweats Jen pulled out of the suitcase tucked under their king-size bed.

As far as she was concerned, her sexy new nightgowns were only window dressing, in case their belongings were searched. Jen preferred her cotton scrubs for bed. Until tonight.

"Partly," she answered, after swallowing a near-shriek. For a few seconds there, she had forgotten he was in the room.

"Sarpantine thinks he's too sophisticated to come after a woman in her bedroom. Especially if her husband is there."

"I felt like he was trying to eat me with his eyes." Her hands shook and she didn't try to hide it. The ice inside her bones had nothing to do with any chill she caught wandering around in the mist with Blade.

Ray's presence on the other side of the bed usually let her get a good night's sleep. Even if the roof caved in or a few bombs went off. Now, though, she wanted Blade to watch over her while she slept.

But *could* she sleep with Blade on the other side of the bed? Would she wear her comfy warm sweats or that white, virginal nightgown that seemed to rattle him?

Doggone, but she *was* a virgin. She'd been saving herself for Blade—or an unreasonable facsimile. It just wasn't fair that now she'd found him, the masks they had to wear kept her from making one move, saying one word to feel out the territory. That moment of shattered privacy in the maze had only made things worse, because they couldn't follow up on it.

111

And on top of everything, along came Sarpantine. All those stories Ray had told her of his reputation and rape drugs kept rising to her conscious mind.

"Innocence and virtue can be very sexy," Ray offered after one of those buzzing pauses that always made Jen think he could read her mind. Usually it was comforting. But not tonight, when she was sure to dream of Blade.

Just because she didn't risk her life and heart test-driving every man who smiled at her, didn't mean she wasn't interested or aware of men and heart-stopping sex. Jen had simply learned early to be extremely careful. And patient.

"I thought I got rid of my Mary Poppins side long ago." Her attempt at cheerful sarcasm failed miserably and left a sour taste in her mouth, a weight in her stomach.

"Purity always shines through. I should have said 'challenge.' You're a married woman. To men like Sarpantine, marriage equals boredom and rules to break. He couldn't care less about Magda *because* she's available."

"So you think marriage is boring? A trap?"

"Not with the right person. With the right one, it could be an adventure." Ray sat down on the bed so she had to look up at his face or stare at his belt. "You'd never be bored with Blade," he added in a soft voice that sent shivers up her back.

"So now you're playing matchmaker?" Jen struggled to her feet and tried to walk—not run—to the bathroom.

She said a prayer of thanks Worley's guests didn't have to share bathrooms. A vision of Sarpantine catching her in the shower made her skin crawl.

"Like I said, I always take very good care of my wives." Ray didn't laugh or even grin. A totally new shiver took over Jen's skin as she shut the door.

Okay, so Ray approved. His opinion meant more to Jen than she would ever admit. Especially to him, the arrogant know-it-all. Not that his approval meant anything if Blade couldn't reach beyond the roles they played.

*   *   *

Jen came awake instantly when she heard the boat engine's rumble change. She sat up slowly, so she wouldn't wake Ray on the other side of the bed. She had heard the engine in her dreams. It had crept up on the island, slowly becoming audible. Even as she analyzed the change, the sound died.

Ray didn't wake. His breathing didn't even change. A shiver ran up her back and she recalled what he had said about Sarpantine using drugs to get the women he wanted. What if the newcomer to the little island party decided to drug Mark Williams, to get at his wife without interference?

If Ray was drugged, there was nothing she could do about it now. But she could foil Sarpantine's game before he even knew she was onto him. She slid out of the bed and headed for the sliding door, which hung open two feet to allow the night breeze into the room. Now that the rain had stopped, the air was fresh, not chilly. She slid the screen door aside and stepped out onto the balcony. She settled down with her back to the tower wall, looking out over the lake and the lights of Put-in-Bay.

No sound came from inside the room. Either Ray was drugged or he was a heavy sleeper.

Or she had simply dreamed the sound of the boat and she was losing sleep over nothing.

What was wrong with her, that the slightest sound woke her? What kept her from sleeping deeply? Ray was there to protect her, just like always. He was one of the few people outside her family who she fully trusted.

Jen flinched, realizing part of the reason for her restlessness. Snooping into Ray's computer files had corroded that trust. He probably knew more about her background than she did, and he hadn't said a word. That was enough to keep her from sleeping peacefully.

What would Blade tell her to do, if she told him about it? Jen's face warmed as she realized she wanted to turn to Blade for advice, for comfort, for safety. How could she so easily trust him, when she barely knew him? And yet, despite the improbability, she did trust him. Wanted to trust him.

Or did she? After all, she hadn't told Blade that she found out Ray investigated her like he had Magda. If she couldn't reveal that little bit of information, what did that say about this warm, slightly disconcerting sense of security she felt around Blade?

"You're getting neurotic," Jen whispered.

The rumble of a small boat's engine answered her.

Jen knelt and crawled to the edge of the balcony. She pressed her face against the railing, following her ears to the source.

A small open boat eased out into the watery light of the half-moon in the clearing skies. Jen blinked and rubbed at her eyes and stared at the spot where the boat had come from—seemingly from under the island.

Well, wasn't that interesting?

She followed the course of the boat, constantly shifting her gaze back to the emergence point. Jen thought she saw some sort of box sitting in the dull gray metal bottom of the boat. One man controlled the engine and steered, and another man sat with his hand on the box. Probably keeping it from bouncing out of the boat as it hit small waves.

What was in the box? Something important enough to sneak it out of the island at night, obviously. Jen doubted they were crossing the lake to Canada in that small boat. Then again, for all she knew there was a larger boat waiting somewhere in the distance over the water.

She turned her attention back to the place where the boat had appeared and stared, trying to memorize the few visible landmarks. Where was it, in relation to the house? That was proof enough that someone used the tunnels and caves underneath the island. Such knowledge was useless until she found how to get into them.

Jen held her breath as something moved in the darkness. Was that just a bush, dancing a little in the dying storm breezes?

All the ugly curses and filthy language she knew, in several languages, came to mind as Magda emerged from the shadows and walked to the very edge of the island. It was a cliff at that point. Magda knelt on the edge of the cliff face and looked down, over the edge. Jen wished the other woman would fall into the lake, or maybe take pity on the world and jump.

No such luck tonight.

Jen waited until Magda finished her study of the cliff and got up and walked back into the shadows. Presumably, she headed for the house and her own bed. Jen didn't care. She had something important to tell Ray. If this wasn't proof that Magda worked for Worley, then something very strange was going on.

*   *   *

"I should compliment you on your taste in women's clothing." Ray smiled blandly at Blade across the buffet table.

He used that accent that made his sometime-partner think of snooty butlers and drinking tea with his pinkie sticking out.

"Are you setting things up so Mik and Mark can beat each other bloody?" Blade asked in an equally bland voice.

The breakfast buffet that morning sat on the flagstone patio that offered a gorgeous view of the lake and Perry's Monument. The sun shone brightly, making a lie of the rain that had kept them bound to the island yesterday. Not another person was awake and about except them. For the moment. Worley's household staff reflected his paranoia, rarely leaving the guests alone, except in their bedrooms and bathrooms. If not for Ray's handy little scanner, Blade wouldn't have believed that illusion, either. Last night's little meeting, to share what Jen had seen, wouldn't have been possible without that scanner. Blade was still kicking himself over the fact that he and Ray had both slept through the arrival and departure of the boat. It said a lot for Jen's precarious adolescence that she was a light sleeper and could tell what sounds belonged and what didn't in an unfamiliar place.

Just for a moment, Blade dreamed of making Jen his partner, for life. Work, play, and pleasure. It made him ache, and woke him faster than triple shots of espresso, straight into a vein.

"No, just saying you did a good job with her wardrobe. Jen hates what she calls fuss and feathers. She's actually wearing the clothes you helped her pick out, and cheerful about it, not grumbling and throwing things around every morning."

"She does that a lot?" Blade smiled, liking the image. Jen wasn't afraid of punctuating her arguments with minor carnage.

"I bought a black bikini for her and she threatened to make me wear it—around my throat." He glared when a snort escaped Blade. "I especially like the nightgowns."

"Which ones?" he asked, before he could stop himself.

"You didn't help her with that?" Ray whistled, soft and low.

"I needed some air." Blade took his platter of eggs and pancakes to a table. He didn't want to see the mockery on Ray's face. Or worse, the pity.

Maybe he would finally tell Ray Anguilano had been sniffing around. That would knock the know-it-all air right out of him. Or had Jen mentioned that to him already?

Blade didn't think so. Jen wouldn't tell Ray about Anguilano, because that would mean confessing she had been snooping through his computer files again. The thought of Ray's dismay at learning his security *was* breakable cheered Blade immensely.

"So you never saw them. Well, I wouldn't either, if I hadn't checked the closet. She sleeps in her sweats," Ray added, when Blade swiveled back around and stared at him. No pity or teasing in face or voice.

Blade swallowed hard and refused to ask. He didn't want to know, really. Especially if Jen had bought the black and red one. It was more Magda's style, and he couldn't stand that. "Where's Jen, anyway?"

"Getting ready for Sarpantine's first attack. And here's the lucky lady with the target painted on her...back." He stepped around the buffet table and held out his full plate as Jen came through the patio doors. "Madame, your breakfast is served."

"Why do you keep trying to get me fat?" Jen scowled at Ray and stepped around him, well out of his reach and his plate.

"Who asked the cook for extra desserts and brought a five-pound bag of chocolate chip cookies with us?"

"That's way too much. Besides, we have different tastes." She wrinkled up her nose at Ray's plate of eggs, fried mush, hash browns, and sausage. "I like what Blade has on his plate," she said as she stepped over to the buffet table. She smiled at Blade, but he didn't much notice.

All he could think was that he wanted *her* on his plate.

That led to another thought. That outfit was supposed to *protect* her against Sarpantine?

Then his next thought was... Had he picked that out for her? If he did, he needed his head examined.

Jen wore a royal blue top that clung to her like a second skin, with straps somewhere between spaghetti and nonexistent. Her scarlet shorts peeked out from under her shirt, which brushed the tops of her thighs. If she had any underwear on, it wasn't evident. Her white sandals laced halfway up her calves, with heels high enough to make a circus stilt walker envious. Her fresh-scrubbed look, sans any makeup but pale pink lip-gloss, contrasted loudly enough with her outfit to make his head ring. Her itsy bitsy ponytails were the finishing touch.

Seductive innocence just took on a totally new meaning.

Blade kept his mouth shut. The cave man inside him fought with the knight errant he had always wanted to be. Did he want to pick her up and run away with her? To some dark place to rip her clothes off? Not that it would take very long.

Or did he want to carry her away to lock her in a stone tower until she got some common sense? Either way, it involved touching her. Blade didn't trust himself.

"You approve?" Ray settled down at the round glass table with

Blade.

"Sure, if she's bait for a serial rapist," he growled.

"Which Sarpantine is."

Blade choked on his mouthful of eggs.

"Here," Jen said, and shoved a glass of apple juice in front of him. She sat down next to Ray and watched, frowning, until Blade drank.

"That's nowhere near enough." Ray glared at her plate.

The gold leaf sailboat pattern showed clearly. The only obstructions were a triangle of toast, four orange segments, and a few crumbs of scrambled eggs.

"I'll barf."

"Dilution is important."

Blade slammed the juice glass onto the table to remind them they weren't alone. What sort of conversation was that, anyway?

Martha scurried out onto the patio with a bowl of cherries in sauce and another of whipped cream. She smiled at the three guests and puttered around the buffet table. Jen, Blade, and Ray exchanged glances; back to their roles. Blade stifled a sigh and wondered when he would get his questions answered.

*   *   *

Whatever the boat had picked up last night, Worley had been hiding it from his guests, including his security team. Blade nearly cheered when their host showed up halfway through breakfast to announce that some unexpected business had come up, and since he would be unable to entertain them as planned, would the Williamses be kind enough to go to work ahead of schedule?

Ray and Jen had been ready to get to work on the security system the day they arrived on Gibraltar Island. Blade wished he could join in and help them survey the entire island, but that would break his cover story wide open.

Sarpantine didn't come to breakfast that morning, which pleased Blade to no end. Worley explained that his new guest had endured a rough crossing last night and was sleeping in. Blade wondered if Sarpantine had been involved in smuggling out the box Jen had seen on the boat.

Then, when Worley sat down next to him at the table, Blade realized their host wore makeup around his left eye. That supported Blade's theory that Worley indulged in makeup to hide his age and excesses, along with the wig and the girdle he could hear creaking when the fat man sat down. Where had Worley gotten the black eye in the last eight hours?

The logical explanation, considering how he reacted when Sarpantine arrived, was that Sarpantine had punched him. Maybe he wanted something Worley didn't have? Had they argued about the contents of the box that left last night? Or the painting?

Blade wished he was working with Ray and Jen as they surveyed the windows and doors, mapped the hallways, examined the treasure room Worley finally opened to them, and did sonogram readings on the structure of the house. As a team, they had a lot to discuss, and very little privacy in which to do it.

Still, their mission was back on track. Blade had to be grateful for that. Plus, Jen wore jeans and long-sleeve shirts while she worked, which temporarily protected her from Sarpantine's advances.

With Worley tied up on business, Jen and Ray busy with their security surveys, and Sarpantine blatantly uninterested, that left Magda bored and ready to sink her claws into Blade. He resorted to trying to learn to handle Worley's sailboat. This allowed him to sail around the island and take pictures of possible entrances to tunnels under the island. Blade was a miserable sailor, but the fact that his feeble attempts kept him free of Magda, who hated the sun and water, suited him fine.

"The problem is," he confided to Ray before dinner that evening, "I'm starting to pick it up." He stepped up to the half wall and leaned against it, looking out over the docks and the sailboat that had been his salvation and bane most of the day. Blade wanted to just stand there and enjoy the sunset, but he didn't know how long they would have this privacy to confer before the staff or Worley descended on them.

"You're a fast learner. That's how you stay alive," Ray said with a tired grin.

"Yeah, but Magda mentioned she wants me to take her out on the lake tomorrow."

"Not good."

"Tell me about it. How about you making a play for Vampirella and I work overtime on Jen tonight?"

"She's Gloria, not Jen." Ray said. He turned, putting his back to the view and narrowed his eyes as he studied Blade. "You can't keep the two separate, can you?"

"I can't see Gloria, that's the problem."

"Uh huh. Let me warn you, old buddy, be careful how you treat Jen.

I don't want her hurt."

"This coming from the man who uses her as bait for a pervert like Sarpantine?" Blade wanted to spit.

"We've taken all the precautions we can, short of closing up shop and running."

Blade sighed and nodded. He knew Ray was right.

"I don't want you playing games with her heart."

It took all Blade's control not to remind Ray that *he* was the Casanova of the Inner Circle. Ray had ten notches in his headboard for every sweet young thing Blade had dallied with over the years. He heard the unaccustomed vehemence in Ray's voice and it drained away his angry response.

"She's had it rough all her life, always looking out for everybody else, with nobody to look out for her. Jen needs someone to depend on, who'll always be there. You never stay anywhere longer than a few months. The only constant in your life is that mountain cabin of yours, and how often do you go there?"

Blade nodded, mentally responding, *Not nearly enough.* He had daydreamed of taking Jen there, stargazing with her, hiding from the world, just the two of them for months at a time.

"Don't take this the wrong way, old buddy, but you're just not good enough for her." Ray slapped Blade on the shoulder and walked back inside.

"I could be," Blade whispered, so that no one heard him, not even the wind gently sighing over his shoulders.

Maybe he was the proverbial rolling stone, but that could change. He just needed someone as an anchor and constant in his life. Someone, not something, though Ray was certainly right, his cabin was his only constant point. Blade knew he would look forward to coming home every night, if Jen waited for him.

Blade grinned and turned to look back over the lake. He rested his elbows on the half wall and his chin on his fist and muffled a chuckle. Jen wouldn't be waiting for him. She'd be right at his side through the day. All the more reason to hurry home every night to celebrate their successes together.

Just who did Ray think he was, saying Blade wasn't good enough for Jen? He pounded the wall with his fist. He had the resources, the skills, the determination to take care of her as she deserved.

Still, Blade had to admit Jen really didn't need anyone to take care of her. She did just fine on her own. She was an independent, intelligent, feisty lady. She would probably resent a white knight coming along to sweep her off her feet and build a castle to protect her. Blade gladly admitted he needed Jen in his life, but did she need him?

CHAPTER 13

Magda was strangely quiet that evening. Blade worried. The Magda he had come to know and loathe should have griped and whined all during dinner about the way Worley abandoned his guests. She should have threatened to leave. She should have tried to slither all over Ray and Blade when they came into the dining room, and afterward when the group convened to the ballroom. When someone finally asked her what she had done all day, she only said she had been working on a book idea.

"She's wearing long sleeves, and she has different nail polish," Jen muttered to Blade when they pretended to study the flowering vines climbing one wall of the ballroom. "Maybe she was down in the tunnels again, scraped her arms and broke some nails and had to replace them." She grimaced and fluttered her fingers, displaying the fake nails she had protested wearing.

"Good idea. But why would she be..." Blade turned, sensing the shadow sneaking up on them before he heard Sarpantine's soft footsteps. How could a man so tall walk so softly in hard sole shoes on a hardwood floor?

"Someone would think you two were unsociable." Sarpantine wore that benevolent, too-cheerful smile that Blade wanted to wipe off his face. With a two-by-four. "Gloria, dance with me?"

"I can't. Danville will certainly testify that I'm a complete klutz." Jen giggled and wiggled her fingers at their host. Worley offered up a half-hearted chuckle and smile.

"Excuse me if I find that hard to believe. Such a pretty little lady merely needs the right partner." Sarpantine stepped back and swept her an elegant bow that made Blade grit his teeth. "Let me teach you. Ecstasy waits on the dance floor."

Especially if you can get her to drink something you spiked beforehand, Blade growled silently.

"Thanks, but no." Jen minced her way across the floor in heels almost as tall as Magda's, and settled down next to Ray. He wrapped an arm around her shoulders. Blade had wanted to do that all evening. "I've been working all day. I want to sit still and enjoy some good music and go to bed early. We have a big day ahead of us tomorrow. Lots of work to do."

"Yes, indeed. How charming that such a lovely lady is so talented and intelligent." Sarpantine's glance slid over Magda. She avoided the man's gaze.

"I'm starting to think our host set you to work simply to deprive me of your charming company," Sarpantine continued as he settled down into a chair next to Worley.

Blade actually felt sorry for the fat man, who began to sweat profusely.

The sooner they found the painting and got off the island, the better Blade would feel. Sarpantine all but hung over Jen during dinner. Offering to fix her a drink, trying to touch her hand, her arm, her hair. Jen usually had a good appetite, but tonight she picked at her food, leaving two-thirds of it on her plate. Blade wished Sarpantine had a room on the second floor instead of the first, even if it put him closer to Jen. It would be easier to fake an accident when he heaved the lecher off the balcony.

*   *   *

Blade couldn't sleep that night. He left the door open so he could hear activity in the stairwell, and walked the balcony, staying away from the sliding door of Ray and Jen's suite.

When he heard Jen crying, he thought he had finally grown tired enough to hallucinate. His feet carried him around the balcony to the sliding door before he could think about it. Blade found Ray sitting on Jen's side of the bed, holding her while she shivered and gasped and hid her face in her hands. Tears slipped between her fingers, silver in the moonlight.

"Good, you're here." Ray tipped his head, gesturing for Blade to come inside. "Hold her while I get something to calm her down." He glared when Blade hesitated.

Jen didn't seem to notice when she transferred from one set of arms to the other. Blade was glad she wore her cotton scrubs that left so much to the imagination. He turned her so her head rested on his shoulder and imagined Jen relaxed just a little. One hand came off her face and she clutched at his shirtfront. Her sobs quieted and her trembling slowed.

Ray knelt on his side of the bed and pulled a long black case like a traveling toolbox from under it. He unzipped it and pulled out three plastic vials.

"Handy dandy mad scientist kit?" Blade muttered. Despite himself, he glanced at Ray's side of the bed. He forgot to breathe for a moment when he realized the blankets weren't even mussed. Ray hadn't been in the bed all night.

"Forewarned is forearmed," Ray responded, mimicking one of their instructors from their training days. "Just in case Sarpantine or one of his ugly brothers decided to show up before we got out of here, I wanted to be ready."

"Precautions," Jen managed to say in a creaky voice. She relaxed her death grip on Blade's shirt, but didn't pull away from him. If anything, he thought she snuggled a little closer.

"Universal antidote." Ray sprinkled powder from each vial into a glass and stepped into the bathroom to fill it with water. "Unfortunately, one of the base ingredients is a variant of a compound that unlocks the subconscious."

"Meaning?" Blade took the glass from Ray and held it so Jen could drink. Up close, it smelled acidic and looked a hazy violet in the moonlight.

"Bad memories." Jen wiped her mouth and took the glass from him so she could down the last third of the mixture. She winced, shuddered, and blindly reached to set the glass down on the floor. Blade took it from her.

"You need to talk about it," Ray said, his voice warm with concern Blade had never heard him use on anyone before.

Something growled deep inside and Blade was surprised to realize it was jealousy. He had always admired Ray, sometimes resented his ease and skill with the ladies, but never really felt any jealousy until now.

Jealous. Yet there seemed to be nothing going on between Ray and

Jen, romance-wise. Certainly nothing physical while the job was in progress. Blade sensed a closeness and partnership between Jen and Ray that excluded him. He hated it.

"Why make her go through it again?" Blade had to ask. He reminded himself that Jen held onto him, even though she had stopped crying and shivering. That had to count for something.

"To get it out of my head," Jen said.

She sighed and seemed to tense up for a moment, like she would leap from his arms and start pacing the room. Blade drew her a little closer against his chest and tried to will his warmth and strength into her.

"There was this guy, when we were kids. He had a camera and candy bars. He used to follow my sisters around." She opened her eyes and met his and Ray's gazes. "You know."

Blade felt his stomach twist. He knew exactly what a stranger with a camera and candy bars would want from girls living on the street.

"He followed Amber home. He said he'd take care of us and we'd never be hungry or cold if we'd...play with him." Jen swallowed audibly. A shiver ran through her and Blade wondered if she would be sick. "If we didn't, he'd tell the police and we'd get split up and sent to foster homes and never see each other again. We found a new home, but he followed us."

Blade didn't want to hear any more of this, didn't want to know what sort of brutality and sickness Jen had endured.

"He caught Mari, but we broke her out when he went away. He hurt her," she said in a harsh whisper. "So we cleaned out his house. We found pictures he took of other kids and we sent them to the police and we found another place to hide. We watched him, and we set up traps all over the place. The boys wanted to beat him up and castrate him for what he did to Mari, but we knew we couldn't get away with it. So we learned to get evidence and make things hard for people like him, and help the police stop them. Sarpantine reminds me of him," she ended on a sigh.

Jen seemed to deflate, leaning even more completely into him. Blade held her, fighting the angry shudders that rose up from deep inside him. He rested his chin on the top of her head and wished he knew the words to say to make her feel better, to drive away the nightmares and erase those painful memories. He lifted his gaze and met Ray's. The bleak hurting he saw there was a match for what he felt, and Blade knew they were united in this area. It didn't matter to him that Ray loved Jen too. She deserved all the love and protection they could heap on her.

"She's out now," Ray whispered. He gestured at Jen's dented pillow.

"Nuh uh," Jen murmured. A tiny smile caught a corner of her mouth. She let them lay her down on the mattress, and curled up on her side when Blade tugged the blankets up around her again. She caught hold of his hand when he rested it on her shoulder a moment. "Don't go."

"Better stay," Ray said. He picked up the glass and went into the bathroom to rinse it.

"You're one tough lady," Blade said.

"You're tougher." Jen managed to open one eye. She sighed. "We had each other. You had nobody."

"I went for the adventure. You're doing something great, helping kids. Why you do it makes a whole lot more sense now."

"Love kids." Her voice dropped to a sleepy rumble. Blade knew she'd be truly asleep in only a few minutes. "Want lots of kids someday. All my own." She tried to open her eyes again, but her lids just fluttered before she gave up. "Silly, huh?"

"Wanting kids isn't silly. You'd be a great mother." His voice caught in his throat.

Jen didn't respond, and he knew she had finally fallen back to sleep. Blade wanted to kiss her cheek, to ensure she had good dreams this time, but he didn't dare. Ray took the chair facing the foot of the bed and settled down to keep watch over Jen. That questioning little lift to one eyebrow stopped Blade cold.

Did Ray challenge him, or mock him? Or did he try to remind Blade of what he had said earlier that evening, that he wasn't good enough for her?

Blade got up and stood over Jen, watching her sleep for a few moments, then retreated out through the sliding door to his own room. He didn't get much sleep, and when he did, it was to dream of Jen, playing with children on the mountain meadow leading to his cabin.

*   *   *

I hate this. I hate this. I hate this.

Jen rested her bare elbows on the raw stone wall that looked out over the docks and kept people from going over the edge into the lake. She didn't know who she wanted to toss over first—Ray, Blade, or

Sarpantine.

Or maybe she should start with Magda, because the scarlet snake wouldn't leave Ray or Blade alone. As if her smirking and sneering during breakfast weren't bad enough, Ray had declared he needed a break from working on the security system today, and asked her to give him a tour of the island. Jen knew it was for the good of their mission, to find all the possible hiding places for the painting, but she still felt abandoned.

So now Magda thought she had scored one on simple little Gloria. Even knowing Magda hadn't won anything didn't help Jen defeat her frustration.

Definitely Ray needed tossing. He didn't show it, but Jen knew he laughed at her. He *had* guessed her purely physical attraction to Blade, and he was going to torment her for it. Jen the Untouchable, the Ice Queen, he had called her on previous jobs, when not even the hottest staged encounter had raised her pulse. Did he think because *he* couldn't get a reaction from her, she would never have the hots for anyone?

Ray was sick. He had to be sick. If he suspected she was a relative, he still played games with her and wouldn't tell her his suspicions, there was something seriously wrong with the man. Did he honestly think she needed his help to notice Blade? Did he think she needed assistance to get hot for someone?

Volcanoes were chilly, compared to how she felt about Blade. Especially after some of her dreams of him.

Definitely Sarpantine needed to be tossed. He hadn't taken the hint from her brush-offs last night. His gallantry at breakfast was almost laughable, until she reminded herself that his MO was to get close to a woman so he could drug her and then swoop in for the kill. Could he bring her some coffee? A sweet roll? Some jam for her toast? Gloria simply must try the buckwheat pancakes. Could he fix some for her?

At barely nine a.m., he wanted to drug and seduce her? It was almost funny, when she knew his motives and game plan. To see the frustration in his eyes, like coals slowly fanned to life. Especially when she let Ray feed her a taste of his buckwheat pancakes dripping in cherries and whipped cream. Hilarious, until she caught a glimpse of Blade's face.

Talk about volcanoes.

Even though she knew it was all an act for Sarpantine's and Worley's benefits, the air temperature rose ten degrees each time Blade looked at her. It was as if he shouted that he wanted to touch her. To pull her into his arms and devour her with caresses and kisses. Jen *had to* remind herself he was only playing a role, or she would have slithered over the table, in imitation of Magda, and thrown herself into his arms.

And then Blade just walked away when he finished eating, as if he had nothing else on his mind.

Last night he had been so sweet, so protective, so comforting. She had been able to let go of the memory-nightmare because Blade held her.

He didn't even try to kiss her. They had plenty of chances and he didn't take one. Was there something wrong with her?

Maybe Blade was just as mentally sick as Ray, playing games with her heart and hormones and then just walking away.

"I'm going to kill him," she told the wind.

It didn't matter that Blade had agreed to go check out all means of leaving the island, he had walked away, leaving her alone on the patio not half an hour ago. Sarpantine could return at any moment to slobber and leer with no one to stop him.

It was all an act, Ray's plan, and that's what made her so angry with all three men. How could Blade just play with her feelings like that? Didn't he know how even one smoldering glance could knock a girl off her feet and collapse her into a puddle of need, rife with extremely risqué daydreams?

Blade probably played games with hearts all the time in the line of duty. It meant nothing to him, and as long as they were pretending to be Mik and Gloria, he obviously expected it to mean nothing to her.

Well, it did. For the first time, soulful, hungry glances and steamy sighs affected her down to her marrow.

Ray wouldn't have suggested the ruse of an affair if he thought it would bother her. How could he know she'd never given her heart away? How could he know? She hadn't suspected that the first time she relaxed her defenses, they would blow apart as if hit by a tsunami.

Could she blame the protective antidote Ray made her take this morning? It affected her dreams, could it affect her emotions?

No matter what the explanation for how she felt now, Jen refused to admit to either man how much she ached, how every meaningless word, touch and gesture scraped her raw inside. Never. She'd pretend with all the creativity and energy she had. She'd put on the best performance of her life.

Too bad the spying world didn't give out Oscars.

"My dear lady," Sarpantine drawled. He sauntered across the pavement from the French doors of the ballroom. It had only taken him an hour to find her. Either he was lazy, or he had never dealt with a bored, abandoned wife before. Was he so sure of his victory he prolonged the chase?

Or did the arrogant louse expect her to come hunting *him* after a few double-entendre compliments?

"How wonderful to find you all alone. It's so difficult to talk without that dreary husband of yours getting in the way. Does he turn every conversation to computers?"

"It's how we make our living." Jen hoped she'd get her chance to toss Sarpantine over the wall after all.

"Yes, but there's more to life than making money. Lovely as it is," he added, his voice dropping to a silky caress.

"Oh, no, I love working on the computers with Mark. It's so fulfilling." She batted her eyelashes and tipped her head back and gave him her most vacuous smile.

Any moment, he was going to give her some line along the lines of finding true fulfillment with his help. He would sadly inform her that her husband neglected her and Guy Sarpantine had come to her rescue because she had captured his heart the first time they met. Then, according to Ray's debriefing, he'd offer her something to drink, just before he led her off to a secluded, dark, sound-proofed spot. Where he would proceed to have his way with her and she would be totally unable to resist.

In his poisonous dreams, maybe.

Ray said kneeing slime balls in the family jewels only got them angry most of the time, rather than making them curl into fetal balls, like in the movies. This was one slime ball Jen would gladly experiment on until she got the technique right.

"Computers fascinate me," Sarpantine murmured. He rested an elbow on the top of the wall, just above waist height, and leaned his weight into it. "I would love to learn what it is about them that brings such brightness to your lovely eyes."

Jen blinked, momentarily thrown off balance. Who said he could change the script?

"Mark could teach you. He is a teacher, anyway. That's how we met."

"Yes, I'd heard that."

Jen fought not to back up a step—or three—or she might start running. How had Sarpantine learned their made-up history? Had Sarpantine done research on all the guests, just as she and Ray did? Had he come ahead of schedule because he suspected a threat to the painting?

"However..." Sarpantine reached out to stroke one long, elegant, tanned finger up Jen's bare arm. "The teacher makes all the difference. Don't you agree?"

"Oh, sure." Jen fought not to yank her arm away. A tingle of burning prickles followed the trail of his finger. "I mean, I liked computers a lot, but then I took my first class with Mark and—whammo—love at first sight." She attempted her fake Gloria giggle, but it caught in her throat.

"Is this a private orgy, or can anyone join in?" Blade bounded up the stairs from the docks and skidded to a stop only a few steps away.

He had been down at the docks all this time, Jen realized. If he had arrived with the swirl of a cape, the flash of a sword, and a rope to swing them both away to safety, she couldn't have felt more delighted to see him. And she *could* let it show.

"Mr. Sarpantine was asking me to teach him about computers. Just like you did yesterday." Jen managed a giggle and bounced over to Blade. He grabbed hold of her hand and the warm pressure of his touch sent bubbles into her brain. "He could take lessons with you, couldn't he?"

"Pretty lady, the only lessons I want are private." Blade raised her hand to his lips.

Jen's knees wobbled as he turned her hand to kiss the palm.

"But—well—I mean, Mark could get a lot more done with two students at one time."

Was her brain going to stay stuck this way? Not that she didn't enjoy it. She'd never felt so fantastic. What was it about Blade's eyes that turned her hollow and light and wobbly?

"My dear Gloria." His rumbling voice sent answering ripples through her chest and downward. "Some lessons are best conducted in private, where we can be both teacher and student."

"Oh," she whispered. Her head swam a little. The deck felt a little too warm for only ten in the morning.

"My thoughts exactly," Sarpantine said, startling her. She had honestly forgotten he was there.

Wake up, stupid!

"And in answer to your question, yes, this is private." Sarpantine grabbed Jen's arm just above the elbow. The burning prickles returned.

Jen could have sworn she felt something coating his hand. Like...plastic?

"Whether it becomes pleasure, or even the orgy you so graciously suggested, is all up to *my* sweet Gloria." He leaned closer. The peppermints on his breath made Jen's stomach jolt.

"That's right, it *is* up to Gloria," Blade said. He slid his other hand down Jen's arm, keeping a tight hold on her hand.

For just a moment, she had an image of the two men starting a tug-of-war with her in the middle, both rope and prize. Instead of getting angry or feeling amused by the idiocy, her stomach decided to do a full gainer with a double twist.

The flagstone paving under her feet rippled. Going up and down in waves. Like a rope-and-board bridge over a high chasm.

A bridge about to break.

Jen hated falling.

Except for falling into Blade's eyes. She wanted to fall into his big gray eyes forever.

Blade would catch her. He had held her hand during that roller coaster ride, hadn't he? He kept her from feeling like she would fall forever and be sick until there was nothing left inside her.

Something's wrong. Bad big time wrong.

"Sweet lady?" Sarpantine whispered and leaned close enough his breath brushed her ear.

"Gloria?" Blade frowned. He knew something was wrong.

"I can't breathe." Jen's insides twisted again, wringing out like a dishrag, as if she would lose her breakfast from both ends simultaneously.

"Lean on me, my dear." Sarpantine slid his hand across her shoulders, where her low-cut, spaghetti-strap shirt left her skin bare.

The prickling sensation streaked across her back. It transformed into a throbbing, nauseous headache that blasted into life behind her eyes and dropped a bomb into her stomach.

Contact drug, was her first thought.

I'm going to kill Ray, was her second.

The bomb went off and breakfast demanded a return trip.

"Mik?" she whispered, then turned her face to Sarpantine and stopped fighting her insistent stomach.

CHAPTER 14

"I'm going to kill him," Blade snarled as he took the tower steps two at a time to get to Ray and Jen's room.

Gut instinct told him it was *Ray's* fault Jen had heaved all over Sarpantine and then collapsed backwards into his arms.

"Take a number," Jen whispered, and pressed her face deeper into his shirt. It sopped up her cold sweat. Another wave of shivers rolled through her and she moaned deep in her throat.

That was so much like the sounds he'd daydreamed of inspiring in Jen, Blade nearly stopped. A shiver rolled through him that had nothing to do with cold. His forward momentum kept them going and he stumbled out onto the landing where two doors divided the tower between Jen and Ray's suite, and his. He almost took her to his room, but instinct also told him Ray would know what to do. Jen needed help. Ray had better be here, still getting ready for his island tour with Magda.

Blade kicked at the door. It barely budged. He turned to maneuver so he could open the door without letting go of Jen, and nearly fell inside when Ray yanked the door open.

"You didn't." Ray groaned, as close to confused as Blade had ever seen him. "I told you, don't let Sarpantine feed—"

"Contact drug. Gloves," Jen said on a raspy whisper.

"Shower." Ray ran across the room and flung the bathroom door open. He turned the shower on full blast and stepped back.

Blade set Jen in the jade green tub, getting himself doused across face, shoulder, and arm before he was sure she was secure and wouldn't slide down and drown.

"You too," Ray said. He gestured at the tub and steaming stream of water, stopping short of actually pushing Blade in.

"But—"

"You heard her. A contact drug. She sweated all over you. It hasn't hit you yet, but it will soon if you don't wash it off. Now."

When Ray used that rock hard tone, Blade knew better than to argue. He toed off his shoes, peeled off his sopping shirt and tossed it across the back of the tub, and settled in gingerly next to Jen. She clung to the side, eyes closed, and took short, panting breaths, probably fighting not to heave again. The tub was big enough for both of them, plus Ray, without anyone touching.

"Here." Ray held out the ice bucket from the little wet bar installed in each of their rooms. "She won't get any better until the drug is washed off or diluted. That's how the antidote works." He filled a glass with water and handed it to Jen. She downed it, visibly fighting nausea to do so.

"Is this the same antidote that gave her nightmares?" Blade nearly dropped the bucket. Ray glared at him and he started dumping buckets of warm water over them both in turns. "You're a menace, you know that?"

"You'd better take some too." Ray filled another glass of water for Jen and gave it to her. A nasty sparkle lit his eyes when Blade opened his mouth to protest. "Unless you want to turn into a raging sex fiend right here in the bathtub?"

Blade opened his mouth to say of course not, he'd never want that to happen. Then he looked at Jen, with her skimpy, silky clothes plastered to her skin, nearly transparent. Her underwear lines were evident now, to Blade's relief, but the cloth outlined every curve, every crease, every dip.

He was already a sex fiend when it came to dreams of Jen, but at least he could control himself while he was awake.

"Soap." Jen's voice sounded stronger, less miserable. She sat up a little straighter and put her face into the warm shower spray. "If it's got an oil base, have to break down the oil."

"Good thinking." Ray tossed them a bottle of shower gel.

The label said raspberry. Blade muffled a groan, imagining what he was going to smell like when this was over. Raspberry was fine, all over Jen, but not all over him.

Unless he got that way from having her all over him.

Maybe he'd better start scrubbing, fast.

"I'll get the antidote," Ray added. "You two, scrub. No time for false modesty."

Wordless, Jen picked up the washcloth hanging over the side of the tub. She held it out and Blade squirted gel on it. He watched for a few moments as she rubbed the lathering gel down her arms, across her face.

"He touched my back."

"You sound a lot better," Blade offered. Then he realized she held out the washcloth. "Uh—"

"Thanks." Jen managed a thin smile. She scooted closer to him and turned so she could present her back to him.

Blade dabbed with the sudsy cloth. His brain filled with images of rubbing suntan oil all over Jen's back. Would she wear a bikini, tankini, or one-piece bathing suit? A moment of thought told him Jen was a one-piece kind of girl.

He imagined rubbing the oil down her back, sliding his fingers under her straps, stroking under the edge of her suit.

"Drink," Ray said, cutting into the daydream before Blade got hotter than the shower water filling the room with steam.

He held out a whiskey tumbler full of a murky olive drab liquid that swirled and fizzed. Shades of Dr. Frankenstein's laboratory. Or was that Dr. Jekyll?

Blade didn't want to drink it, but if he was starting to react to some drug Jen had sweated onto him, he needed it. He took a deep breath and downed the salty, gritty glassful. He would have held his nose to block what was sure to be a rancid taste, but Jen was watching him.

"If I get sick—" He belched. "Sorry. If I get sick, that means I'm safe?"

"Nausea means your body neutralizes the drug as it attacks your nervous system." Jen took the cloth from him. She stood, wobbling— she wore her spike sandals, and they were never meant for bathtubs— and rinsed once more under the spray.

"Sure you're safe now?" Ray helped her step out of the tub with one hand, and yanked a jade green bath sheet off the wall pegs with the other.

"Starving." She managed a soggy smile as he wrapped the sheet around her.

"She's better." He grinned and watched her leave the room. When she slammed the door, shutting them into the bathroom, he turned that grin on Blade. "She has a cast iron stomach and a killer sweet tooth, but you'd never know by looking at her."

"You didn't answer my question." Blade rubbed the remainder of the raspberry scented sudsy cloth over himself, anywhere Jen's sweat might have touched him.

Had he let Sarpantine touch him? Maybe while they were starting that tug-of-war over possession of Jen's arm? He couldn't remember much of anything after Jen heaved and Sarpantine staggered away, pale and gagging.

"My friends who whipped up this little gourmet delight can't tone down the side effects of the antidote without losing the scope of its protection." Ray sat on the edge of the tub and turned off the shower. "How do you feel?"

"Don't worry. I'm not going to redecorate the bathroom any time soon."

"No reaction to seeing Jen in wet clothes?"

Blade opened his mouth to respond no, then the very casualness of Ray's tone woke up a few suspicious brain cells.

"I'm not going to knock down the door and start raping and pillaging, if that's what you mean." That earned an exasperated sigh from Ray. "I'm fine. No change."

"Okay, let's try it another way. How do you feel about Jen without the help of drugs?"

"None of your business. Besides, I thought you wanted me to stay way from her." Blade stood with all the dignity he could muster, stepped out of the tub, snatched up his shoes and his wet shirt, and exited the bathroom.

"You're bad off," Ray said with a chuckle.

A yelp and a sandal that missed his nose by an inch drove the response from Blade's lips. He froze, caught by the after-image of Jen in hot pink panties and bra, diving behind the bed.

"Sorry." He started back to the bathroom, but he didn't need to face Ray's smug grin so soon. Blade settled for turning his back.

Total silence.

He was willing to risk another shoe in his face for a glimpse of Jen in her underwear. What if she had passed out?

"Are you okay?"

"This is worse than a dozen brothers," Jen grumbled. He hoped those sounds of movement meant she finished dressing.

"Could you tell me when you're done?"

"Why don't you go to your own room and change your clothes before you get pneumonia or something?"

"Oh. Yeah."

Good idea. He wished he'd thought of it. Jen probably thought he was hopeless.

*   *   *

Three hours later, Worley found Blade in the gymnasium, trying to sweat away frustration. He had run the treadmill until his knees threatened to buckle. Now he worked on abdominal crunches. He had worked up past his usual morning routine and lost count around the agony point.

"My friend..." Worley mopped his forehead and sat down on the bench opposite the sit-up station. He managed a shaky grin when Blade gave him a sideways glance and never interrupted his routine. "How are you feeling?"

"Never better," Blade grunted.

"You're worried about Gloria." His host chuckled when Blade did pause for half a second. "I know the signs of a man in love. I've resorted to the weight room many times, until I was so exhausted I couldn't even dream of my lady love."

It had probably been twenty years since Worley was in love, Blade decided, after a glance at the man's bell-shaped girth.

"Might I suggest sailing as a less...strenuous escape? Nothing like letting the wind take you far away. Out on the lake, nothing but water in every direction. Very calming. Soothing. And you do enjoy the sport, I hear."

"I've been out of practice," Blade muttered. "Too busy. No time to relax."

"Then you must take the time to relax. Until the Williamses are done setting up my new security system, I will not need your help with my new treasure."

"And you're still telling me to keep my hands off Gloria. Well, let me tell you, I know Sarpantine's reputation and his MO. I bet Gloria got sick because he drugged her. He had his hands on her, just before she blew. Tell *him* to keep his paws off the lady, why don't you?"

Worley froze, eyes wide. A waterfall of sweat spilled over his forehead and into his eyes. He couldn't talk until he had taken a dozen shallow, panting breaths.

135

"I…I had not realized." He attempted a smile. "Yes, I should talk to Guy. He will understand. He is as concerned about the safety of my new treasure as I am."

Yeah, Blade mused. *I'll just bet. You think he's going to take it right out of your hands. Bet that's why you want people around, so he doesn't bully you into handing it over.*

Worley stood and headed for the door. "Please, my friend. Consider everything here available for your enjoyment."

Blade decided Worley didn't choke on those words because he was too upset to realize what he had just said.

Everything Blade could want for an enjoyable afternoon *was* on the island, except privacy and time to talk to Jen, to get to know her, to find out if he hadn't imagined that hunger he thought he saw in her eyes. From the moment he first saw her, there was a connection—though he was the first to dismiss the idea of soul mates and destiny. Kindred spirits, maybe closer to him than any partner he'd worked with over the years.

If he couldn't have some privacy with Jen, then some privacy just to think and not be Mik Poling would be very welcome. He didn't know diddly about sailing, except what he had picked up in the last few days. He could just take off, wander back and forth out there in the wide open water where he could see the islands and nothing but water until Canada. Just him, the water and wind and only the gulls for company.

Or wait a minute…

"Sounds good," Blade said, pretending he couldn't have cared less. "How soon can a boat be ready if I feel like going?"

"There's one waiting right now. The green one. I'll have the sail put up, ready to just slip the lines and head out. The wind is perfect right now. Don't waste any time."

No, Blade decided as he did one more crunch for luck. He wouldn't waste any time. Or the privacy.

When he knocked on the door of Jen and Ray's room half an hour later, his overindulgence at the gym was starting to catch up with him. But, he had showered and changed his clothes and anticipation soothed most of his growing aches.

"Who's there?" Jen asked, her voice a quavering whisper.

"Mik. Just checking if you're feeling any better."

The door flew open and Jen grabbed him by the shirtfront, dragging him into the room before he could even brace himself.

"I guess you're feeling better." He barely kept from stumbling across the room to the opposite wall.

"Sarpantine's been up here twice, offering to keep me company. Ray is downstairs with Worley, playing up to Magda and telling everybody how disgusting I am when I'm sick. I'm pretending to die. It's a good thing he stole something from lunch for me or I'd starve. Plus I'm bored, because he took his computer with him." She crossed her eyes and flopped down on the end of the bed. She wore another shorts outfit, but this one looked more like Jen than Gloria; jeans shorts and a French-cut T-shirt in a swirling pattern of greens and blues.

"Sea air is good for invalids," he offered.

"We're on a lake."

"Okay then, how about sunshine and fresh air and a relaxing sailboat ride?"

"Just the two of us?" She sat up, and Blade dared to flatter himself there was interest in her eyes.

"And a bunch of sea gulls—or is that lake gulls?" He bowed and offered her his bent arm.

"Whatever they're called, as long as they don't fly overhead, I'm fine." Laughing, she slipped her hand through the crook of his arm and they were on their way.

After a brief stop for her sandals. And another stop to leave Ray a note, so he wouldn't think Sarpantine had kidnapped Jen. And pausing to make sure no one could see them sneak down the tower stairs and out the side door. The last thing they needed was for Sarpantine or Magda to try to come along.

The docks were deserted. That suited Blade. The sailboat was up and ready to go. It was the smallest of Worley's fleet. Blade estimated four people could ride in comfort, but what did he really know about sailing? He counted on the tiny outboard motor to keep him out of trouble. How bad could it get, when they were almost within shouting distance of Put-in-Bay? He could swim, Jen could swim, and there were life jackets in all the boats. Blade had made sure of that this morning when he checked out their escape options.

"All right, here we go."

Blade made a show of settling Jen onto the edge of the open pit in the center of the boat, where the passengers sat and put their gear. He loosened the lines holding the boat, then took a long step down into the pilot's seat. The boom creaked as he released the rope holding it in place, and tried to swing about.

Jen ducked, but she laughed as Blade caught the swinging bar with the sail attached, and kept it from going anywhere near her. In moments, they had left the docks with the wind at their backs. They kept silent as they left the shadow of Worley's island and headed toward open water. The wind picked up.

"I supposed sailing is one of those skills they require you to learn at the Agency?" Jen said, breaking the silence first.

"Never learned."

"Wait a minute—we're out in a sailboat and you don't know what you're doing?"

"I'm a fast learner. Besides, we have the outboard as a backup."

"Oh." She studied him, her face unreadable.

"Besides, I thought you knew how."

"Never even sat in a sailboat until I got here." Jen laughed.

"Not a survival skill either?" Blade kept half his attention on a motorboat skimming past them, and the ferry leaving Put-in-Bay behind it.

"Swimming is a survival skill. Sailing is a luxury."

"Never know when you'll need it."

"Like now?" Jen scooted around the edge of the pit to get closer to him. "I'm not worried. I trust you."

"You do?" He grinned, feeling a new warmth spread over him. "How much?" He winced as the wind slapped at his face.

"Enough not to wreck us. Enough to get us out of this whole stupid mess alive if something goes wrong. I mean, you got me away from Sarpantine this morning."

"You got yourself away from him. In case you didn't notice, he was already running by the time I caught you."

"I trusted you to catch me." Her voice throbbed through him. Jen tilted her head to look up at the mast, gilded with fading sunshine and spotted with cloud shadows. "I think I trust you more than I do Ray."

"Smart choice," he said, trying not to choke on what would emerge as a touchdown cheer if he let go.

"Survival skill. Gut instinct. Ray's one of the good guys. I thank God to have him on my side when things get rough, but there's something about him. He holds back. Some part of him is always coolly watching and assessing and figuring out how to make it work. And then he starts throwing around advice like—" Jen swallowed audibly and looked away.

"Advice like what?" Blade wanted to reach over and squeeze her shoulder, to steady her and just for the pleasure of touching her. But the wind picked up, slapping little wavelets against the sides of the boat and rattling the rigging. At least, he thought it was called rigging.

"Oh...personal stuff. Sometimes you wonder if he has a heart, and you hope and pray for the day some woman knocks him flat. I almost hope he opens up and holds out his heart, and she doesn't notice. For a while. Make him sweat a little." She shrugged and managed a stiff little smile.

Blade's heart sank. For a long, breathless moment, he felt hollow and yet heavy enough to sink the sailboat.

Had Jen fallen for Ray at the beginning and he had never noticed? Or had he played with her before discouraging her?

"I'll kill him," he muttered without realizing he said it aloud. Until it was too late.

"No, let *her* do it." Jen managed a rusty little laugh. "Do you—you thought he and I—No way, not for a million bucks." She laughed again, and the sound held music. "Like I said, survival skills. I knew from the beginning not to let my heart anywhere near Ray. He's a sweet guy, really. Especially when it comes to kids. He's going to make a great daddy. Just not my type, you know?"

"No?" Blade knew he wore the stupidest grin that ever split his face, and he didn't care. "Ray's an idiot."

"Hmm, I wouldn't say that."

"Letting you get away."

"Oh?" She scooted close enough he could catch her raspberry scent. The fitful breeze swirled it around to him and more cloud shadows covered them. "You think I'm worth keeping?"

The boom yanked hard against the rope Blade held. He looked up and tightened his grip instead of answering her. Another gust of wind caught the sail, yanking the rope from his hand and spinning the beam around the mast.

"Duck!" He flung himself forward and grabbed Jen's shoulder, slamming her down against the deck as the beam passed overhead.

Jen offered a breathless little laugh and huddled there for a few seconds. She turned on her side and watched the beam, then flipped completely on her back. She lay close enough her hair touched his leg.

"Maybe I should just stay here for the rest of the voyage," she offered as he caught hold of the rope and yanked the sail and beam—boom?—back into place.

For a moment there, the sailboat had started to turn, despite the keel and Blade's hand on the rudder.

"I thought you said you trusted me." Blade grinned, even though he felt alternately sick and relieved. Sick at the opening he had lost; relieved he hadn't totally screwed up.

Worth keeping? If he could, he'd snatch Jen up and carry her away to his cabin in the middle of the Appalachians. The most secure place he could imagine, short of nuclear war.

First, he had to make sure she was interested. He'd seen instances where one lover had imagined the beloved felt the same way and had been wrong. That led to disaster for them both. Just because Jen flirted with him now, with no audience, that didn't mean she was interested.

"I trust you completely, body and soul." Jen stretched like a cat, getting comfortable on the shadowed fiberglass surface.

"You shouldn't trust anybody with your body."

"Why, Mr. Blade Hampton, did I just hear you—"

The line holding the beam snapped with a cracking sound that cut through the growing rumble of the wind. Blade twisted sideways to avoid the sweep of the beam—then realized what a disaster they would have on their hands if he didn't get hold of the sail and control it. He raised his hand just half a second after the beam passed over him and snatched at it. And missed.

"Something's very wrong," Jen said.

"Tell me about it." He stood in the cockpit and turned around, hoping to catch the sail on its next sweep. But the perverse beam stayed out over the water, out of reach.

"It was cut."

"What?" He took the chance to look down at her. Jen was half in the cockpit with him now, and she held up the end of the rope.

Sure enough, the synthetic fibers weren't frayed or melted or stretched by unusual strain, but cleanly cut. Part of his brain started calculating what it would take to cut this thickness of rope, and the mental skills needed to cut it enough to not be noticeable, to make the rope usable for a short time.

"We've been set up. *I've* been set up. Nobody knew you were coming out here." He sat and reached for the engine ignition.

"Worley doesn't have the guts." Jen scooted over so he had room to maneuver in the cockpit.

Blade wished he could enjoy the warm pressure of her leg against his. Maybe later, when they were out of danger, he could find some place just as private.

"No, but somebody could have heard him offer me the boat." He frowned when the engine didn't respond to his repeated stabs at the button.

"My bet's on Magda."

"Why?"

"Besides jealousy?" She watched him raise the little hatch that gave him access to the motor. "What's wrong?"

"Doesn't want to start." He sprawled across the deck to look into the pit where the passengers sat.

"What are you looking for?"

"Toolbox." He groaned when he saw what wasn't under the edges of the pit.

"What's wrong?"

"The life jackets are gone."

"What?" Jen started to climb over to the pit to join him, but Blade put up a hand to stop her. "Who would take out all the life jackets?"

"Someone who hopes I can't swim." Blade ducked back down, praying the toolbox had been ignored.

None of his prayers were being answered today.

"Gas tank is empty," Jen informed him as he sat up again.

Blade closed his eyes and counted to ten. It amazed him right now that he had survived as long as he did in the espionage game. Look what a rotten, fumbling mess he had made of things, just trying to get close to Jen. Nothing dangerous, nothing with the fate of world peace resting on his shoulders, just some private time to open up a little and find out if she felt anything remotely like he did. And he blew it. Not only didn't Jen need him to protect her, but she had more common sense. What kind of an idiot took a girl out in a sailboat when he had barely learned how to sail?

The obvious answer was, a guy thinking with his hormones instead of his brains. Did he really think one afternoon of privacy would have her falling into his arms?

"Should have thought of that." He sighed and heaved himself back into the cockpit, after casting another despairing glance at the sail. It stayed tauntingly out of reach.

He stopped and stared, his gaze going beyond the sail. North and upwards. The slate-colored sky looked ready to boil. Where had those clouds come from?

"Worley told you everything was ready. You trusted him," Jen offered.

"Stupidest mistake green kids wouldn't make." Blade refused to look at her as he slammed the engine hatch closed.

"Hey, I'm not green, but I trusted him too. Worley needs you. He wouldn't attack you." Jen rested her hand on his arm.

"He's been warning Mik away from Gloria. He can probably find an appraiser before he can find another security genius."

"Oh."

Maybe somebody suspected he was a fraud. Maybe Sarpantine had set him up, to get him away from Jen.

If they hadn't been so careful to sneak out of the house, somebody would have seen and come after them. Of course, if this was Sarpantine's game, the man had already found she was gone and raised the hue and cry to find her. The island wasn't big enough for her to avoid him for long.

Jen gasped as the wind gusted down and across the boat, hard enough to whip icy spray on them. Blade yanked her down onto the floor of the cockpit and leaned over her, shielding her from the worst of it with his body.

"Yow. Thanks. That storm was kind of sudden."

The storm had blown over the lake in a matter of moments. Blade had the sneaking suspicion he should have known it was coming. *If* he knew anything about sailing. Whoever had sabotaged the boat probably knew about the incoming storm and did this to keep him from returning to shore in time.

And he was the booby who got caught in the trap. With Jen.

"Sorry." His voice caught and his smile was a stiff grimace.

"It's not the best first date I've ever been on, but it's certainly not the worst." Jen patted his knee.

"First date?" For just a few seconds, Blade didn't hear the rising wind or even feel the buffeting against his back.

"That's why you asked me to come out with you, right?" Jen tried to smile, sitting at his feet, and Blade swore he saw a glimmer of childlike uncertainty in her eyes. "Actually, I don't have anything for comparison."

"Should have found a better place to be alone with you, but yeah." He swallowed hard, unsure whether he was going to choke or shout in glee. "First date."

"Next time, let's try a movie. Lots of greasy popcorn and lemonade. A romantic movie."

"Romantic?" He felt like cheering. "Like what?"

"I don't know. When's the fourth Terminator movie?"

"You are my kind of girl." Blade leaned down and brushed a hurried kiss across her forehead. Nowhere near where he wanted it to be, and certainly not long enough. Jen's eyes sparkled—no, they smoldered like coals—when he straightened up again.

Just in time to see the beam come slamming around in a full three-sixty, to smack him right across the forehead.

For an eternal moment, Blade couldn't feel anything, couldn't see anything, couldn't hear anything. Then his whole world was Jen screaming his name, Jen's hands grabbing at his clothes, and the pain that spiked through his body and shattered him, separating his head from his shoulders.

Blade hung onto consciousness with all the grit and nasty stubbornness he had learned in the Marine Corps and his years in the Agency. It seemed he'd only managed to get his lungs working again when something cold smacked him across his entire body and enveloped him. Lake water.

He was overboard. The boat had capsized. Where was Jen? Flailing, he forced his eyes open, forced himself to see, to heave himself out of the water, to find her.

"Hold still!" Jen shrieked right in his ear. She dug her fingernails into his shoulder and the minuscule, sharp pain cut through everything else that turned his body to cement.

Water splashed across his face and he choked when some went into his mouth. Blade groaned when the crossed signals in his brain straightened out, and his eyes started working.

He lay on something hard and streaked greenish-gray over a white, sloping surface. Bracing himself, he raised his head. Wind slapped more water into his face, but he got a good look around. The stinging of lake water in his eyes was a negligible pain compared to bone-deep bruises and the shattered feeling in his head.

"Coming around?" Jen called above the roar of the wind.

Blade turned his head too quickly, looking for her. Through the blackness trying to fill his vision and the swirling nausea that indicated the king of concussions, he found her. He groaned again as their entire situation became clear in a flash of humiliating insight.

Not all that blackness was in his eyes, but from the clouds that pushed the day toward midnight. Jen hung in the water, holding onto the side of the overturned sailboat. He lay sprawled like old laundry across the only part of the sailboat above water. Blood ran in a thin, watery stream down the curve into the gash where the keel belonged.

A splintered board three inches wide stuck up at a twisted angle from the slot; all that remained of the keel board. Fiberglass shouldn't splinter like that. It wouldn't splinter like that, unless someone had tampered with it.

"Somebody wanted you out of the way really bad," she said when she caught him staring at the shattered board.

Blade nodded, ignoring the pain of that injudicious movement. The wind shrieked louder, wrapping an Arctic fist around him. He shivered.

"Can you hold on if you get into the water?" Jen asked. "It's warmer in the water than out in the wind."

He would have thought of that, if his brain ever kicked back into gear long enough. Blade bit his tongue hard enough to make it bleed, to silence the groans as he maneuvered off the bottom of the boat and into the water.

Jen scrambled to grab hold of him, her fingers thin and sharp, digging into his shirt as he slid into the water and kept going down. For a few seconds, it took all his concentration just to move his legs and kick hard enough to get his head above the surface. Jen guided his hands to the ropes she had twisted through the gaps in the sailboat's side.

She was right. The water was much warmer than the storm winds. Blade closed his eyes and concentrated on simply holding on, keeping his mouth and nose above water. He flinched a little when something slid up along his leg. Eyes fluttering open, he found himself nearly nose to nose with Jen, and realized it was her leg bumping his in the water.

He had dreamed of being this close to her. Now, he couldn't even enjoy it. What had he ever done to deserve this torment, and why did it have to catch up with him now, of all times?

"How are you feeling?" Jen had to raise her voice to be heard above the wind and the slapping roar of the waves.

"Getting there." Blade nodded and forced a grim smile.

He wanted to say he felt like a prize idiot, a moron so caught up in adolescent hormone fantasies he couldn't keep from getting popped by the beam like in a Three Stooges movie.

"I was going to tie you to the boat, but I couldn't be sure it would stay afloat or it wouldn't roll over or something. What do I know about boats?" She tried to shrug. A wave slapped her in the face and she gasped, spluttering through the water.

"More than me." He moved closer, craving the warmth of her that radiated through the storm-tossed waters.

144

Jen let out a tiny shriek, her legs flailing against his.

"Please tell me that was you!"

"Just me." He pivoted a little, bringing his legs against hers again.

"I hate being like this." Jen tried to smile, but her lips trembled. She had suddenly lost half her color.

Why? She had weathered the capsizing and his injury and everything else like a trooper. Why did the collision of their legs underwater scare her like that?

"What?" Blade tried to chuckle, though the effort hurt his head. "You don't enjoy the challenge of hanging onto an overturned boat in the middle of a storm?"

"If I want challenges, I'll do crossword puzzles in ink."

"You don't already?" It was getting easier to tease her with every passing moment. The pain didn't recede, but at least he could push it aside if he had something else on his mind. Like staying closer to Jen, sharing warmth, trying to make up for failing her so badly right from the start.

"Ray does the crosswords in ink." She stuck her tongue out at him, and groaned a moment later when another wave slapped her face while her tongue was still out. "Oh, gross!"

"Nobody said Lake Erie was fit for human consumption." Blade pressed his feet around her ankles. Jen didn't flinch away.

"It's not that." She closed her eyes for a few seconds. He could have sworn she was embarrassed. "I have an over-active imagination."

Yeah, and he could tell her a thing or two about his imagination, just being pressed close against her in the water.

"I hate not being able to see what's below us, you know? Not knowing what's going to come swimming up from down in all that murky water." She shuddered, and the movement telegraphed into his body. He definitely felt a little warmer.

"I guarantee, there are no sharks or killer squids in Lake Erie."

"Oh—you." Jen started to stick her tongue out at him, then flinched and seemed to think better of it. "Good thing there aren't, with you bleeding. Though it seems to be slowing."

"Head wounds are always pretty fierce, but they close up quick too."

"Good."

"So...you don't like being in deep water?"

"Deep, fine. Not being able to see, like I said." She paused as an especially high wave lifted them and the boat. "If I wanted a roller coaster, I would have gone back to Cedar Point."

"How about that for our next date?" slipped out before he could think.

"Please tell me you aren't a roller coaster freak?"

"Not really."

Today, Blade felt like an idiot and a wimp. Why not go for broke and confess all his flaws? That way, she wouldn't be surprised by anything if she hung around for very long. If she hung around at all, after today.

"Good. I'm not a coward, but I figure, why put myself through it voluntarily? I do like that water ride where you're in a fake log."

"Okay, but you sit in front. If you don't mind getting wet?"

"Not really." She rolled her eyes, and they both chuckled. "Don't," she blurted, when he started to release her legs from between his feet. "It feels...safe, with you so close."

"Okay." Blade hoped she couldn't feel how his pulse picked up speed, the longer they pressed against each other. How could he tell her that he was probably the last person she should feel safe with, without repelling her? Or would she be flattered? He prayed for it. "So, I'm driving the monsters away?"

"Big time. Sometimes, I even hate swimming in pools. That filter drain in the deep end, you know? That grill over it? I have this nightmare of it flipping open and *things* swimming out to get me. Like in those horror movies they show at midnight. Where these teenagers who are just too stupid to *breathe* on their own go swimming in a tank at a secret scientific base, and something living in the tank eats one of them."

"Thanks a lot. Now you've got me imagining things." He grinned, ignoring the ache through his skull when his words brought a muffled chuckle from her.

Blade shifted his hands in the rope, to move around closer to her. The movement of the waves gently rubbed their bodies together in the water. Nothing erotic about it, though he was sure if he let his imagination run wild it could be. He much preferred underwater contact to be in a hot tub, with a good bottle of wine and no awkward clothes getting in the way.

He wondered how long it would take before hypothermia got to them. How long was this storm going to last, anyway? Where was Worley's island? How far were they from Put-in-Bay? Or had they drifted over the border to Canada? They weren't that far out into the lake when everything fell apart around them. He couldn't see anything, with the gray sky and the clouds hanging low over the lake and the waves lifting them high and dropping them down into gray-brown troughs. They could be miles out at sea, instead of in the middle of a lake within an hour of shore.

"Are you okay?"

"Hmm? Fine." Blade brought his thoughts back to Jen.

"You're getting quiet. Don't go falling asleep on me. I don't think I could get you back up on the boat if you did." She tried to smile and her lips turned white with the strain. That told him she was scared.

What kind of a useless idiot was he, to make her worry? She wasn't supposed to be the hero. He was supposed to take care of her. It wasn't right, to force her to be the strong one, the observant one, the one who got them through this debacle.

In all honesty, Jen was too self-sufficient to ever need him. She might like him. They seemed to have the same taste in movies. She enjoyed verbal sparring and held much the same assessment of Ray. That didn't mean Blade had a chance with her.

Maybe a few nights of wrestling and laughter were all Jen would give him before she got bored and disgusted by his inadequacies. Until now, that had been more than enough for Blade. Leave them smiling, leave them with good memories, get out before they started making demands and expecting something from him he couldn't give. That had always been his motto.

But with Jen, he wanted to go beyond steaming up the windows in the back seat of his car.

The thought of her moving on to someone else—*staying* with that someone else—ate a hole through him like acid. Heck, the thought of who might have already kissed her and made her laugh and moan irritated him like sand in his carburetor.

Had he only imagined she implied she'd never had a date? Maybe that knock on the head was making him hallucinate. How could Jen have lived so long without someone claiming her for his own and making her feel precious and appreciated?

"Blade?" Jen reached up to stroke his face. "Are you still with me?"

"Yeah, for all the good it does you," he growled.

"You—" She glared at him and wriggled loose of his grip on her legs as she struggled for words. "You—man!"

Blade blinked hard, wondering what he had missed.

"Of all the pig-headed...you're mad because you couldn't be Mr.

Macho Hero?"

"I almost got you killed! You'd be halfway back to the island by now, if you didn't have me to worry about. Heck, you wouldn't even be out here if I hadn't dragged you along."

"I came because I wanted to be with you, you moron!"

"Oh, thanks. Now I know how you feel about me." Inside, an entire stadium cheered a major touchdown. "I'm useless."

"I've been too busy worrying about you to be scared. I don't think that's useless at all!"

Blade took a deep breath, a gusher of words on his tongue, but as they rose to the top of a wave a light hit him full in the face. Through the wailing of the wind, he heard the roar of a boat's engine.

CHAPTER 15

Heinrich piloted the largest of Worley's three power launches, and Hanson tossed Jen and Blade the line with the life ring on it, to draw them to the boat. Blade nearly went under, pushing Jen up the ladder despite her insistence that he get on board first because of his injury.

He regretted that when Sarpantine met Jen at the top of the ladder and enveloped her in an enormous blanket. He kept his arms around her, despite Jen's struggles to get free and stand on her own. Blade's foot slipped on the last step of the ladder in his hurry to leap into the boat and yank Jen free. Magda caught him, nearly blinding him with another blanket. He stumbled as she shoved and guided him down the narrow passageway into the boat's cabin.

"I'm fine!" Jen growled.

Several knots of tension inside Blade loosened, just knowing she was nearby.

"Mik's hurt—he got clobbered by that stupid sail bar or whatever it's called," she insisted. "He's bleeding."

Magda yanked the blanket down and shoved Blade into the nearest seat. She had a first aid kit in her hands so fast he could almost believe she pulled it out of thin air.

"Let me go!" Jen shrieked, playing Gloria at her dizzy nastiest. "I want to take care of him." She yanked her arms free of Sarpantine and darted across the cabin.

Magda brought her to a stop by nearly clotheslining her with an outstretched arm. "You listen to me, little girl, and listen good," the

149

vamp writer growled. "Do you know triage? I *do*, so I take care of Mik. Unless you want him bleeding to death or blacking out?" She didn't wait for Jen to whimper an answer, but turned back to Blade and ripped open an antiseptic wipe. "This is going to sting."

"Can't hurt worse than anything else," he muttered, earning a thin-lipped, grim smile from her.

Was he just knocked silly, or had her oozy accent faded? Magda's odd little absences took on a whole new meaning. Jen was right, and she was more than just a nosy, irritating, slinky guest. Magda claimed to be fascinated by the island and wanted to explore it for background for her next Anastasia Peach book. What if it was something else? What if Magda prepared to double-cross Worley?

"Where's Mark?" Jen wailed.

Blade glanced over in time to see Sarpantine jerk back away from her as if stung—spilling hot coffee down himself. Blade grinned. Jen had timed it perfectly to avoid drinking anything Sarpantine had touched.

She continued to wail, growing louder, drumming her heels against the floor and demanding her husband's presence. Finally Sarpantine snapped.

"Your precious husband is scouring the island. He insists you wouldn't leave without him. I guess he isn't as smart as he thinks he is," he tossed over his shoulder as he stomped out of the cabin and up onto the deck again.

"Almost wish I hadn't agreed to come rescue you two," Magda purred. "You don't really need your hunky hubby if you've got Mik dangling, do you, Gloria?"

"I have no idea what you mean," Jen sulked.

"That's probably true." She pressed a little too hard as she smoothed the bandage over Blade's forehead. "Want me to kiss it and make it better?" she murmured when he winced.

"Ah...no, thanks." He wanted Jen to kiss it. And his lips. And anything else that struck her imagination.

"Didn't think so. Pity." Magda squeezed his shoulder, snatched up a raincoat from one of the benches lining the cabin, and sauntered back onto the deck after Sarpantine.

"Think he's hunting?" Jen whispered, as she scooted over next to Blade.

He didn't have a chance to answer. Through the moaning of the wind, he heard Ray calling, pretending panic. The big boat rocked as it came up against the docks. They had to resume their roles, though their false personas were as uncomfortable as their lake-soaked, dirty clothes.

*   *   *

"The good news is, the boat wasn't bugged," Ray said, coming into the bedroom.

"Bugged?"

Jen turned back from looking out the balcony door. The sun, perversely, had decided to shine again. The clouds that an hour ago looked heavy enough to smother her now shredded and faded before her eyes. At Ray's words, something inside her dropped. All the way to the ground floor of the tower.

"We weren't exactly careful about what we said," she admitted.

"I figured. So it's a good thing the boat wasn't bugged."

"They thought Blade was going out by himself."

"And wanted him dead. Or scared off." He settled down on the edge of the low dresser and watched her catalogue her bruises and scrapes. "Kind of a busy day for you?"

"Tell me about it. How's Blade doing?"

"That gash is mostly bruise. He won't let us send him to the mainland to get it sewn up. He's worried about you."

"Me?" Jen turned her head so he wouldn't see the big grin that took over her face. "Why?"

"You know Blade. If he doesn't get to be a Boy Scout at least once a day, he goes into withdrawal." Something reserved in Ray's tone made Jen wonder what he had on his mind. "I think Blade likes to worry about you, especially."

"Yeah?" She closed her eyes, reliving that soft kiss on her forehead.

Not exactly what she had been hoping for, but it was a good start. It meant Blade was interested. Jen had thought her heart would stop, that she had made a big mistake when she talked about their first date, but he hadn't been scared away. He even seemed to like the idea.

If only the sailboat hadn't capsized and he hadn't insisted he was to blame. What was it with white knights, that they couldn't lay down their armor once in a while?

For all she knew, capable, strong, independent women scared Blade. Jen didn't want to spend the rest of her life pretending to be something she wasn't. She couldn't cling and coo like Magda did, when she tried to get a man's attention. She certainly didn't have the

151

curves or the guts to wear the things Magda did.

Jen honestly wanted a man who would watch out for her—someone reliable, strong, and responsible. Being put on a pedestal or ending up the princess in the tower would bore her silly.

"You did a pretty good job out there," Ray said after a few seconds. If he had expected her to say or do something, Jen had no idea. She refused to look at him until she was sure she had her face under control. "Saved the day, according to Blade."

"Oh, yeah, Wonder Woman." She stuck her tongue out and crossed her eyes.

"Nah. You don't have the figure for it."

"Oh, thanks very much for noticing." Now she could look at him, letting mock indignation take over her face. "We called her Blunder Broad in junior high. How in the world could anyone catch criminals in a bathing suit and high heels?"

"You're more subtle, for one thing. You get a lot more done from the shadows than somebody running around with flashy moves. Besides, I prefer Marvel over DC."

"Well, a new side of you emerges. The connoisseur of comic books." She went to the closet to decide what to wear to dinner. Not that she wouldn't enjoy spending the rest of the week in the thick, jade terrycloth robe she had found in the bathroom.

"I think we have to face facts that we have enemies here."

"Someone guessed we're fakes?"

"I'm hoping someone acted out of jealousy, or fear, of Blade's progress with you. He is making progress, isn't he?" Ray studied her for a few seconds. Jen had no idea what her face showed, but he nodded as if satisfied and continued. "Let's hope they only think *Blade* is a fake. I'm going to push Worley to shorten his timetable, so I can get my delicate little bride away from this deathtrap island. The sooner we get our hands on the Dordt, the sooner we fly."

"With the two of you acting like mother hens, I've got nothing to worry about."

Jen's fingers lingered on the white negligee set, hanging at the back of the closet. Ray hadn't said anything about it. She wished she had reason to wear it, but had to face facts that it was there only as window dressing.

"I think I'll concentrate on the painting and leave you to Blade. We don't want overkill." Ray grinned cheekily when she turned to frown at him. "Get some rest, Mrs. Williams. We'll both play cat burglar tonight, and you need all your strength."

"Relapse time?"

"I'll have them send up a tray for you."

"And put you on a silver platter for Magda?" She batted her eyelashes at him. Ray let out a bark of laughter as he headed for the door. "We must play every card in our hand, mustn't we, Mr. Williams?" Jen felt her spirits raise a little, imagining Ray playing up to Cousin Magda. She hoped he squirmed in misery.

"You're the best wife I ever had." He swept her a grandiose bow as he pulled the door open.

Jen sighed as the door clicked closed, leaving her alone. She turned back to the closet and stared at the clothes hanging there. Most of them, Blade had picked out for her. Except for the white lacy confection.

Or maybe he *had* picked it out. She grinned, remembering how big his eyes got when she held it up to herself. The way he hurried out of the store. If that wasn't an indicator that she had found the perfect outfit...but what good did it do, hanging in her closet and Blade nowhere around to appreciate it?

She hadn't even tried it on yet. Why not now? She was sure to be alone for the next few hours. She had plenty of time to ransack Ray's computer and get all the information he had found on her and her mother, and any other relatives he suspected existed. Just in case she never got another chance, she would copy everything to her computer, first. That would keep her busy until the supper tray came. Besides avoiding the problem of Ray interrupting her and finding his computer was warm from use, it would allow her to read at her leisure.

Before she did that, though, she would try on the negligee. She would walk the balcony that circled the tower and pretend to be a fairy tale princess, just for a little while.

*   *   *

Blade knew he had fully recovered from the knock on his head that afternoon. So why had Ray ordered him to play sick? Dinner would start soon. Didn't Ray know he had to be there to protect Jen from Sarpantine?

"I hate this," Blade muttered, and slammed himself down into the easy chair facing the balcony doors.

Pacing hadn't helped to work off his nervous energy. The exercise hadn't soothed his headache, either. Blade wished the storm had lingered. He hated looking out over that peaceful lake and remembering what a mess he had made. Sure, Jen softened things by telling him he kept away her nightmares, but what good did that do? Blade's idea of driving away nightmares was to hold her while she slept. Not that he'd ever get a chance, now. Jen probably thought he was a pitiful excuse for an agent, let alone a man worth her time. Not even for a brief fling.

Not that he wanted a brief fling. He didn't want a limited time option on Jen, but permanent, full-time, all-rights-included access.

A flicker of something white on the balcony caught his attention. Blade went on alert. He needed a weapon. Whoever had sabotaged the boat might be back to finish the job. The closest weapon at hand was a hair dryer or belt. Even his shoes weren't heavy enough to do damage. Not like those spikes he had talked Jen into buying.

Blade grinned at that thought.

Why not? The woman he wanted had to save his worthless hide— why not borrow her shoes to defend himself?

Blade backed slowly for the door, keeping an eye on the wisp of white flickering in the air at the edge of the doorframe. He slid across the landing between their rooms. It was a matter of moments to enter Jen's room and find her lethal sandals. Blade grinned in nasty anticipation and stepped through Jen's open sliding door to sneak up on his visitor.

"They don't go with your pants," Jen said from behind him.

Blade snapped around, ready to grab her and race back to the safety of her room. He froze.

Jen wore that pristine white lacy creation she had showed him when they went shopping.

While he tried to get his breath back and prayed his tongue didn't drag on the balcony pavement, Blade finally saw the whole picture. That movement was Jen, walking around the balcony. Technically, he had borrowed her shoes to attack her.

What he wouldn't give for her to attack him right now.

"Ah...would you believe I'm protecting you?" he offered with a wide grin. Blade wished the sunset was more spectacular, so he could blame it for the crimson heat rising in his face.

"Maybe." She smiled and leaned against the railing. "Did Ray badger you into staying up here and playing wounded hero?"

"Sort of." Blade held out the shoes to her. "I thought I was alone and someone was sneaking around so..."

"You did say these would make great weapons. So far, the most damage they've done is to my ankles." She smiled as she took the shoes and tossed them through the open door.

The movement made her lacy robe flutter and cling to her body. She turned just enough to put the sunset directly to her back, so every curve became outlined in brilliant, sparkling silhouette. Blade knew he stared and didn't care. It was the most he could do to keep from drooling.

"Do you like it?" Jen's voice dropped to a whisper. Blade could barely hear over the rising thudding of his heart.

He swallowed and nodded. White suited her. Pure and light, untouchable. It turned her skin to gold and made her dyed hair glow like coals in the sunset. Even the crimson, gold, and purple sky framed her perfectly. Like a snowflake, an ice sculpture that would melt at the slightest unworthy touch. He groaned.

"What's wrong?" She took a few steps closer to him.

"Are you crazy? Wearing that outside where anyone can see you?" His voice cracked.

"Who? Besides you, I mean. Everybody is heading for dinner, and we're facing away from Put-in-Bay. It'd take a pretty strong telescope to see anything from the other shore."

"That's beside the point. You're barefoot, you're not even wearing a belt for a weapon. You can't defend yourself."

"I could. I have a lot of skills you know nothing about." A tiny smile caught one corner of her mouth.

Blade groaned. He could just imagine some of her skills he *did* want to experience. And teach her more along the same lines.

"There are some things a woman just can't defend against. Especially when you look the way you do and it makes a man feel the way—" Blade swallowed, refusing to complete that line.

"The way you do?" Jen whispered. "I think I can protect myself." She took two steps closer to him.

"Can you protect yourself against me?" he growled.

Despite his better sense and years of training to avoid unstable situations, Blade stepped closer. If he could scare Jen, maybe he could save them both?

Jen stared up at him, her smile glowing in her eyes, which seemed to get bigger. Blade felt his knees wobble. In another minute, he would lose his balance. He clutched at the railing and leaned closer to her.

His aching imagination said her gaze touched the emptiness inside him and promised fulfillment that went beyond physical hunger. He imagined her mouth would taste like honey and wine. Her hair would be silky smooth, so soft he would barely feel it tangled around his fingers. Every long, lean line of her would press against him, fitting perfectly, like they had been made for each other.

"What if I don't want to protect myself?" Jen asked in a whisper so soft, Blade had to lean closer to hear it.

"Jen—"

"I know we're missing the movie and popcorn, but is this our second date?"

"You're going to drive me crazy." A chuckle hovered inside his chest, where everything grew tight and smoldered.

"That makes two of us. You think Ray's playing matchmaker?"

Blade froze. Hadn't Ray warned him away from her? Or did Ray play them against each other, pushing Jen toward him while he warned Blade away? That sounded like the psychological games Ray liked.

"Do you mind? I don't," Jen admitted, and looked away.

"If I don't kiss you pretty soon, I'm going to explode."

She blushed and refused to look at him. Her hands trembled on the railing and she looked out over the lake.

Blade realized he didn't like it when he wasn't in charge, the aggressor. That wasn't a nice revelation, but he didn't have time to go into self-analysis. Jen was here, right now. She shivered a little, standing close enough to him he could feel the heat from her body. She didn't laugh at him, didn't run.

She didn't mind that Ray played matchmaker with them.

Jen flinched when he grasped her shoulders and turned her away from the railing to face him. Her mouth trembled, just a momentary tremor, and she caught her breath when he slid a finger under her chin to tip her face up toward him. More than the sunset gleamed in her eyes when she met his gaze.

When he slid both arms around her and drew her up against him, Jen stumbled. Blade chuckled, the sound muffled as he brought his lips down on hers. He curved one hand down around her waist to press her close, the other up around her neck and under her hair, to tip her head at just the right angle.

Her lips tasted of strawberries, soft, cool. They warmed as Blade moved his mouth across hers. He threaded his fingers through her hair for a better grip and she gasped as he brushed her lips with his tongue. Jen held still as he slipped inside her mouth, hyper-aware of every sensation—the edges of her teeth, the warmth, and sweetness.

She held too still. Blade nearly retreated, positive she would bite or push him away. He waited, softly stroking his hand down her back. His pulse tripled its pace as his hand curved over her bottom. Without thinking, he pressed her closer to him.

Jen touched the tip of his tongue with hers, but the electric shock of contact died under a greater discovery. Blade inhaled, feeling like a drowning man as he drew his head back.

"You're not wearing any underwear." His voice didn't even sound like his own.

Jen just shook her head, her eyes wide and dazed. Her lips glistened and looked darker from the pressure of his mouth.

"Are you asking for trouble?"

"Not—trouble—if I want it—you. Is it?" She took a deep breath, as if she hadn't breathed since he started kissing her. The movement pressed her closer against him.

"Jen, why do I get this feeling..." Blade felt his face burn. The weighty combination of feelings roiling through him nearly suffocated him.

What a way to go.

"Is that the right way?" she whispered.

"Right way?"

"With our—our mouths?" Jen hunched her shoulders again and started to push away. She refused to look at him.

Blade clutched her closer without thinking. He couldn't think, as suspicions came crashing to the front of his mind.

"You've never— But I saw Ray kiss you."

"It never counted before. I mean, it was never real before." Her whole body vibrated against his. He couldn't stand it if she feared him. "He never did that to me," she whispered, as if ashamed to admit it.

The smart thing was to let her go. If a single kiss could affect her that way, what did it do to her to be pressed so close, she felt every reaction racing through his body?

Fortunately, at times like this, Blade knew he wasn't smart. He squeezed her bottom tighter, lifting her up against him. Any closer, and she'd have to wrap her legs around him. His other hand tangled in her hair and gently moved her head around so she had to face him.

"How real can you take it?" he whispered.

Jen's smile, tentative and sleepy slow, was all the answer he needed.

She clutched at the front of his shirt with one hand and slid her other arm around his neck. Her lips parted as he brought his mouth down on hers and she tipped her head back, making it easier for him.

The tension that turned every fiber in her body tight as a harp string was anticipation, he knew, not fear. Through the hungry thudding of his heart, he felt hers hammering against his chest. As if not even flesh and blood separated them.

"That," he whispered as he lifted his head many long minutes later, "is what our first kiss should have been."

"And nothing to knock you off your feet this time."

"You already do that, Mrs. Williams." Blade felt her grimace through her whole body at that little teasing remark. He was glad. The masquerade wore on her as much as it did on him. "It's real for me too. Pretty soon, we need to figure out how real we both want it to get."

"What exactly—"

She stopped, breathless, as he slid his hand between her robe and gown and moved up her back. Her eyes closed and she tipped her head back in response to the caress of his fingers through the lacy fabric. Blade took advantage of it to run kisses down her throat, making her purr.

"Oh...I guess you both are feeling better." Sarpantine paused, framed in Jen's balcony door.

Blade's first impulse was to push Jen away and put himself between her and Sarpantine. He clutched her closer instead. It'd take a duel to the death to let Sarpantine get between them now.

"It was rather unfair of you, my dear, not to let me know how things stood." Sarpantine took a few steps closer to them.

"Stood?" Jen slipped her arm around Blade's waist.

"I'm not the sort of man to poach in another man's territory. Very unsporting."

"But I'm married. You didn't seem to think that was any problem."

"All's fair when it comes to married women. A silly little piece of paper doesn't mean anything. An affair of passion is something no civilized man should threaten, don't you see?" He looked her up and down, one eyebrow raised in appreciation. He chuckled when Blade turned to put himself between him and Jen.

"But—" she began again.

Blade squeezed her waist, to silence her. Sarpantine's double standards knocked him breathless too, but trying to argue with him might ruin their cover stories.

"I wish you every happiness, dear Gloria. However long it lasts." He nodded and headed for the balcony door. "Whoever *he* really is," Sarpantine threw over his shoulder as he crossed the bedroom to the hall doorway.

Jen stiffened. "Do you think—"

"Can't take the chance. Get changed and think of something on the way down." He set off after Sarpantine, cutting through Ray and Jen's room.

*   *   *

Jen nearly tore her dress as she slipped it on. Her hands shook from fury and disappointment and the last dregs of the thrill that Blade's every touch sent through her.

Blade was in danger. Sarpantine knew he was an imposter. Despite what her common sense shouted, another thought insisted on being paramount.

Sarpantine had interrupted them just as all her daydreams and hungry yearnings finally promised to turn into reality. She could easily kill Sarpantine tonight. With her bare hands.

Jen had killed before, to protect her adopted family. The first time, her enemy had been a two-bit pusher who used rape and pain to establish dominance. Sarpantine was the kind of man the street-dwelling low-lifes aspired to become. Jen knew she could kill him with no hesitation, because he threatened Blade.

That realization shook her. Maybe she loved Blade?

"Save it for later," she counseled herself as she pulled on a pair of panties. Pale green, for luck. "Right now, all that matters is saving Blade's neck."

*   *   *

Sarpantine moved fast. When Blade reached the bottom of the stairs, he heard the man call greetings to the other guests in Worley's music room, waiting for dinner to be served.

Blade almost wished he'd held onto Jen's shoes, to club Sarpantine and punch a hole through his skull with the spiked heel before he could open his mouth.

Only someone seriously warped saw no harm in seducing a married woman, with drugs, but thought it uncivilized to interfere in an adulterous affair.

Not that he wasn't grateful. Blade knew Jen was safe from Sarpantine as long as it looked like they were fooling around.

But if he married Jen, would she become fair game again?

Blade almost stumbled. *Married* to Jen? Why did that idea keep coming back? Where did it come from?

Probably the same place that made him want to carry her off and not come up for air for a few years. That mountain cabin of his looked better all the time.

Get back on track! he silently scolded, and entered the music room.

Sarpantine perched on the back of a half-circle couch, engaged in conversation, as if he didn't care if Blade came tearing after him. He ignored Magda, sprawled across it playing "eensy weensy spider" with her fingers, up and down Ray's arm. Ray ignored her while listening to Sarpantine. Worley sat on the far edge of the couch, totally ignored. He seemed relieved.

"Ah, and there he is, risen from the dead," Sarpantine said as he turned around. He flashed that too-bright smile. "Come in, my friend. Tell us, how is that bump on the head?"

"Fine...I guess," Blade said slowly.

"I'm curious. Did you forget how to sail before or after you hit your head?" He stepped over to the sideboard where decanters and an entire bar's worth of glassware waited.

"Forget?" Blade put on a smile and tried to look like he couldn't have cared less. "I don't know much of anything about sailing, actually. I was counting on the motor to get me out of trouble, but the tank was empty." He looked to Worley, feeling not one flicker of guilt for putting his host on the hot seat.

"Everything was ready," Worley said in a raspy voice. "My people double-checked before I invited you to use the boat."

"Anyone with experience would have been able to handle those problems without breaking a sweat." Sarpantine poured himself a snifter of brandy. "Rather odd, considering that my old friend Mik loves sailing. It's one of his passions. We spent an interesting two weeks exploring the Baltic just a few months ago, believe it or not."

"I don't believe you." Blade knew better than to play along with someone who claimed to know his false identity. It was too easy to trip up someone who pretended nonexistent memories.

The room seemed to hold its breath. Magda's eyes glittered with something that normally would have made Blade nervous. He had other things to occupy his attention right now.

Sarpantine burst out laughing. He nodded, raising his brandy in salute, then muffled his mirth long enough to take a whiff of the fumes and sip.

"Excellent year, my dear host." He nodded to Worley. "And

excellent move, whoever you are. I never did take a vacation on the Baltic, with or without Mik Poling. But we *are* friends. You're a reasonable facsimile, but you aren't Mik. Who is an excellent sailor. I wonder who put together your dossier on him, so that particular detail was left out."

"What in the world are you talking about?" Jen demanded.

Everyone turned to stare at her, poised in the doorway. Blade wanted to applaud, even as the knight errant part of him wanted to shout for her to run.

Her hair hung loose and tangled, as if she had just leaped from bed. Her cheeks had an unnaturally bright flush and her eyes had dark smears around them, as if she had passed a restless evening or been frightened. She leaned into the doorway as if her legs were weak. She wore her simplest sundress, blue gingham with lace edging, and was barefoot. It made her look young, defenseless, and innocent.

"Mark, what's going on?" she continued, and put a little whimper of confusion in her voice. On cue, Ray hurried to meet her and wrapped an arm around her shoulders.

"I simply pointed out that I am acquainted with the real Mik Poling," Sarpantine said. "It might be polite of this gentleman to tell us who he really is, before we apply pressure."

Jen made a little gasping sound and she clutched at Ray's hand. "He's not who he says?"

"Look, we came here to put together a security system for you, Worley. Not get caught up in some argument over identity," Ray said. "How about Glo and I leave until you get this little problem cleared up?"

"I have a better idea," Sarpantine purred.

CHAPTER 16

Jen felt Sarpantine watching her as she worked on her notebook computer. His gaze felt like a solid weight. She had never felt as threatened by him, as polluted by his attention. One wrong move now, the slightest hint that she tried *not* to uncover Blade's true identity, and Sarpantine would attack. Being fondled and drooled on were the least of her worries.

Long ago, she had made her peace with the chance that she could be killed in her efforts to defeat the world's monsters. She knew Ray had taken full responsibility for his life and would never blame her if a mistake threatened, harmed, even killed them. She knew there were people who would sexually abuse her before they killed her, and she had developed a mental wall to—hopefully—hide behind when that day came.

But failure on her part now could doom Blade. Jen had no armor in that particular area because she had never needed it. Blade made her laugh even as he made her hotter than a griddle. She wanted to know all the things he liked and loathed, what kept him awake at night, what he liked to do to relax, and all his fondest childhood memories. She wanted to know where he got the tiny scar by his mouth. She wanted to know how a man trained by the Agency broke away and went freelance and spent his life helping people.

Now, she might never get a chance to know, thanks to Sarpantine.

Ray's contacts had given them the background on Mik Poling, but should she have done her own research? Would she have uncovered

Poling's love of sailing and his friendship with Sarpantine? Why didn't Ray know the two were friends?

Jen clenched her fists on the keyboard.

"It's okay, baby doll," Ray soothed. He reached across the space between them and stroked up her arm. It would have been soothing, if she still didn't have the memory of Blade's kiss burning like witches' brew in the back of her mind. "Tired? It's been a pretty rough day, hasn't it?"

"My head hurts," she whimpered, seizing the opening he offered her. "I think I'm getting a cold."

Jen glanced over her shoulder at Worley and Sarpantine, who kept an eye on Blade while they worked. Magda was nowhere to be seen, and she was grateful for that.

"It'll all be over soon, my dear," Sarpantine soothed.

Did he plan to take Blade's place on the balcony, once they got rid of him? Jen shuddered and promised herself she'd burn that nightgown before anybody but Blade saw her in it.

"Okay," Ray said. "All set." He looked up from the scanner he had transferred from Worley's office system to the equipment they had brought with them. "Ready, honey?"

"Let's get this over and done with." Jen decided she could play petulant now. "I want to go to bed."

Preferably with Blade, to finish what they had started out on the balcony, but what were her chances of that?

Concentrate, Jen scolded herself, and tried to push the memory of Blade's kisses to the back of her mind.

She'd never even suspected that part about sticking his tongue in her mouth. Startled, she had almost pushed him away, terrified he was just as gross as the boys in third grade who tried to peek at her underwear. Then Blade had pressed her hips tight against his and a flare shot up from deep in her belly and his tongue stroked across hers to make her shiver, hot and cold.

"Glo?" Ray prompted. He frowned at her and Jen wondered if he could read her mind.

Back to work. Still, despite her resolve to narrow her focus, her hands shook a little as she typed the commands into her computer. She scanned the inkblots of Blade's fingerprints and pretended to transmit them, while Ray pretended to hack into FBI and CIA files. She would do whatever Ray told her to do, and prayed he was as good at the shell game as he claimed.

"Transmitting," Ray reported. He crossed his arms and sat back. "Could take a while. How do things look on your end, Glo?"

"I have no idea what I'm looking at."

Ray chuckled in his smug Mark persona. He rattled off translations for the codes and files supposedly being transmitted and opened, and the levels of security being breached.

It was all a load of bunk. Jen had no idea what sort of information Ray had sent to her, but the snatches of code she did understand coincided in no way, shape or form with what he said. She suspected there was *some* communication going on; Ray had sent something out and a response was coming through. Maybe a call for help? There was no way this little retrieval mission could be upgraded to a national security crisis, could it? She still hoped for the cavalry to swoop in. Even though he was retired, Blade was still one of theirs. Didn't they owe him?

"Okay, enough is enough," Blade said, standing.

Worley nearly fell out of his chair. Sarpantine jerked his hand out of his pocket and revealed a gun.

"You want to know who I am, what I'm after?" Blade bared his teeth in a fierce grin that was half challenge, sweeping the too-plush office with his gaze.

"That would be very civilized of you," Sarpantine said, nodding.

"The name's Munroe Hampton. Born in Pittsburgh. Folks died when I was a kid, passed around to a bunch of relatives who only wanted the state's money, been on my own since I was fourteen. Got busted for stealing for the first time when I was fifteen."

Blade didn't look at her as he rattled off a list of offenses that built up in severity from shoplifting food from the corner grocery store to stealing school buses. Jen was almost surprised to hear he hadn't dealt in drugs, prostitution, and pornography.

"Five years in the Marine Corps," Blade said, surprising her enough to flinch.

He *had* spent five years with the Marines. Ray had told her.

He told about flying into Beirut to kidnap the daughter of a government official. In Ray's version, Blade had led the team that *rescued* the hostage daughter of a diplomat.

Jen dug her fingers into the seat of her chair as it dawned on her that Blade told the edited truth about his own life. This was no false identity for him to fall back on, but his entire painful past, with all the grit and darkness that had shaped him into the man she had glimpsed in these last few days. The man who had been worried about her safety even as he fought not to rip away her nightgown.

At least, Jen hoped he had wanted to rip away her nightgown. She wasn't ever going to find out that answer if Blade's current ploy didn't work.

*　　*　　*

"So what was that all about?" Jen asked Ray when they finally went up to their room, after midnight.

"Exactly what it looked like." He glanced once more at the palm-sized scanner as it cast a pale green beam around the room. He nodded, pleased by the data on the screen, closed it and put it back in his pocket. Jen tended not to trust anything that smacked of James Bond gizmos, but if it made Ray happy, fine.

"If I knew what it looked like, I wouldn't be asking, now would I?" She dropped down on the end of the bed. "That was his life story, wasn't it?"

"With some modifications. The truth is always the best weapon, because you don't have to keep patching it over like you do with lies." Ray tossed his glasses onto the dresser and peeled off his shirt.

For the first time since they had discovered what a good team they made, his unthinking ease in her presence irritated Jen. She wanted him to be self-conscious. She wanted him to be disgruntled that the merest hint of muscle and washboard abs didn't turn her into a mongrel in heat. Ray acted like they were an old married couple who found more zing in the crossword puzzle than each other's bodies.

"If your cover got blown, would I hear something close to the truth about you?"

"There is no truth about me." He grinned cheekily and headed for the bathroom. "My sources will send back the same story Blade spilled. And Sarpantine's people will come back with the same information. Probably some time tomorrow morning."

"Why did he tell the truth?"

"He knew his next false identity wouldn't work. Not with Sarpantine. There's something else going on. It's obvious now that he and Poling were in this from the beginning, and he changed his plans when Poling went missing. So why didn't he blow the lid off Blade's game the moment he arrived?" Ray shook his head as he stepped into the bathroom. And stopped short.

He let out a soft wolf whistle, picked up her discarded negligee and stepped back into the bedroom. His crooked grin warned that no matter what she said, he wouldn't believe her.

"I was getting ready for bed and I realized Blade was in trouble and I came down to help him." Jen forced herself to meet his gaze. She knew better than to look away when she told basically the truth. Highly edited truth.

"Once upon a time, they lived happily ever after," Ray muttered. "It's all the story in between that's the good part."

"You were hoping something would happen when you conned both of us into staying up here."

"Evidently something *started* to happen, but Sarpantine interrupted." Ray rubbed his fingers through the lace and tossed it to her. "Did you have any fun?"

"Frustration is no fun at all," she admitted.

"I really planned on needing to use Blade's room tonight." He stepped over to the bed and squeezed her shoulder. It was a comforting touch.

Jen had an awful urge to fling her arms around him and cry on his shoulder. And more horrifying, she suspected Ray would let her. She hated feeling like one of the hopeless and helpless. Still, when Ray pressed her for the details, she told him exactly what had happened. But only from the moment Sarpantine caught them in the clinch.

"It doesn't make any sense," she said when she finished. Jen hated how her voice tried to turn into a wail. "Why is it okay for Gloria to have an affair, but not for Sarpantine to steal her from Mik? The guy is warped."

"Yes, but his warped sense of honor kept him from telling Mark his wife was fooling around behind his back," Ray said, nodding, staring at an invisible, distant point. "The question now is, does Sarpantine have a warped sense of honor, or does he keep that knowledge as a weapon if Blade's allowed to stay?"

"Allowed? How about buried?" Jen said with a snort.

"Blade's trickier than you'd think. He'll probably use his dark past to convince Worley to hire him."

"So Sarpantine could use the affair against him anyway."

"Not if I have anything to do with it," Ray said with a nasty grin. "It could work for us, actually. Time to change tactics. Tomorrow, you hunt, and I distract."

*　　　*　　　*

166

Blade knew things could be a lot worse. He had been in worse situations. He could have been tied to the dock, to let the restless lake batter at him all night and soften him up for further questioning. Instead, he was locked in this nice big pantry. Warm, actually. He had even made himself a nest of sorts, with a couple throw rugs under him and a roll of paper towels for a pillow.

Sarpantine had been impressed by the sordid details in his past. Blade couldn't find any other explanation for that gleam of interest in his rival's eyes. Now, would Sarpantine decide his dark past made Blade a valuable tool, or someone who needed to be disposed of and taken out of the way?

He couldn't help wishing for Jen, curled up beside him. Even knowing she was safe, Blade couldn't stop wishing she was right here. Who was he fooling, thinking he could do a better job of protecting her from Sarpantine and his mad scientist potions? He was the one locked up, and Ray was with Jen.

Still, he wanted her. Wanted to go back to that kiss. A fantastic kiss as far as first kisses went. First, as in more than one. First, as in a long, long string of kisses that would go on for the next fifty, sixty years. Maybe longer. Jen could make a man with a death wish change his mind.

Blade held his breath, sensing movement in the hallway between pantry and kitchen. Who was out there?

His hungry imagination hoped it was Jen, sneaking down in some misguided sense of duty. Or lust. He would settle for lust. Blade knew Ray would stop her, if he hadn't already come up with a better plan to set him free.

So who did that leave, sneaking into the kitchen at that time of night? Blade heard a single, hushed footstep.

How about Magda? He wouldn't put it past that alley cat in heat to come after him. It was a given Sarpantine didn't want her, Ray was too busy playing concerned husband, and she wasn't desperate enough to turn to Worley.

For all he knew, she had been sneaking downstairs every night to seduce Heinrich or Hanson. Blade threw aside that theory a second later. Magda treated the two chunky men like they were invisible.

More likely, that was just Worley coming down for a midnight snack. Though why he would bother tiptoeing past was beyond Blade's imagination.

His head still hurt from the sailboat attacking him. Thinking and theorizing just made the dull throbbing worse.

He took down a second roll of paper towels to try to make his pillow bigger, then curled up on his side and listened to the night music of the house. Muffled through the walls, Blade heard a heavy door creak open in the area of the kitchen.

There was a door leading outside from the kitchen, but there was an alarm system linked to it. No one could go outside unless they disarmed the alarm. Anyone who could disarm the alarm wouldn't need to sneak.

There were three more doors in the massive kitchen, not counting the walk-in freezer and refrigerator. Two were simply more big closets. The third led down into the cellar, a remnant of the university's research station. Why would someone go down there? It was nothing but dust, grime and damp, and filled with sheet-draped discards from Worley's treasure trove.

Could the hidden entrance for the boat dock be in the cellar? Was there another delivery tonight? Maybe Worley was trying to sneak something past Sarpantine. Blade almost felt sorry for the pathetic fat man, and wondered if Sarpantine would blacken Worley's other eye when he found out.

He waited, listening through the creeping night hours for the door to open again and the hushed footsteps to come back past the pantry door. If the mysterious walker ever did, Blade wasn't sure. The next thing he knew, the door opened and morning sunshine and the smell of cooking trickled through past Worley's bulky shape.

"Did you think about my proposal?" Blade asked as he stretched and got leisurely to his feet. Worley didn't answer, just gestured for him to come out.

"We're still trying to decide what kind of a liar you are," Sarpantine said, as Blade stepped into the hallway. He lounged against the opposite wall, looking bored and impeccably dressed. He, obviously, had spent a comfortable and secure night, judging by his well-rested and groomed appearance. "If you truly are interested in a job, you won't do anything stupid."

"Yeah," Blade muttered, when the man turned his back to them and stalked down the hall. "Stupid like getting caught in bed with the girl *he* wants, who doesn't want him."

Worley glanced at him, his eyes wide, and some color returned to his chunky face. Blade noticed and repressed a grin. Worley had been pale and off his feed ever since Sarpantine showed up. Maybe Blade could use that.

"So, you working for Sarpantine, or what?" he asked.

"This is my island. Guy is a friend," Worley said after a few moments, during which his mouth worked and angry secrets glittered in his eyes. But just for a few moments. He gestured down the hall and they started walking.

"Yeah, a friend who maybe wants a bigger cut of something more than you're willing to give him?"

"I think he was going to let you keep right on pretending to be Mik Poling, but he caught you with Gloria." A tentative smile lit his flabby face. "You two really are together?"

"As together as we can be with that geek husband of hers breathing down her neck. The guy's oblivious, but he's still got enough brains to guard a pretty little package." Blade winked, and Worley's smile widened a few degrees. They continued through the house, heading for the patio past the ballroom.

"I think Guy wants to romance her into giving him the secrets of my new security system. If you can keep him from getting to her, you're hired." He made a show of putting the safety on his pistol and sticking it into his pocket.

Worley's pants pocket wasn't made for pistols. It sagged and made him look even fatter than before, and rather pathetic.

"I did come looking for a job. Any kind of job. And after getting the low-down on my resume last night...well, you know I can do just about anything. Cat burglar. Security. Forged documents. Bodyguard. You name it, I've probably done it."

"You've killed? Not just in the military, but outside?"

"Oh, yeah. Whatever you need, I'm your man. Just don't give me any reason to think you're a stupid pig like my last boss. I had to leave real sudden." Blade forced a grin. Let Worley think what he wanted about that explanation.

From the momentary hitch in Worley's stride, he took it as a threat. Blade almost felt sorry for him. The man was surrounded by friendly enemies.

Sarpantine waited for them on the patio, along with breakfast. The buffet was smaller than yesterday's, but Blade couldn't find fault with it. Scrambled eggs, bacon, ham, pancakes, stewed apples, and cherries to put on the pancakes, whipped cream and butter, and pitchers of juice sitting in a basin of crushed ice.

"It seems you've earned a reprieve, Hampton," Sarpantine said. He waved a sheaf of glossy thermal fax paper at them before tossing it on the table and stomping over to the buffet.

"Reprieve?" Blade decided to smile. He needed a new persona now. Why not a wise guy?

"It seems every detail of your story checks out. And then some." Sarpantine stared at him a moment longer, lip curled, before devoting himself to filling his plate.

"Does that mean I have a job?"

"I guess so." Worley gave him a wobbly grin and wiped sweat off his forehead.

Yeah, to act as a buffer between you two. Blade settled down at a table on the other side of the buffet. Common sense said to put as much room as possible between him and Sarpantine.

Worley did the same. Neither one made any move toward the food until Sarpantine sat down. Blade grinned at his new employer and gestured for Worley to go first.

Definitely there was something wrong between Sarpantine and Worley. The wobble in the fat man's legs meant he was scared, not just nervous. What had happened overnight, while Blade cooled his heels in the pantry and depended on Ray to keep a bullet away from his vital organs? He mentally catalogued the escape routes off the island, and followed Worley to the buffet.

"Is Hampton your real name?" Ray demanded, skidding to a stop in the doorway leading from the dining room.

Oh, great. Blade slowly turned, holding the scrambled egg spoon. He nearly burst out laughing.

Ray's hair was mussed, standing on end in spots. His glasses sat crooked. His sweater was buttoned crooked. He wore a pea soup sweater with an orange sherbet polo shirt and neon green sweatpants. The perfect picture of a fashion-handicapped computer geek, who found out in the middle of getting dressed that his wife was fooling around behind his back.

"Yeah," he finally said, and coolly turned his back on Ray.

"You leave Gloria alone, Hampton. I saved everything we dug up on you. I can hang you just like that." Ray-Mark snapped his fingers, but didn't quite make it.

"You and whose army?" Blade kept on filling his plate. He took a scoop of cherries, betting on Ray's love of flash and his own growing need to really let loose and irritate Worley by playing on his almost prissy sense of neatness.

"She was crying half the night, telling me how you played with her and promised to take her places and told her lies about being Mik Poling." He grabbed Blade's arm, yanking the plate out from under the second scoop of cherries.

Blade almost cheered as the bright red glop hit the patio tiles and splattered on the white tablecloth, his shoes, and Ray's pants.

"She says Sarpantine came after her last night when she was supposed to be sick, but you got there first and you two started fighting over her."

"Oh, come on now, when I fight over a girl, you'll know it. And I don't have to fight over a silly little bird like Gloria. There's plenty for everybody."

He knew it was coming, but Blade still didn't see Ray's fist come straight for his eye until almost too late.

The plate went one direction and he went the other. Ray's fist hit the outside of the socket. Blade rolled away, knowing that was going to hurt like the devil's own when he finally slowed down enough to feel anything.

Ray followed him, his face twisted in a rictus of fury that was almost laughable.

Blade backed away, taking glances in all directions so he wouldn't back into something painful—and kept an eye on Worley and Sarpantine. He noticed Ray did the same, and neither Jen nor Magda were anywhere to be seen. He couldn't care less about Magda, but Jen had to be busy doing something.

A distraction. Of course. They were still using the affair as a distraction. He grinned and launched himself at Ray, determined to put on a performance that would win him an Oscar in the Slime ball Hall of Fame.

Ray stumbled forward, bent over as if to ram him like a bull. Blade resisted the temptation to snatch up a fallen napkin and flap it at him. This could almost be fun. He sidestepped at the last moment and hooked his arm around Ray's neck. The forward momentum and impact almost knocked them both off their feet. Blade bit his lip against laughing and dug his heels in. They skidded a few steps, then started to pivot.

"Where's Jen?" he whispered as they struggled, their heads nearly knocking.

"Reconnaissance." Ray snuck in a jab to his ribs.

Blade grunted and shoved him away. Okay, so he was right. Now, how to prolong this little demonstration and keep the audience from getting bored? Or worse, interfering?

He danced away from Ray's renewed attack, slapped his hands on the edge of the buffet and vaulted over it. Ray slammed into the table, making the steam trays clatter and chime dully against each other. Blade snatched up the pitcher of tomato juice and emptied it straight into Ray's face.

He tossed the pitcher over his shoulder. Worley gasped. The pitcher hit the patio tiles and the thick plastic shattered nicely.

The pineapple juice followed. Ray ducked this time and it splashed Worley's feet while he went for the platter full of little paper butter cups. Blade barely had to duck to make the missiles pass over his head. Grunts and plops and the sound of shuffling feet and displaced patio furniture told him Ray had aimed at Sarpantine. The two ex-agents exchanged winks and dove for their next missiles.

Blade barely felt the scorch in his fingers when he snatched up handfuls of pancakes from the warming pan and slung them. He ducked when Ray's return volley, using plates like Frisbees, knocked the steam tray right off the table.

"Gentlemen—" Worley began.

"Keep your slimy hands off my wife," Ray growled. He stayed still as the bowl of apples in sauce bounced off his shoulder. Most of the contents baptized his sweater. It was an improvement.

"If she wasn't bored, she wouldn't need me, now would she?" Blade taunted, and sidestepped a splattering arch of cranberry juice. Too bad. He liked cranberry.

"Gentlemen, surely there's a better way—"

Sarpantine burst out laughing. Blade didn't like the sound of his laughter. Evidently, neither did Ray because he let the pitcher of orange juice slide back into the basin of ice and stepped back from the table. For a few seconds, the three watched Sarpantine laugh so hard he slid down in his chair and his face turned red.

"What in the world is going on here?" Jen demanded, appearing as if on cue in the doorway. She gaped at the mess smeared across the patio, her mouth hanging open like the ditzoid Gloria was supposed to be when not talking computers.

Blade barely missed it, and he was watching for it. Jen made a little OK sign with her right hand before clenching it into a fist. She slightly shook her head. Ray nodded acknowledgement. Blade slid into the nearest chair, relieved to know Jen had finished her mission and hadn't been caught.

"Guy?" she pleaded, turning to Sarpantine, who couldn't get his laughter under control.

Sarpantine wiped tears from his cheeks, stood, and staggered for the nearest door. He waved her away and retreated indoors.

CHAPTER 17

"All right, Mark, just what did you do?" Jen jammed her fists into her waist and stomped over to where Ray slowly wiped at the glop coating his clothes.

"I didn't do anything, honey." He offered her a wimp's smile and turned to look for his fallen glasses.

Jen turned in a swirl of lime green sundress and looked at Blade. "What happened to your eye?"

"My eye?" Blade touched it without thinking, and winced. "Oh, yeah, my eye."

"Did that big ox hurt you?"

"Gloria—" Ray began.

"Get out. Leave me alone. You're a stupid, jealous brute and I don't want to see you for the rest of the day!" Jen stomped her feet for punctuation to her fishwife shriek.

Blade turned his back and bit his lip to keep from laughing. Both Worley and Ray beat a hasty retreat.

"I thought he was going to pull his punches," Jen whispered, once she and Blade were totally alone on the patio.

She snagged a clean napkin and scooped up a handful of crushed ice. The ice pack she pressed to Blade's now-throbbing eye smelled faintly of apple juice.

"Usually he does. Guess he figured he needed the realism."

"When he said he was going for his pound of flesh, I didn't think he'd take it out of you." She settled next to him, still holding the ice

174

pack to his eye.

"Pound of flesh?" He groaned.

"Did I press too hard?"

"No. Not you. Ray. He wouldn't say that unless he was calling Shylock. Something must have happened."

He frowned, vaguely aware of her sweet strawberry scent, the warmth of her leg lightly pressed against his and the inviting way the neckline of her dress gaped out a little when she leaned over him like that. Any other time, Blade would be hard pressed to keep his hands off her. Especially when they were guaranteed privacy for a good while.

"He contacted someone and sent information on Sarpantine last night, while he pretended to research you." Jen offered a shy smile. "Did you really do all those things you confessed to last night?"

"And then some. A few exaggerations to get Worley's attention, but..." Blade shrugged. And winced when the movement pressed his bruised flesh harder against the ice pack.

"Sit still, stupid."

"What did you find? I figured you and Ray set this up to let you do some hunting."

"And take a weapon out of Sarpantine's hands. If he couldn't hold the secret of our affair over you, he'd waste time looking for something else to control you. Anyway, there were two rooms we figured were most secure, most likely to hold the painting. Ray searched one yesterday while everybody else was rescuing us. I searched the other just now. Empty as Tut's tomb."

"That doesn't make sense."

"Lots of goodies hidden away, but not the Dordt. If I had found something, I'd be fussing over Ray right now and calling you a big brute. Thank goodness, I didn't find anything."

"What?" Blade took the ice pack from her hand and sat back. "Did he hit me harder than I thought?"

"If I turned away my...my lover, and went running back to my husband all repentant, Sarpantine would start his campaign again. No thanks. My slime quotient has gone off the meter. We have another problem, anyway." Jen shrugged. That uncertain little smile came back. "You had a rough time when you were a kid, didn't you?"

"I got over it." He had no idea what that warmth in her eyes meant, the little catch in her voice, but he liked the feelings it generated in him.

"That's the thing. Not many people are strong enough, smart enough to get over it. Most people would just use it as an excuse to become slime and punish everybody else for their problems."

"Yeah, well...thanks...I had help."

While Blade would have loved to sit there and wallow in her admiration, maybe take advantage of it with a few kisses, there were more important considerations.

"We're running out of time," he said on a sigh, and stood. "If Ray called in Shylock, then he thinks something big is going down. We have to find the Dordt before the Feds get here. Otherwise, everything becomes official record and the senator's secret is out."

"Oh. Yeah." She nodded and slid off the table. For just a moment, they brushed against each other. Blade thought he'd been slapped with live wires. Jen's eyes looked starry.

What would it hurt to steal just one kiss?

"Have either of you seen Magda?" Sarpantine demanded as he stomped back onto the patio.

"Magda?" Blade looked around, half-expecting the woman to slink around the edge of the patio. "No. She sleeps in."

"Usually. But it looks like her bed hasn't been slept in at all," he growled, and stomped back inside.

"That's the other problem," Jen whispered. "If Magda is missing and the painting isn't where we expected it—"

"Then the two of them are probably together."

*   *   *

No boats had left the island. No boat had visited during the night. Jen thought it rather amusing that Worley tried to deny his household staff patrolled the island at night.

Fact: the painting was still in its hiding place yesterday.

Worley wasn't a man who put something away and simply left it there until he needed it. He probably visited it every night to touch it and gloat. Someone—Magda?—followed him to the hiding place and took advantage of the distractions yesterday to take it.

Fact: Magda had gone up to her room last night and the housekeeper had brought her a slice of torte to nibble on while she read. Or so she claimed. The book was still lying on the floor. Along with a strangely modest, white cotton nightgown. Her luggage was still in her room. The only things missing were Magda herself, and the painting.

Worley had pressed them into searching, against Sarpantine's glowering and hissed remonstrances. Everybody had set off separately, with the understanding that no one was getting off the island until Magda and the missing item had been found. Jen came back downstairs after changing into jeans and sneakers, and found Blade heading for the kitchen. When he explained about hearing someone sneak down into the cellar last night, but hadn't heard anyone come up, she agreed with his theory that he had heard Magda going into hiding.

"Did Ray ever make you watch any of those Marx Brothers movies he loves?" Jen whispered. She and Blade crept down the creaky stairs that led from the stainless steel kitchen to the grimy, shadowy cellar.

"I'm not that stupid." He flashed her a grin. "Sorry. Wrong choice of words. Let's just say I've never let myself get roped into it."

"Okay, so I was bored, we were snowbound, the place had cable and it was better than getting whipped in chess for the eightieth time. Especially when he refused to play poker."

"Ray refused to play poker? Amazing." Blade reached for the string hanging from the dust-coated light bulb at the foot of the stairs and pulled it. Naturally, the light didn't come on. That left them with their flashlights. "Why not?"

"When he ran out of money, I suggested strip poker."

"You didn't." He grabbed hold of her shoulder, just hard enough Jen knew that suggestion had shaken him. She felt like laughing, but she couldn't breathe, either.

An image of playing *Blade* at strip poker flashed through her mind. Jen knew she might just deliberately flub a few hands and let him win. Not enough to be embarrassing. Not before she took him down to his briefs. Was he a thong man?

"I did. He cheats, did you know that?"

She took a deep breath of the damp cellar air. In the ineffectual beams of their flashlights, the joists were gray-brown, coated with years' worth of dust and grime. The same color as those streaks of dirt she had seen on Magda's clothes. Blade's theory looked more probable all the time. The floor was cracked cement or the original packed dirt, hidden under at least two inches of neglect and sediment.

"I'm not surprised. You must be good, if he was afraid to play you."

Blade's hand tightened on her shoulder. Did the thought of her seeing Ray in his underwear bother him? Good.

"Anyway," she continued, "in one movie, a painting vanished, and fakes kept reappearing in its place. Kind of like here."

"I'd like to just burn the whole place down and settle the question once and for all," Blade murmured. He swung his light around the room, revealing it was long enough the beam couldn't reach to the end. Dim gray-brown light barely penetrated the dirt-crusted windows from outside. The air felt thick with decades of grime.

"Be careful what you wish for. Think this is the original cellar?"

"Probably." He released her shoulder and stepped to the right. Jen followed him, repressing a sigh of regret.

Bundles swathed in burlap and plastic sheeting created ghostly outlines in the dimness. A few testing pokes sent clouds of grime into the air. Or worse, didn't disturb the layers of sediment. Magda couldn't have hidden anything down here without leaving a trail. Besides, the woman seemed so fastidious. She probably had a shudder factor about cobwebs and dark, dirty places that matched Jen's shudder factor for murky water. Jen hoped so. She could handle darkness and cobwebs.

"Bingo," Blade muttered.

He caught hold of Jen's hand and guided her flashlight to a narrow aisle between stacks of wooden crates. A few streaks in the grime revealed the raw wood. He guided their doubled beams of light to the floor. Small, triangular, scuffed wedges in the layers of dust were footprints. Someone with small feet, walking on tiptoe.

Blade held Jen's hand as they headed down the aisle. She held her breath, the better to concentrate on the warm tingling that spread up her arm from his touch.

After a dozen steps, the darkness closed around them like a muffling blanket. The narrow gap between the crates wasn't very comfortable, but it had its advantages. Jen had *lived* in holes far less inviting. And without Blade's company.

They came out into an alcove in the basement that was half rough-finished cement and half natural rock. Damp oozed through the air and Jen could almost feel it collect on her face and weigh down her hair. Stairs hacked into the gap in the natural rock led down into a dark pit reaching under the foundations of the house.

She had read that the Lake Erie islands had been home to Native American tribes, who used the tunnels and caves as homes. The tunnels and caves housed Admiral Perry and his men, and runaway slaves in the Underground Railroad. For all she knew, this darkness led into a cave under the island. Maybe that cave opened onto the lake, and had a boat waiting.

Blade likely had the same idea. He tugged on Jen's hand and led her down the steps. The slashing of their flashlight beams revealed the steps were damp and clean; no footprints to be seen. The damp made the stone slick, with no banister to grab for balance. Jen stumbled twice. Blade caught her both times. Then Blade fell, going to one knee. He let go of her hand to try to catch himself, and slammed his other hand against the rough-carved, glistening wall. The flashlight died with a sharp crack and Blade tumbled down four more steps, to land with a soft splash in the darkness.

Jen knew better than to run, but it took all her control not to fling herself down the steps after him. She swung the beam around in time with the rapid thudding of her heart.

Blade lay sprawled on his back, propped up across the bottom two steps, one knee bent to point up at the low, bumpy ceiling. The other leg lay straight out in water that looked black. Fortunately, it was shallow enough only to go to the instep when the toe of his boot pointed up at the ceiling. Blade groaned and levered himself up on his elbows, and then sat up. He slid down another step before he caught himself. Wincing, he looked over the hand that had held the flashlight. Jen saw a glimmer of glistening red. Blade licked at the cut, then pressed his hand against the back of his head.

"Let me look." She settled herself on the step, shivering a little when damp immediately oozed into the seat of her jeans. Blade moved himself around to present his back to her.

It took all her control to brush his hair aside until she found the spot he had pressed with his hand. Had Blade's hair felt this silky and warm last night? Had he smelled this good, a combination of pine and some unidentifiable spice and warmth that filled her head and made her breathless. Jen wanted to run her fingers through his hair and rest his head on her lap and brush her fingers over the fine stubble that shadowed his face. She had been angry Sarpantine hadn't even let Blade shave this morning, but now she didn't mind. It gave new definition to his face.

"How bad is it, doc?" Blade asked. The slight break in his voice shocked her out of her angry, hungry daydreams.

"No cut. Just a lump the size of Detroit." She smoothed the hair down over the spot and tried to swallow the regret that threatened to choke her.

"Don't," Blade said, when she withdrew her hand. He caught her fingers and pressed them against the back of his head again. "That feels good."

Jen swallowed hard. His hand certainly felt good on hers. She liked the weight of him pressing back against her knees.

"You know, before my mom died, she used to kiss my booboos and make them better." He chuckled, a ragged sound.

Holding her breath, Jen leaned down and pressed her lips against the back of his head. She knew she had to act, listening to her gut before common sense took over.

"How's that?" Her voice cracked. His hair felt good, warm and clean and silken against her face. Jen wanted to take handfuls of it and never let go.

"Maybe it works better from the other side." Blade shifted around, dangerously fast for the slickness of the steps.

"Other—" She couldn't breathe, suddenly finding herself inches from Blade's face.

Blade knelt on the step below Jen, his hands pressing her knees apart as he leaned in close enough she felt his body heat, a physical force pushing her into the steps. Blade braced himself against the rough wall with one hand and caught the back of her head with the other hand. His eyes were enormous, burning with dark fire, so she thought she would fall into them.

And he just stayed there, waiting, that taunting little, hungry smile gleaming in the darkness. She could see it even when her hands went limp and she nearly lost her grip on the flashlight. That smile tugged at her, like a winch and rope that pulled her insides into a tight knot.

She was ready this time as his mouth touched hers and his tongue teased her lips apart. She still flinched as the warm, salty sweetness of his mouth overwhelmed her, but Blade didn't hesitate, didn't draw back. Jen held onto the flashlight, wrapping that arm around his neck to support herself. Blade brought them upright so he took most of their weight on his knees, there on the slippery steps. Jen welcomed his heat soaking into her damp, chilled body, and clutched at his shirt with her free hand. It didn't even matter when she forgot to breathe.

A tiny giggle escaped her when Blade drew back days later, gasping for breath himself.

"All better now?" she whispered.

"Better?" Blade frowned, and she decided to take that dazed look as a compliment. Then he smiled and nodded. "Best cure-all in the entire world." His smile grew wider. "I can't believe nobody ever kissed you properly before."

"That was proper?"

"You have a problem with my technique?" His voice echoed off the water, the damp stone, cracking a little with indignation. Mock indignation, she dared hope.

"I meant proper as in decent. Civilized. A gentleman." Jen leaned in close enough to feel his heart thudding against hers. "Instead of like a hungry beast."

"Is that a complaint?" Blade laughed when she could only shake her head. "How come I'm the first? Not that I'm complaining, you understand."

"Never been...real before."

"Real, huh? Let me show you real, Mrs. Williams," Blade growled. He tightened his arms around her, and let out a yelp as his knees slid out from under him.

They ended up lying in the black water. Blade took most of the damage, since he pulled Jen on top of him as they slid down the steps. She had heard his head whack at least two steps and that terrified her.

"Blade?" Jen slid off him, getting herself thoroughly soaked from the hips down until she finally got herself upright. "Are you all right?"

"I have a black eye, a wrenched shoulder, and three dents the size of Texas in my head. This whole situation feels like a reject Scooby-Doo episode and all I can think about is you in that white nightie and ripping it off you. How all right do you think I feel?" His voice rose until it rang against the wet, dripping tunnel, each word echoing muffled a dozen times over.

Part of Jen knew she should analyze those echoes and try to decide how many openings and passages lay beyond the blackness. She knew she should be grateful she hadn't dropped the flashlight in the water or broke it. All she could do was kneel in the water and stare at the dark bulk of him as he pulled himself upright against the steps. The waves of heat from his words drove away the chills and her breath.

"Jen?" Blade whispered, when minutes ticked by and she still couldn't speak. He reached through the dark and turned the flashlight in her hand so it illuminated her. "Did I scare you?"

She shook her head. Everything turned sparkly bright when he shone the light in her face. She suspected she had tears in her eyes, which was stupid. She never cried.

Then again, she had never wanted a man to touch her before. Not a real man, flesh and blood instead of a hero out of some classical novel or adventure movie. The only men she allowed near her all her life were either family, they belonged to other women or they were too busy keeping other people alive to be a threat to her.

"What do I get to rip off you?" she finally managed to say.

Anything else would shove the floodgates wide open.

Blade laughed. He reached over and gathered her close and held her on his lap. He laughed until his voice deafened her and his arms wrapped so tight she started to lose feeling from her chest down. Or maybe that tingling sensation wasn't from lack of circulation but something else moving through her?

"Now is not the time or the place," Blade finally said, pressing a kiss against her ear. He flicked the tip of his tongue along the curve, making her jump nearly out of his lap.

"We have a job to do," she admitted on a sigh that came from the sudden, aching hunger digging a pit inside her.

Life just wasn't fair.

She braced herself, but it still hurt when Blade lifted her off his lap and set her upright on her knees. She shivered, feeling the cold from her soaked clothes and the damp air. Blade gripped her hand and took the flashlight from her other hand as he stood. He swung the beam around to study their surroundings.

The water ran past them just fast enough to see movement. Jen estimated it was five inches deep at the most, maybe three feet wide. Narrow enough she could cross it in a running leap, but why bother, when her shoes were already soaked through?

The mental image of Blade kissing her bruises away was an appealing one, and warmed her a little.

On the other side of the water, more stairs led upward into blackness, at such a steep angle the flashlight beam couldn't penetrate. To the right and left, the water ran through a natural tunnel, maybe two feet high. Jen didn't relish the idea of crawling through that. There were worse things in horror movies than scientific experiments living in dark tanks of water. Her imagination started to lift details to her conscious mind—tentacles reaching from crevices in the rock, slime and quicksand and piranha-like creatures. Jen held tight to Blade's hand for the strength to push the images back into storage.

She was going to concentrate on G-rated movies from now on.

Or maybe not. Blade's words about her nightgown kept echoing through her head.

"Upward and onward," Blade murmured and released her hand before he started across the water. He stretched out his arm, effectively keeping her from following. He didn't slip, didn't step into any sinkholes, and he pretended a sigh of relief as he guided Jen across after him

"You like playing knight in shining armor, don't you?" she whispered as they started up the steps.

"It's an ego trip, that's all," he said with a shrug. "I mean, you've proved you don't need anybody to look after you."

Something in his voice stopped her from shooting off a smart remark. Jen wove her fingers through his and tightened her grip. She decided silence was the best course of action.

The best course of action from this point *was* silence, in more ways than just their personal interaction. For all they knew, Magda had a gun.

They reached the top of the stairs and the flashlight beam revealed the tunnel curved to the left and sloped down gradually. The ceiling lowered with every step, until Blade walked hunched over and Jen had to worry about scraping her head. She told herself repeatedly that bats couldn't live in caves and tunnels this small. Could they?

"Down," Blade grunted, and wrapped his arms around her as he dropped to the rough ground.

They landed in a puddle, Jen on the bottom this time. She closed her eyes, not even feeling the mineral chill soak into her clothes. Most definitely, she had felt something swoop past and the squeaking of furry, fanged radar.

"You okay?" he whispered, his breath hot in her ear.

Jen nodded, then realized how stupid that was in the dark, with the flashlight beam pointing back the way they had come.

"Fine." Her voice caught and croaked when she tried to laugh. "We really have to stop meeting like this."

"You're dangerous, lady." Blade finally got up on his hands and knees and levered himself off of her.

Too late, awareness of their differing anatomy pressed together flooded through Jen. She was glad for the darkness, and trembled as he pulled her to her feet.

"Dangerous?"

"A distraction." He choked, and Jen realized he tried to muffle a chuckle. "You could have gotten me killed on a dozen missions. Good thing this isn't life or death."

"Yeah. Good thing." She let him lead her for a few more steps, further into the darkness. "Was that a compliment or a complaint or a warning?"

"Compliment." Blade squeezed her hand. "And a complaint that we're not—"

Jen saw the glimmer of light up ahead and bit back the question, *not what?*

A voice crackled through a burst of static. The damp air and the faint echoes warped the sound so Jen couldn't make out what was said. A radio? She held her breath and Blade stopped them, so they held still and waited.

And waited.

No response.

Finally the person on the other end repeated the question. Still no response. Blade squeezed Jen's hand twice and started forward. She had no idea what he meant by that signal. They were going to have to work together longer than this for her to understand such things.

Working together for a long time sounded fine. Pillow talk wouldn't be boring, to say the least.

Later, she scolded herself as they moved around the corner and into the light. After the dim yellow beam of the flashlight, the harsh, white light of the camping lanterns scraped at her eyes until they adjusted.

A radio sat on a makeshift table of boards and crates. It was high-tech enough that the dials and gauges were liquid crystal, glowing softly red in the shadows at the edge of the lantern glare. Someone had set up a cozy little camp in the cave, with a cot, camping stove, and jugs of water. The floor was sand, and Jen saw footprints leading around the next bend in the tunnel. The ceiling was higher here too.

"Feel the wind?" Blade whispered, after she pointed out the footprints to him.

She paused a moment and indeed did feel air movement. Jen nodded. Blade gestured around the campsite.

"Search. I'll see what's ahead." He shut off the flashlight and turned it around in his hand like a club as he left.

He walked on his toes and hugged the wall as he crept around the bend. Jen noticed he cast two shadows, forward and back. Meaning there was more light ahead. Maybe, judging by the air movement, the door out of the tunnel caves?

Jen went to work, careful to touch nothing where she could leave usable fingerprints. For the first time since this farce had started, she was grateful for her acrylic nails. She used them like tweezers to pick up or pry things open.

Judging by the supplies, whoever had set up this camp didn't intend to stay long. A few cans of soup, some beef jerky, dried apples, and raisins. One bowl, one spoon, one fork, one knife, and one pot for cooking over the stove. The plastic storage box under the cot revealed two changes of clothes and a first aid kit. Jen carefully lifted the jeans and sniffed them. They reeked of the heavy perfume Magda wore.

The radio crackled again. Jen scooted over on her knees and listened to the voice. It was a man's, harsh with static, asking for an update. Nothing revealing. Nothing to identify who was supposed to give the update, or who waited to receive it.

Jen got down on her hands and knees and looked into the crates that supported the radio. They held a few books, extra batteries; probably for the radio and flashlights. No ammunition, either loose bullets or loaded clips. That was good. The less she had to deal with guns, the better.

A scraping sound echoed through the cave room. Jen got up too quickly to remember the low ceiling and banged her head. She bit her tongue to keep from crying out, and turned to face the opening of the tunnel. It was probably just Blade coming back to tell her he had found nothing.

But what if it wasn't? She turned to duck around the bend in the tunnel, to hide in the darkness.

And came face to face with Magda, dressed in black sweats and hiking boots, sans makeup, her hair pulled back in a ponytail and jammed under a baseball cap. Her sweatshirt hung over a gentle landscape, where a bust of Valkyrie proportions used to reside. She was so changed from the slinky creature encountered at the dinner table, Jen nearly didn't recognize her. Except for her scent.

She also carried a gun.

CHAPTER 18

"You should have stolen the painting when it was easier to leave." Jen's voice bounced off the tunnel walls, to emerge flat and tinny in the pebbly alcove where Blade stood.

He turned so fast he twisted his already aching ankle. Muffling a curse, he hobbled back down the tunnel. Behind him lay a cave mouth that opened right into the lake. The dock was metal, dented from use, crusted with algae and lake weeds and rusty from neglect. A handy little two-man boat waited. Judging from the sleek newness of the motor, Blade didn't doubt it would make little sound when it headed across the lake.

"Some things can't be helped," Magda said with a chuckle.

Her heavy, seductive drawl had vanished. Blade grinned, delighted to find that assessment had proven correct. Maybe everything about Magda was as false as her accent.

"Timing is everything. And knowing when to cut your losses. Do you mind if I sit?" The cot creaked, meaning Jen sat without waiting for Magda's permission. "Do you have aspirin or anything? I have got one killer headache."

"You're a wonderful actress, Gloria. Is that your name? Not many airheads I know would be so relaxed with a gun pointing in their cute little faces."

Blade peered around the bend in the tunnel. Magda leaned back against the wall by the radio, arms crossed so she could keep the gun leveled on Jen, who sat on the end of the cot and rubbed the top of her head.

"When did you become Magda Torrene?" Jen countered.

"Become?"

"Clever of you to hide Mary Margaret Tortelli under incorporation, so no one could know it's a pen name. When did you pick up the makeup, padding, and accent?"

"Self-defense. The public Magda is a persona I created to protect myself from overly-enthusiastic fans and keep my boss from firing me. The slimy creep would love to have Magda waltz into the office, but then he'd expect her to be constantly in heat, like Stacy Peach. Know what I mean?"

"Mary Margaret certainly doesn't deserve sexual harassment," Jen murmured.

"You're telling me." She chuckled. "It's kind of fun, being two people. When I finish signing autographs, I pop into the bathroom, change my clothes, remove the rubber enhancements, wash off my makeup and voila, ordinary housewife."

"Who carries a gun and knows about these tunnels, and slithered in here to steal a fake painting."

Blade straightened with a jerk, nearly bashing his head against the low ceiling. Why had Jen revealed *that* secret?

Magda took a step forward and actually lowered the gun. "You never saw the painting. How do you know it's fake?"

"How do *you* know it's fake? How do you know I'm not trying to scam you?" Jen returned with a grin.

"If you know it's fake, you know where the original is?"

"I don't care about the real one. I just want to get the fake out of here and back to my client. And so do you."

"Senator Carlisle?"

"Not Senator Carlisle," Blade said as he stepped forward to join them. He raised his hands and offered up a non-threatening grin when Magda pointed the gun at him. "The owners of the real Dordt, I'm guessing. Jen, remember how ticked Ray got when we found out the new owners had hired a PI? They weren't even supposed to know the fake had been stolen."

"You know politicians." Jen slouched against the wall. "One man's secret is another's press conference."

"You work for Senator Carlisle?" Magda chuckled. "I work for the VanderHueys."

"The owners of the original." Blade sat on the cot next to Jen.

"You're their PI. We moved up our schedule because we were afraid you'd show up and ruin things."

"And to think all along, we could have been double-teaming Worley." She grinned wider.

"You want to put that gun away? I get itchy when I'm on the wrong end of those things. Even if the safety is on."

"Oh." Magda shrugged and tossed the gun next to the radio. "Well, isn't this cozy? I assume this is all an act, the criminal appraiser and the computer security team?"

"Mik is real, but the real Mik is in federal custody."

"What about your husband?" She licked her lips, reverting to her seductive persona. "Please tell me he's the ringleader and not a pigeon. It's just not fair when someone that tasty is a couple fries short of a Happy Meal."

"Ray is all yours." Jen waved her hands, effectively giving Ray over to Magda's tender mercies.

Blade was more grateful for that little bit of silliness than he could quite express, even to himself. He wished he could be there when Ray got desperate enough to tell the truth to Magda. He hoped she walloped him good, when she found out they could possibly be relatives.

"Tell you what," he said. "We'll trade you Ray for the painting."

"Oh." Magda's cat-in-the-cream smile dropped right off into the sandy floor. "Problem."

Jen sighed. "Where's the Dordt?"

"I haven't the foggiest." She dropped down on the end of the crate table and scowled. "I was ready to lift it last night and Sarpantine caught me red-handed. He's slimy, but smart. Let me do all the work, picking those locks. Then he sailed in with a bottle of wine in one hand and a gun in the other. Offered me a toast to our new partnership and no alternative."

"I hope you didn't take the drink." Blade wouldn't wish Sarpantine's potions on anyone.

"I've heard about him." Magda shuddered. "I opted to keep control of my senses and my pulse, thank you very much, and handed over the painting. He wasn't even disappointed that I turned down his drink. What is with that guy?"

"He has some warped sense of honor," Jen offered. "You don't trust him, so you're hiding until the coast is clear?"

"Until I get reinforcements."

"Ray sent for reinforcements too," Blade said. "How good are yours?"

"More PIs. You?"

"Federal."

"Ooh, playing with the big boys." She managed to hold onto her grin for all of five seconds. "What are we going to do?"

"We need a big distraction," Jen muttered.

"I have this delicious little black and red peek-a-boo number I could loan you," Magda said. "On your figure..." She cast an appraising glance at Blade and her grin widened. "It could be a free-for-all, once they get a good look at you."

"Maybe I should give Sarpantine what he wants," Jen said, nodding.

"No. No way in the world. You are not going anywhere near him. If I have to tie you up and leave you—" Blade stood so quickly, he slammed his head into the ceiling.

*   *   *

"What are you doing in here?" Sarpantine asked, stepping into Magda's abandoned bedroom.

Jen let out a little shriek that was only half-feigned and turned, spilling the contents of the drawer. All Magda's lacy, see-through lingerie cascaded to the floor. Jen's nerves were so tight, she didn't have to pretend to be startled. Her blush felt completely natural as she held onto the red and black lacy bit of fluff Magda told her to use.

"Just—looking." She pressed her hand to her chest.

The movement draped the negligee to display the sheer cloth and hip-length hem crusted with black rhinestones and red marabou.

As if guided by remote control, Sarpantine's gaze dropped and followed the line of the outfit. He very slowly licked his lips and took a long breath before raising his head and looking Jen in the eye again.

"I thought maybe—you know—I could look around here and maybe find something." Jen tossed the outfit onto the bed. She swore Sarpantine whimpered. "The sooner we can get off this island, the better. Mark is such a stupid-head and Mik or Munroe or whoever he is...I don't know why I thought he was cute. Older men are much more fun. He didn't kiss all that good, either." Jen sauntered over to the bed and flopped down—making sure Sarpantine could still see the negligee.

"You're not happy with your lover, my dear?" he crooned.

"We never even got that far." She pouted.

Did he drool? No wonder he had to use drugs to get women.

"Disappointed?"

"More than you could possibly know." Jen sighed. That was one hundred percent truth. "Well, there's nothing here. Are you sure Magda didn't get off the island?"

"Positive. Every boat is accounted for." He stepped closer. "You seem a little...depressed."

"What I am is achy and tired. Mark and Danville and that Hampton jerk are still hunting, and I hope they stay out until tomorrow night. I—" she bounced up off the bed. "—am going to take a long, hot bubble bath. That's one nice thing about this place. The tubs are big enough for a dozen people."

Sarpantine definitely drooled.

To fight nausea, Jen concentrated on her mission—get him so focused on her, he would ignore everything else. Including strange noises coming from his room.

"Maybe I should try this. Magda won't mind, do you think?" She picked up the negligee and held it against herself. "It's not wrong to want to get some help, is it? I mean, when we were first married, Mark was really hot in bed. Every night. Now, it's just snore city after the fourth time."

"Fourth?" Sarpantine choked.

"We used to be able to go all night." She giggled. "Mark switched to teaching afternoon classes, because he missed so many morning ones. Maybe this'll put a little spice back, you think?" She sighed and turned to saunter out the door.

*   *   *

"She's good," Ray whispered.

He and Blade waited in the darkness of the walk-in linen closet between Sarpantine and Magda's rooms. As soon as Jen led Sarpantine up the stairs, they could emerge and get to work.

"Too good." Blade clenched his fists until his nails dug into his palms. The only alternative was to leap out and strangle Sarpantine.

Not a good idea. Sarpantine had a reputation for using a dead-man switch to booby-trap his caches if he were killed or even knocked unconscious. And a delayed timer. They could be halfway to their goal and it would all blow up around them.

Blade knew with his head that the best weapon was to use the man's weaknesses against him, but why did *Jen* have to be the bait? Other than the fact that the two women staff worked for Worley and Sarpantine ignored Magda. Every fiber of Blade's body cried out against the mental image of Sarpantine putting a hand on Jen's bare skin. Even if it was just to touch her hand.

It was Ray's fault they were here. Ray's fault Jen was stuck playing bait bimbo to lure Sarpantine up two floors so they could search his room. Maybe he should just strangle Ray instead. Would he have the time? Reach through the darkness and grab Ray so fast he didn't have time to resist. Break his neck if he had to. Then race upstairs and throw Sarpantine off the third floor balcony, onto the rocks. With luck, Sarpantine would linger for a while, giving them time to get off the island before his booby-traps went off. The mental image had a certain charm to it.

Especially if Jen had that black and red number Magda told her to use. No court in the land would convict him, if they realized what was at stake. What red-blooded American male would blame him? He had to protect his lady.

The only problem was—and Blade's temperature and pulse started to drop—Jen *wasn't* his lady. Not by any stretch of the imagination. Those few kisses they had managed to share were only a prelude to the real thing. Like appetizers that made him more ravenous, instead of helping him endure until the feast.

"Okay," Ray said. He waited. Blade did nothing. "Go on."

"What?" Blade turned around in the darkness. Ray was between him and the closet wall. He could still body-slam him.

"They're upstairs."

"They are?" He muffled a groan.

What was wrong with him? So worried about Jen, so stinking jealous of the necessity for playing on Sarpantine's libido, he had paid no attention to the unfolding of their plan.

"You'd better hope Jen likes the cave man routine. You're not going to be any use to anyone until you've had her in bed for a week." Ray pushed past Blade and reached for the closet door.

Only their time limit kept Blade from flinging Ray against the wall and pounding him into a bloody paste. If he wasted time beating up on his ex-best friend, that was more time Jen was in Sarpantine's clutches.

Maybe once they were on their way to the mainland, he could tie an anchor to Ray and heave him overboard.

Five steps took them to Sarpantine's room. It was locked. Ray brought out his handy-dandy lock pick kit and they were inside in ten seconds flat.

*　　*　　*

191

"Ooh!" Jen squealed.

She staggered backwards and sat down hard on the toilet seat. The faucet thundered and peach-scented bubbles filled the jade tub. Steam misted through the room and Sarpantine braced himself against the door with both arms, watching her with wide, bright eyes. His lips looked wet. More drool?

Somebody should take this guy to a doctor. Preferably several. Preferably in prison.

Jen had felt Sarpantine watching her, but until he said or did something, she had to pretend to be oblivious to him. She had fussed around the bathroom, pulling out towels and a neck rest. Not a sound or move from him.

She played with the water temperature and drizzled in more bubble bath until the suds were thick and white and twice as deep as the water. She took off her shoes and socks. The man didn't even have the decency to groan.

Knowing she would have to start taking off her clothes soon or risk making him suspicious, Jen picked up Magda's borrowed outfit. She held it up to herself and turned to the mirror. That let her finally see Sarpantine.

"What are you doing here?" she squeaked.

"I just want to help you, my dear," Sarpantine crooned. From anyone else, the sound might have been mesmerizing. Or soothing, at the very least. From him, it only sounded oily.

"Help?" She clutched the negligee against her chest.

Sarpantine's eyes got wider and he swallowed loudly.

"You sounded so very...lonely." He crept into the bathroom and settled down on the wide edge of the tub. "It saddens me to see such a lovely, fragile creature so unhappy." He dragged his fingers through the bubbles and paused to contemplate them. With a sigh, he flicked the bits of white froth into the air and turned to her again. "I would like to offer my help. I believe I could make you very...happy. For tonight. And maybe tomorrow, your troubles won't look quite so bleak."

Yeah, I bet. When a girl wakes up from a night with you, the bubonic plague probably looks good.

"How could you make me..." She licked her lips and sighed. "Happy?"

"Love makes the world go 'round, my dear. Let me love you tonight, and you will never regret it." He slid off the tub and reached over to close the bathroom door.

"Well, let me think about it, okay? I mean, I just got this bath going and I don't want to waste it." She giggled and turned away, hoping he took it as shyness.

"Have you never made love in the bathtub, my dear?"

"You can do that?" A mental image of tangling herself with Blade under those mounds of bubbles filled her mind for one hot, tantalizing moment. She smiled. If Sarpantine thought that smile was for him, that was his problem, not hers.

If he took that smile for acceptance, it became her problem.

She wished she had turned Ray down when he asked for her help on this "simple" retrieval mission.

"There are many things we can do, to fill the night."

"Oh." Jen nodded. "I guess that could be fun."

"Ecstasy. Paradise." Sarpantine held out his hands. "Let me help you out of those uncomfortable clothes."

"Uh uh." Jen scooted beyond his reach. "You take off your clothes first. I like to watch."

She prayed she wouldn't throw up, and Blade and Ray would finish their task and come bail her out.

"Well, who's the little fireball?" He chuckled and settled down on the tub again, and bent over to remove his shoes.

Jen settled on the counter and prayed his shoelaces were knotted.

He wore loafers.

It didn't help to know that if Blade were sitting there, she would knock him into the tub and they would undress each other under all those sweet-scented bubbles. Pretty hot for a girl who'd never been kissed properly until Blade came along.

Sarpantine tucked his socks into his loafers. He let his gaze travel up and down Jen, as if he could see through her snug jeans and green polo shirt. The sensation of slime coating her skin made her nauseous.

"Are you sure you wouldn't like to help me—" He stopped, his mouth hanging open, and sat up straight.

Jen held her breath, trying not to laugh as the bleats of an alarm trickled up the winding stairs. From the way Sarpantine's smug face paled, that sound meant nothing good.

For him, anyway.

For her, it meant a reprieve, and a reason to keep living.

He cursed under his breath and staggered for the door.

"Where are you going?"

She had to delay him as long as possible, to let Ray and Blade get away with the painting.

He ignored her and almost ran into the door before he got it open. When she caught hold of his shirtsleeve, he cursed and batted her hand away.

"Aren't you going to teach—"

Sarpantine swung and would have knocked her across the bathroom if she hadn't dodged. His eyes blazed like a maniac's and an angry red flush made her think of a blood blister about to explode. She let him go and prayed those few seconds she gained would help Blade and Ray.

Jen scooped up Sarpantine's shoes and followed him to the landing to toss them after him. One nearly hit him on the top of his head. Sarpantine cursed as he ran. Jen doubted he even noticed the shoes.

Chuckling, feeling giddy over her reprieve, she went into the bathroom and turned off the faucet. Much as she longed to relax in a hot bubble bath, Jen knew better. With luck, they would be off Gibraltar Island before nightfall.

Downstairs, the alarm continued to bleat and Sarpantine swore louder with every pulse that passed. It made wonderful background music as Jen started packing for the exodus.

When she went into the bathroom to retrieve her shoes and socks, she saw Magda's negligee, where she had dropped it on the counter. Jen grinned at herself in the mirror, put her shoes and socks on, then picked up the scrap of red and black. She studied herself in the mirror as she held it up against herself, smoothing it over her hips.

"Not your style," Blade said, appearing in the doorway. He watched her in the mirror.

"What happened?"

"Are you all right? He didn't get very far, did he?"

"I'm dressed and no barfing. Good sign, right?"

The intensity of his concern, the anger underneath it, made her heart thunder and drove the breath from her lungs. How would it be if Blade worried about her like that all the time? It took effort to bring her mind back to business.

"So, what happened?"

"He had an alarm rigged to the bottom of his bed. Effective, unless you're dealing with people who know how to disable atomic bombs. Bad place to hide a supposedly valuable painting." He shrugged and took a few steps into the bathroom, still watching her in the mirror.

"You got it?"

"First place we looked. It took all of ten minutes and Ray was out the door. We didn't let the alarm go off until we wanted it to. Ray's halfway across the lake with Magda, right this minute, heading for her contact in Sandusky. He'll come back with the sheriff or whoever he can get hold of. In the meantime, I'm staying right by your side every minute to protect you."

"Did you warn Ray he'd need protection from Magda?" Jen tossed the red and black negligee aside. Blade's gaze stayed focused on her, not the wisp of rhinestones and fluff.

"She told me the brainy geek act turned her on. I think Ray is going to end up with a partner whether he likes it or not. If she doesn't kill him, first."

"Where does that leave me?"

Blade moved so fast she lost her breath. He grasped her shoulders and lifted her up to sit on the counter. Now their heads were almost at an even level. He pressed her knees apart so he could lean against the counter, and braced himself with one hand against the mirror behind her. He lightly touched her lips with his index finger, then his hand curved around her jaw to tip her head up to meet his kiss.

His hand left a trail of fire and ice in its wake as it moved through her hair, then down her arm, around her back to clutch her close against him. Jen wrapped her arms around Blade.

She forgot to breathe as all sensation pooled in her mouth, in the dance of Blade's lips and tongue taking full possession. She stared up at the ceiling and saw stars around the edges of her vision as he trailed hot kisses down her throat, then back up to nip at her ear. He laughed when she squealed, not sure if she liked the spike of electricity that jolted through her at the unexpected sensation. Then he claimed her mouth again as his hands smoothed over her body, pulling her so close she thought they would melt into each other. All Jen could do was clutch at him, dig her fingernails in and wrap her legs around his hips.

She wished she knew what to do, to show him how he made her feel.

"Perfect," he moaned into her mouth. Then laughed, when she flinched at the first feel of his fingers sliding up her back, under her shirt. "Nobody ever touched you there?" His breath was warm in her ear, sending electric tingles through her middle.

"Nobody but a doctor," she whispered. Jen shuddered, shaken by the newness, wanting to savor every moment of this experience. Her breath caught when Blade delicately dragged his fingertips around her side, following the curve of her ribs.

"I think it's time for a full physical exam, Mrs. Williams."

"Stop..." Jen felt him flinch and she laughed. "No, not that. I mean, stop calling me *Mrs*. The job's over, isn't it?"

Blade drew back and just looked at her, his eyes wide and dark. A slow smile crept over those strong, warm, yet amazingly soft lips.

"We should celebrate." He raised one hand to brush strands of hair out of her eyes. It amazed Jen to realize she had started to sweat. "A long, hot bath and champagne, to start out."

"I don't do champagne."

"No?" He frowned just slightly.

"I like to keep my wits about me every second. I don't want to miss a single detail," she added, dropping to a whisper.

"Uh huh. My kind of girl." He drew back a step, dropping his hands to her hips, and looked over his shoulder. "We have a big, hot bubble bath waiting. We sure didn't do it right the last time we were in the tub together."

Jen managed a dry little laugh, but his words started a chain reaction of questions and considerations. Sometimes she hated the way her brain worked, though her tendency to analyze and step back and dissect everything had kept her alive.

They had ended up in the tub together the first time because of Sarpantine's drugs.

Sarpantine wanted sex with her in the tub.

Now, so did Blade.

"Jen?" Blade leaned close again and brushed a soft kiss across her upper lip, then another across her bottom lip.

It vibrated through her more deeply than the hot, hungry kisses that left the imprint of her teeth against her lips. But that didn't stop her brain from whirling through the analysis.

What was the difference between the two men and their goals? Besides Blade's lack of slime? Blade made her hum inside, while Sarpantine made her want to retch.

Her common sense finally kicked in. Jen mentally slapped herself, but she couldn't stop the process. She had trained herself to think hard about any life-changing decision. It meant survival. She couldn't turn off her brain now, despite the clamor running through her body.

After seeing the mess friends had made of their lives, giving everything to a man just because he knew the right words, the right touch, the right smile, Jen had promised herself she would wait. A long time. Forever, if she had to, until she was absolutely sure of a man.

No matter what her heart and body said about Blade, no matter what Ray had told her about his former partner, how much did she know about him? Enough to risk her health, heart and soul? In just a few days' time?

Jen had long ago decided she was an "all or nothing" girl.

But she had the awful feeling if she didn't give all to Blade, as soon as possible, she would be nothing.

She shot the last man who gave her an ultimatum like that.

"Blade." Jen licked her lips, finding her mouth suddenly dry. Her heart jolted hard when the simple action brought flames to his eyes. "What are we about to do?"

"You're a big girl, Jen. If you don't know..." He tried to laugh. The sound caught in his throat, like it was sandpaper. A few of those flames left his eyes.

"That's just it. Are we going to make love...or are we just having hot, wet sex?"

It would be love for her, but what if Blade only saw sex? It would leave her in the same situation as girls she pitied. Like her friends, whom she had defended by killing. Jen refused to let that happen. Even for Blade.

Oh, please, make him the kind of guy who wants forever.

Blade stepped back. His fingertips trailed down her thighs to her knees, until he moved just out of arm's reach. Jen held still despite the cold jolt that ran through her and the whimper that followed like an aftershock.

"You're having second thoughts?" He sounded calm, but shadows like storm clouds gathered around his eyes.

"I really haven't had time for first ones. I mean, X-rated daydreams aren't the same as thinking things through." Jen slid off the counter. She felt vulnerable when she couldn't stand on her own two feet. She hated feeling unsafe around Blade, but until common sense requirements were fulfilled, she couldn't turn it off. "Nobody ever swept me off my feet before." She choked. "Straight into the bathtub."

"Well, not straight." Blade managed a half-smile. "I thought I'd undress you first. Wet denim is pretty tough to manage."

"I'm not the kind of girl to just throw myself at the first gorgeous guy who makes me melt inside."

"You've been doing a pretty good melt job on me since the first time I saw you." He held out his hand and she fought conflicting urges. Run, or wrap her arms around him? Jen gave her hand into his grasp. "I think I know what you're asking, Jen. You want more than a few nights."

"I've never been able to depend on anyone before." She flinched when Blade started to tug his hand free. She held on, weaving her fingers through his.

That had definitely been the wrong thing to say. Why had that slipped out? Why couldn't she just ask him if he loved her?

"I want you so bad, Jen, I'm ready to explode. The first time I saw Ray kiss you, I wanted to deck him." Blade clutched her hand tighter.

She had no idea what to say. Jen feared anything she did say would only make things worse. Why couldn't she just have used her mouth for kissing and let the moment flow where it would? Why couldn't she have just let Blade work his magic on her, know a few hours of fantasy, and worry about reality tomorrow?

Because she hadn't lived this long by letting tomorrow take care of itself. What she did today always determined if she lived until tomorrow, and if she would be glad of it.

In the silence, Sarpantine's howls and curses drifted up the stairs in wisps and jolts.

CHAPTER 19

Crashing sounds punctuated Sarpantine's unintelligible ravings. Worley screamed, sounding like Chekov when the hapless Russian was tortured on a *Star Trek* episode. The total incongruity of the image snapped Jen out of the moment.

"We should rescue Worley," she said, and darted out of the bathroom. If Blade followed her, she wasn't sure. She told herself she didn't care.

He was two steps behind her when she reached the bottom of the tower stairs and Jen realized she did care. Then she saw Worley's bruises and blood and the past half hour evaporated.

Sarpantine struck with lazy, deliberate elegance like the movement of a snake. Jen shuddered and couldn't look away. He didn't hurry, but he somehow managed to keep up with Worley as the fat man staggered and stumbled backwards away from him across the entry hall. Why didn't he just turn and run?

Sarpantine's fist connected with Worley's bleeding chin and the fat man flew a good five feet, to hit the wall and fall. The impact brought a painting down on him. The canvas split to form a square collar.

"What are you doing?" Jen demanded.

Stupid question, but sometimes she had been able to shock people into stopping and really seeing what they were doing.

Then again, did she really want to bring Sarpantine's attention onto herself?

Sarpantine responded with a stream of curses in several languages.

Jen would have been impressed, but she had always believed dependence on profanity was a sign of low intelligence.

Worley climbed to his feet and yanked the painting collar away. He staggered across the floor to her and Blade. His terrified pallor darkened to anger. He shuddered as he pointed a pudgy finger at Sarpantine.

"I've done nothing!" he finally spat—punctuated by a spray of blood and spit. "I went beyond hospitality and—"

"Hospitality?" Sarpantine sounded like he had been castrated. "I've been robbed, you pitiful excuse for—"

"You robbed me first!" Worley turned to Jen and Blade. "He stole the painting from me and then pretended he didn't know where it was. I wouldn't be surprised if he killed that sweet little Magda and put the blame on her. And now he's misplaced my painting and he's blaming me!"

"*My* painting." Sarpantine grabbed Worley's shoulder and spun the fat man around to face him. "It's my painting. If you don't give it back, you'll be sorry you ever set eyes on me."

"I've been sorry for the past twenty years!" the fat man howled, accompanied by more blood and spit. "You trashed my house and broke my face. What more could you do to me?"

"Enough C-4 to send this pitiful hunk of rock to the bottom of the lake. How's that for starters?"

Worley shrieked and flung himself at Sarpantine, fat hands extended like claws.

"As in—bombs?" Jen asked no one in particular.

Blade hooked his arm through hers and moved backwards.

Worley followed Sarpantine across the room, flailing his arms like fat, ineffectual scythes. Sarpantine alternated between laughing at him and spilling more curses. He held the fat man at arm's length by pressing one hand flat against his bowed head.

"Why shouldn't I blow up your silly little island and your tasteless, tacky little castle?" Sarpantine spat. "Did you honestly think I would let anyone cheat me? Especially you?"

"Cheat?" Worley's voice rose another octave, almost enough to shatter glass. "It was my painting. I stole it fair and square! You had no right to take it."

"I take whatever I want," he growled, and shoved Worley away. "What I want, I get. That's the rule. That's always been the rule, and no one gets away with breaking that rule."

With a shriek worthy of professional wrestling, Worley launched himself at Sarpantine from five feet away. He hit him square in the chest with his head. The two men went down, rolling and kicking, biting, and punching.

"That's our cue." Blade grabbed Jen's hand. They bolted.

The front door was locked, with a deadbolt that required a key. Jen wasted a few precious seconds wishing she had taken lock picking lessons when Ray had offered.

The library was next, but it had leaded glass windows. Blade threw himself at the closest one and it barely squeaked when he hit it with his shoulder and bounced. Jen reached for a heavy chair to throw through it.

"No time." Blade grabbed her hand and led her out into the main hallway again.

*   *   *

Where next? Blade shuddered, realizing the sounds of Worley and Sarpantine's battle had vanished. Which man was dead? Or had they taken their struggle to another part of the house?

He remembered Sarpantine's words about the C-4 and his gut told him it wasn't an idle threat. A lunatic like Sarpantine *would* follow through. It was a matter of his twisted honor.

"Dining room?" Jen tugged on his arm.

Blade took the lead in three steps. He pushed aside the twinge of dismay that once again, Jen rescued him. Was he ever going to be good enough for her? Was she ever going to need him?

The aching disappointment of that scene in her bathroom throbbed at the back of his mind. She had never been able to depend on anyone—including him? Why hadn't he said he thought he loved her? Why hadn't he sworn she could depend on him?

The dining room had leaded glass windows just like the library. Blade swore and turned Jen around to leave. No use wasting time trying to heave those heavy chairs through these windows, either. He saw the arched doorway leading into the ballroom, grinned and headed around the long table at a run.

In seconds they had burst into the ballroom and navigated through the first ring of decorative trees and tubs of flowering plants. Only twenty yards of ballroom between them and the French doors out onto the patio.

A bullet skipped across the expensive inlaid wood flooring five steps ahead of them. Blade skidded to a stop and nearly tripped, turning to see who had shot at them.

Sarpantine shook his head and made a *tsking* sound as he sauntered into the room, pointing a gun at them. Worley's blood and streaks of sweat marred his clothes. His collar was half-torn from his shirt. Blade silently cheered for Worley. The fat man had been a more effective foe than he had thought possible.

"Didn't you hear me, out in the hallway?" Sarpantine smirked when neither of them answered.

Blade squeezed Jen's hand tighter in his. He studied Sarpantine's movements, trying to judge the play of muscle and predict when he would shoot again. He had to put himself between Jen and the bullet if it was the last thing he ever did.

Why had he been so stupid? He didn't *think* he loved her. He *knew* he loved her. If he told her, would she believe him? The timing was all wrong.

Would it ever be right?

"I always get what I want, little Gloria. I want *you*."

"The name is Jen Holt, and the last time I looked, women had the right the choose." She stepped out from behind Blade.

Yes, he definitely loved her, loved the defiant strength in her voice, the disdain that twisted her mouth. Even if she stupidly exposed herself to Sarpantine's aim.

"Well, a little spitfire. How nice. It just adds spice to the mix, doesn't it? I still want you, and what I say goes. You're mine until I toss you aside."

"Nobody tells me what to do." Jen actually sounded bored. She glared at Blade when he tried to put her behind him again.

"I've heard that line before. It doesn't work. You're too good a girl, and too smart."

"Too smart to let a scum-buzzard touch her," Blade added.

"Too smart to let her lover die." Sarpantine chuckled, nearly covering up the little gasp that escaped Jen.

Blade knew better than to look at her. He had to watch Sarpantine. It was too much to hope he would be like a cartoon villain and spout some insane, self-righteous speech for half an hour before shooting them. He could shoot at any moment.

Still, Blade hoped the threat to him hurt Jen. Just a little.

What kind of a selfish jerk are you? Do you want *Jen to sacrifice herself to save your miserable hide?*

"Well, what will it be Jen Holt?" Sarpantine purred. He took a step closer and aimed at Blade.

Jen didn't say a word. Blade could almost taste her indecision in the air. His heart dropped down somewhere around his knees, heading for the floor.

What have you become? He shifted his feet in preparation for leaping at Sarpantine. *You actually want a girl to save your life? No wonder she's hesitating—she doesn't know if you're worth it!*

Jen's hesitation in the bathroom suddenly made sense. She didn't feel for him what he felt for her. Blade swallowed the hard, cold, indigestible fact that he was not only Jen's first kiss, but her first fling. He was new and tantalizing and that was the only attraction for her.

He should just be glad she had enjoyed him, and move on when this was over. But, Blade realized, he wasn't that kind of guy anymore. Instead of being allergic to commitments and permanence, allergic to pregnancy and babies and white picket fences, he suspected he could become addicted to the whole scenario. If Jen was in the details.

If he lived that long.

Letting out a kamikaze yell, Blade leaped. He had less bulk and more leg power than Worley. He aimed and caught hold of Sarpantine's hand as the man's finger tightened on the trigger. The two went down. Blade fought to stay on top. Sarpantine bucked and kneed him in the gut and he folded. His hands lost their grip for two crucial seconds and his opponent sent him flying. As Blade hit the floor and scrambled to get back to his feet, Jen raced up behind Sarpantine with a wrought iron chair raised above her head. She swung with her whole body. Sarpantine went down and Jen went sprawling, hauled off her feet by the momentum of the chair. Blade scrambled across the floor, halfway to her before he got his feet under himself. Jen evaded his supporting hands and flung herself on top of Sarpantine.

"He wasn't joking." She yanked aside his mangled sport coat to reveal three tiny black boxes clipped to his belt. Lights flashed and numbers slowly counted down. "How long?" she asked, and staggered to her feet to lean against him.

Blade wrapped his arms tight around her, welcoming the warmth and the hammering of her pulse under his hands. He gave enough attention to the countdown to do some rapid calculations.

"Maybe half an hour. I don't suppose you defuse bombs?"

"That's if we knew where to look. And no, I don't." She shuddered and a choked sound escaped her, and Blade realized she tried to laugh.

Or maybe, she fought to resist the hysterical laughter he felt rumbling inside himself too.

They found Worley half-buried in the splintered wreckage of his beloved reproduction Victorian sofa. Blade didn't feel a flicker of regret; the ridiculous thing was swaybacked and hard and the horsehair cushions scratched through his clothes. Worley wasn't alert enough to resist their questions, but coherent enough to help them find the keys to the boats. Jen led Worley out to the docks and went to warn the staff while Blade ran upstairs to retrieve the computer equipment that couldn't fall into enemy hands. While he was at it, he found Jen's white nightgown and stuffed it into the computer case.

Jen had the middle-sized of the three boats ready to go, the engine rumbling and the lines loosed. Worley huddled on the bench seat at the back of the boat, whimpering when Blade joined them. The four household staff were nowhere to be seen, along with the smallest boat. Blade jumped into the boat. Half a second later Jen gunned the engine and they fled the dock.

"This is the fastest?" he shouted over the scream of the wind battering his face. He stumbled forward to the pilot's seat.

"Speed over size over maneuverability. Worley was no help." She scowled and jerked her head in the fat man's direction. Jen's mouth dropped open and she turned, looking back to the island.

Blade didn't bother looking. He knew he would see Sarpantine racing down to the docks. If they were close enough, they probably could have heard him swearing.

"Want me to—" What kind of an egomaniac was he, to offer to drive? Jen was doing just fine. She was probably a better driver than him.

"I've never done a water chase." Jen slid out of the pilot's seat and held onto the wheel, waiting for him to take over. She tried to smile, and her lips trembled. "Please?"

Blade heaved himself into the seat and slammed forward on the throttle. He didn't care what dangers lay in the shallow water around the islands, they were getting out of there. He had to get Jen to safety.

She finally needed him. Finally, something she couldn't handle for herself.

There was something definitely wrong with him, Blade acknowledged, if he needed a woman to lean on him in order to feel worthwhile.

"Here he comes!" Jen cried, leaning over his shoulder so he could hear her. The boat hit a wave head on and leaped. She let out a little yelp and clutched at his shoulders.

She didn't let go. Blade grinned into the wind and prayed she held onto his shoulders all the way to Sandusky.

They came around the eastern tip of South Bass, Buckeye Point, and turned south, heading for the barely visible docks of Sandusky. Or was that Catawba?

Over the scream of the engine and the howl of the wind battering his face and threatening to rip off his hair and ears, Blade heard another sound. The louder, deeper roar of a bigger, faster boat. He glanced back and couldn't see past Jen. He turned the boat slightly and looked again.

Sarpantine had taken the big boat. Unfortunately, it looked like size and weight didn't count against the boat, because it gained on them and Blade had the engine up to the fastest speed.

He supposed they could throw Worley overboard, but he doubted that would lighten their load and increase their speed enough to be worth the effort.

"Hold on!" he shouted, and spun the wheel hard to the left. Jen's fingers dug into his shoulders and Blade grimaced, welcoming the pain. He wanted her to hold onto him just that tight the first time they made love. If they survived this.

Sarpantine turned, gaining on them and coming up on their right side. Blade swore. If he turned right to head back toward those distant docks, he'd throw them directly into the other boat's path and close the gap even more. He straightened the wheel and ducked low, praying a little less wind resistance would keep Sarpantine from gaining on them.

Wind resistance?

Blade grinned and spun the wheel around again, until he had the wind to his back and then gunned the engine. That put them on a direct course back to South Bass Island. He could ground the boat on the bathing beach under Perry's Monument, which was close enough to the center of Put-in-Bay to suit him. It was a National Parks monument. A dozen rangers would come in handy when Sarpantine came after them. He wouldn't try anything on an island full of tourists.

Or was he warped enough to shoot and not care what happened to himself? Was he the type of lunatic who considered himself invulnerable?

That didn't matter. Blade knew what he had to do—aim for land, crash the boat if he had to, get himself and Jen and Worley onto dry land and lost among tourists. Then find the police and dig in until the cavalry arrived. He'd even be glad to see Shylock.

"Hold on, sweetheart. It's going to be a bumpy ride." Blade took his hand off the wheel long enough to squeeze Jen's hand on his right shoulder.

"Good luck." She pressed a kiss against his ear.

Blade groaned, and it took all his control not to melt into a puddle right there in the pilot's seat. But sanctuary was still several hundred yards away and he could hear Sarpantine's boat gaining on them.

A tiny racing boat, shaped like an arrow, darted across his field of vision from the right. Blade swore and jerked hard on the wheel to the left. Jen's fingers seemed to pierce his shoulders to the bone. Sarpantine's boat roared up from the left. Blade imagined he heard the man's maniacal laughter, just before the crunch and shriek of fiberglass and metal colliding shook the lake bed.

Jen vanished, taking a piece of his shirt with her. Blade struggled to keep his eyes open as sky and water pinwheeled around him. He saw the water coming up and closed his eyes.

He hit the water like landing on a concrete pad. The air gushed from his lungs as if yanked by a vacuum hose. Blade fought not to breathe as the water closed around his head. He kicked his numb limbs, thrashing to the surface just before reflex overrode his brain and he breathed.

Gunshots behind him. Blade scrambled to turn around and inhaled half the lake when he saw Sarpantine's boat bearing down on a dark shape in the water.

Jen! Blade struck out with everything he had left, knowing he couldn't reach her in time. He didn't even have a gun.

Sarpantine stopped shooting as his boat swept past Jen. He turned sharply, coming back for another pass. More gunshots. Jen thrashed and went limp.

Blade roared and reared half out of the water, as if he could leap up and run across the surface to reach her. He thought he heard Sarpantine cackling as the boat turned again.

The engines screamed, suddenly exposed to air. The boat reared up sideways out of the water. The turn had been too sharp, too sudden, the speed too high in the shallower water near shore. As if in slow motion, the boat flipped over. Sarpantine howled as he tumbled into the water and the boat slapped down on top of him.

Blade fought the pull of the waves as he struggled to get to Jen. She lay limply, her head turned to the side, flopping with the motion of the water. He could barely be grateful that the waves seemed to push her toward him. Blade turned her onto her back, hooked an arm around her and headed for shore. He couldn't see any blood, but that didn't mean anything, out in the water.

The rumble of an engine made him thrash, turning to find the source. Blade rubbed water out of his eyes with one hand and nearly cheered when he saw the Coast Guard insignia on the boat that pulled up alongside him. He grudgingly handed Jen over to helpful hands and climbed into the boat, then yanked her free before anyone could do more than wrap a blanket around her.

"I'll do it," he growled, as he stretched Jen on the deck.

He found a pulse, strong and steady. Blade took a deep breath, resisting the urge to sob in relief, and pressed his mouth over hers. Slow and steady, he reminded himself, as he blew breath into her lungs.

Jen's tongue tickled his lips.

Blade froze and forgot how to breathe.

The tip of her tongue pressed past his lips. Her mouth moved, turning their contact into a kiss.

"Jen?" He choked as he sat back on his heels with his heart thundering in his ears. The next moment, he wavered between gathering her close and smothering her with kisses, or strangling her. Jen opened the eye closest to him.

"If you stop now, I'll kill you," she whispered.

Blade leaned down and pressed his mouth over hers again. He kissed her with everything he had, and it took all his control to break away and pretend to take a deep breath and go back for more artificial respiration.

Mouth to mouth resuscitation had suddenly taken on a whole new meaning.

"You'd better move before somebody decides to do CPR," he whispered.

"How is she?" the woman with the Red Cross shoulder patch asked, right on cue.

Jen coughed and struggled to sit up. Blade helped her and leaned her back against himself. He folded her into the blanket, strategically keeping her arms tucked out of sight and trapped against her side.

"She's going to be fine." Blade managed a smile as he looked at their rescuers for the first time. "When I get you alone," he breathed in her ear, "I am going to kill you."

"When somebody's shooting at you, it's smart to play dead," Jen retorted. She wriggled around against him until she was more securely on his lap. That set off a chain reaction through his anatomy, despite what they had been through, that made Blade groan and squeeze her tighter.

What was he going to do with her? He loved her nasty sense of humor and her quick wit and ingenuity. He loved her feisty spirit and her survivor's instincts.

And she had proven once again, she didn't need him at all.

He held her tight and told himself to enjoy what little time they had together, before she came to her senses and walked away. Blade pressed his face against the damp curls of her hair, inhaling her scent even through the lake water that drenched her. He wished the ride could be longer, but they had already come back around the tip of the island and headed toward the main docks. He could even see Gibraltar Island ahead of them on the right.

The radio crackled and the man standing next to the pilot on the deck above them picked up the microphone. Blade could barely hear for the wind whipping in his face and the rumble of the engines directly behind him. He settled back more comfortably against the side of the boat and let the crew give him and Jen more blankets.

"Anyone named Hampton down there?" the man at the radio shouted. He leaned out of the pilot's deck, one foot on the ladder to come down. Blade raised one hand. "Some guy named Anguilano is looking for you. We're supposed to get you on the chopper that's coming in. You up for it?"

"Doesn't matter if I am or not. Shylock," he said, in answer to the puzzled look Jen gave him. "I know I'm retired, but he ignores the paperwork if it isn't convenient for him. When he says jump, I can't even ask how high? Yeah," he called, and waved to the man above him, "all set."

"Did you pick up the other two?" Jen asked. She coughed up a little water and waved away the understandably concerned medic. "The man who was in the boat with us, and the one trying to run us down? Did you get them?"

"Our partners did." She shook her head. "What did you think you were doing? Those were pretty dangerous stunts."

"When you've got a bomb at your back, you don't really worry about things like obeying the speed limit."

"Bomb?" The medic reached out and pressed a hand on Jen's forehead. "Is she—"

A muffled thump reverberated through the air. Blade stood,

208

dragging Jen with him. A plume of smoke rose in the air from Gibraltar. Another thump-roar echoed the first, and a flash of light showed where something had burst into flame. Blade imagined all that wood, the draperies, the reproduction antiques. All gone. A third explosion sent a bang-clatter across the water and he stared as the tower slowly leaned, like the Tower of Pisa, and spewed bricks like confetti.

"A bomb," the medic said, shaking her head.

CHAPTER 20

Ray got on the radio and talked with Blade just as they landed at Put-in-Bay. Chief Anguilano was on the Agency chopper, coming out to supervise personally. Ray stopped just short of ordering Blade to be ready to go as soon as the craft touched down at the little airfield on the south side of the island. He didn't mention Jen, but he did tell Blade not to give Shylock any reason to step out and look for him.

Jen knew Ray didn't want his former boss seeing her. She appreciated his protection. The less Shylock knew about her talents and involvement with Ray's work, the better. But that meant she had to stay behind and not help in the wrap-up of the job. She didn't mind, but Blade didn't argue with Ray about leaving her behind. The Coast Guard medic insisted that Jen rest and recuperate from all she had been through. She couldn't admit she had faked drowning, so Jen kept her mouth shut.

She was glad they put her in a tiny office at the airfield all by herself, so she could watch alone through the old-fashioned Venetian blinds when the helicopter took Blade away. Nobody would see if she totally humiliated herself by bursting into tears.

To top it all off, her body had betrayed her. Jen felt sore all over, threadbare exhausted, and her brain didn't want to leave the grumbling rut she had fallen into.

All right, so she had a really rough day. Going from a sleazoid sex maniac drooling over her to almost making love with Blade to a crazy run for her life, and then getting thrown from a speeding boat and getting shot at—well, it was enough to wear a girl out. She certainly wasn't getting any younger.

Jen pulled herself up off the cot and reached for the sweats the medic had brought for her. Dry, fresh clothes were about the only good news she had received in the last hour. To top it all off, all the equipment Blade had retrieved was currently at the bottom of Lake Erie. It would take weeks to customize another computer the way she wanted it. If only replacing her computer was the largest of her worries. She winced when sore muscles protested being unfolded, and a groan slipped through her clenched teeth as every rib proclaimed its bruised condition. Jen fought tears as she peeled out of her torn, damp jeans and struggled into the sweatpants; blessedly oversized and just made for loafing around. Another groan escaped her as she dropped the remains of her torn shirt and then had to reach behind herself to unhook her bra. If she had gone with the lacy, wispy model Blade had suggested on that shopping trip a lifetime ago, there'd be nothing left of it right now. She wouldn't be contorting herself into painful positions, now would she?

"Need help?" Blade asked.

Jen turned around too fast. Her stiff muscles wrung a pained yelp from her and she tumbled toward the cot. Blade kicked the door shut and leaped across the room to catch her. He kept her from hitting the floor and picked her up to settle her down on the cot again.

Someone had given him a Put-in-Bay souvenir shirt and paint-spattered, faded jeans that hugged every lean line. He wore gaudy neon-pink flip-flops on his feet. He'd never looked better, never smelled better. Jen clung to him a few seconds longer than she knew she should have. She started to let go of him, then the draft hit her skin. She was bare from the waist up.

"Here." Blade twisted free and turned his back on her and snatched up her borrowed sweatshirt to toss backwards to the cot. "Sorry about that."

"Don't be." Jen tried to laugh. Even her lungs felt sore, as if she had inhaled half the lake and most of the sand on its bottom. "If things had worked out differently today…"

Would they be naked together in bed or the tub right that moment? She had finally started to come to her senses, thinking with her brain and conscience, rather than her glands. Jen had too many people depending on her, too much pain and caution in her past, to just throw away the habits of a lifetime for the first man who took her breath away.

"Yeah. If." Blade started to turn around, then stopped. "Are you decent yet?"

Jen was half-tempted to say yes, even though she hadn't even picked up the sweatshirt. She sighed, the sound turning into a moan as she raised her arms and stiff muscles protested with fiery stabs. In the momentary quiet, she heard the whump-whump of a helicopter landing. The window frames rattled.

"Okay." She settled back on the cot, until she could lean against the wall directly below the window. The light fell in stripes across Blade's face and shoulders as he turned to face her, hiding his expression.

"That's my ride." He nodded at the window and stepped closer so his shins brushed her dangling feet. "Feeling better?"

"Nothing a few hours alone with boxing gloves and Sarpantine tied to a chair wouldn't cure."

"Yeah." A grin flickered across his face, too brief to reveal anything. "He's in a lot of trouble, now. Blowing up Worley's island, threatening federal agents and civilians, endangering boating traffic and the safety of a resort town, plus a few dozen warrants out for his arrest in the international community. When we get finished with him, there are a lot of other people waiting for their cut. It's a domino effect. Once he tripped, everything went."

"Then we did good?"

"You did great. I was scared to death for you half the time, and the other half I wanted to strangle you." He sighed. "Or drag you into a dark corner."

"Blade?" Ray called. He sounded out of breath, which meant he had run.

Jen could have laughed over his concern that Anguilano never see her, but she didn't feel like it. Not with the desperation and hurt making Blade's eyes into dark pits that sucked her in.

"In here!" Blade didn't turn to the door. He licked his lips, opened his mouth to speak, but the words didn't come out.

"Let's go, pal. Five more seconds and he's coming after us. He suspects." Ray thumped on the door.

"Just a minute!" Blade scowled.

"Now!" Another thud on the door.

"Maybe you should go." Jen started to stand.

She gasped, not completely from aching muscles, as Blade snatched her close. His mouth closed over hers with bruising force. She couldn't even breathe for several long moments. But at least her body had stopped aching, as if the warmth of his body pressed full length against hers drove away every bruise and strain.

"You're out here in a ten-count or I'm coming in after you. I don't care if you're buck-naked. Might do you some good, if Jen sees you." Ray banged on the door again.

"Would it?" Blade whispered between kisses. A sigh escaped him when Jen couldn't find the breath to answer. Out in the hall, Ray counted down from five. "I should be ready to die about now, but I want you so bad it hurts."

"And I want you," Jen whispered.

"Yeah, but you don't *need* me," Blade said, and released her so abruptly, Jen's knees buckled. "I'm the last guy you'll ever need. You're better off without me."

"Time's up," Ray growled, and flung the door open.

Jen stumbled backwards and fell onto the cot. Ray stared, frozen in mid-stride. He looked at Blade, he looked back at her.

"Sorry," he muttered. "If I could, I'd lock you two in here together for a week, but…"

Jen didn't know whether to burst into hysterical laughter or scream and fling herself at him, fists flying. The wretch *had* been matchmaking, just like she suspected.

"It's okay," Blade said, and slid through the door past Ray without looking back. "Better this way."

Jen closed her eyes against Ray's look of pity. She only nodded when he told her to stay on the island until one of them came back for her. She held her breath, fingers digging into the blanket underneath her, until she heard the door click closed again. She listened to the clatter and squeak of the Ray's boots and Blade's rubber footwear racing down the hall.

"I don't need him?" Fire rose up her throat from her stomach, driving away her aching need for Blade's arms around her. "What the heck is that supposed to mean? Just because I didn't jump into bed with him the first time he whistled, he thinks I don't need him?" She turned around on the cot and lay down with her arms crossed under her head. "Yeah, well, he's right. I don't need him. I'll never need a man. Not 'til the day I die."

A single tear slid from the corner of her eye to trickle into her ear. Jen flinched and turned her head sharply to the side to shake it out.

"Just because he can't be a white knight, he thinks I don't need

213

him? What kind of an arrogant jerk is he?" She shuddered, every muscle aching with the sudden drop in adrenaline. "If I never see him or Ray ever again, it'll be too soon."

Jen struggled to sit up again and searched for the shoes someone had loaned her. Nothing in the world would persuade her to sit and wait for Ray to come back for her. It might be a few hours, or even a few days, until Ray got Anguilano out of the way. She refused to be beholden to him. She refused to follow another order. Who did he think he was, running her life like he had a right? He even had the gall to try to fix her up with someone. Did he think she couldn't choose her own lovers? Did he think he had the right to arrange a marriage for her, like some old-style feudal lord, or the head of a family?

Jen bit back a sob before it choked her. Ray was supposedly a cousin, if Blade's story meant anything. Did that give him the right to treat her that way?

And as for Blade—

She stood and decided to forget about the shoes. What did she need a half-hearted lover and a suspected cousin for, anyway? Tyler was here on the island. She would go to him and he would help her get off the island. She didn't need Ray or Blade for anything.

CHAPTER 21

Ray's fist came out of nowhere. Blade turned just in time to save his eye and his nose, but the impact on the side of his head knocked him sprawling. His coffee mug went rolling and he staggered. He clutched at the porch railing and hung on until the world steadied and the echoes stopped ringing through his head.

"Where is she?"

"Who?" Blade blinked hard, trying to focus.

"Jen. She's not here. Where is she?"

"How should I know? Why would you expect her to be here?" He sagged down onto the porch floorboards and waited for the inside of his head to settle.

"You went back to get her, didn't you?" Ray hunkered down, leaning close enough their noses almost touched. Blade had to fight the urge to punch him.

"She was gone. Nobody knew where she went. I thought she got hold of you."

Blade wondered if it was time to switch from coffee to something that would numb him for a while.

Jen hadn't waited for him. That just proved what he had feared; she had discovered he wasn't good enough for her, and she wasn't going to waste any more time on him.

"I thought two weeks was long enough for you two to come up for air. You've been sitting here, moping the whole time." Ray stood up and stepped back. "You know, there's this new dictionary that just got published," he drawled. He smirked when Blade glared at him.

Blade wondered why he tried anymore. This incident showed just how much his life and mind had gone downhill. He hadn't seen Ray coming from a mile away. Hadn't heard his car coming up the long, steep gravel road from the valley below. Knowing Ray, he had walked, to sneak up on him. He hadn't seen Ray cross the clearing around his cabin or heard the birds go quiet in the presence of an intruder. Blade had simply been too caught up in his own thoughts, wallowing in his misery, so he didn't feel that first footstep when Ray climbed up on the porch that wrapped around the cabin. He didn't sense Ray approach him, sitting on the side that looked out over the ravine.

Blade almost smiled, even as he probed the half-numb side of his face. It was a sign of his low spirits that he barely considered heaving Ray over the porch railing into that ravine.

His mountain cabin was the perfect place to get away from everything, let the tensions melt away and put it all behind him. Usually. Blade had been here a week already with the phone ringer turned off and the answering machine turned on and not a single voice to be heard. Not even his own.

He still couldn't put the fiasco on Gibraltar behind him. Images of what happened and what he could have done differently kept replaying in his dreams.

"Okay," Blade said on a sigh, when Ray just leaned against the post supporting the roof and continued smirking at him. He got up on his feet. "What's the punch line?" He bent over and picked up his mug. Thank goodness for wooden boards and gaps between them; no need to clean up spills.

"The definition for 'Ass' has your picture."

"Pretend I'm laughing." He headed for the door. Ray followed him inside. Blade didn't even feel tempted to slam the door shut in his face.

The entire downstairs was one room, with the kitchen tucked into one corner, his computer desk in another, and his library filling the wall space between the deep-set front windows. Heavy old wooden furniture with thick, shabby blue cushions filled the floor space in front of the fireplace. The loft upstairs had a massive skylight in the sloped roof, and his bed directly underneath it. He could look out on the mountains or stargaze. Blade had dreamed about bringing Jen here, sharing long hours of stargazing and quiet, just holding each other. The memories of those dreams took away the healing power of this last sanctuary.

"Are you going to ask me if I know where Jen could be? Don't you care how she's doing?"

"She didn't wait for either of us. She can take care of herself. Wherever she is, Jen's fine." Blade put the mug down—too quickly, judging by the crackling sound. Another mug broken.

"Yeah, fine, after you walked out on her. How far did the two of you get, anyway?"

"None of your—" He swallowed the rest of his roar of outrage and turned his back on Ray. The anger settled in his stomach and lined his throat like heartburn.

"It *is* my business, after all the hard work I did to get you two together." Ray settled down at the island counter unit that separated the kitchen from the rest of the room.

"Right. After telling me I'm not good enough for her."

"If I told you I wanted you to watch out for Jen for the rest of your life, you'd head for the hills. Reverse psychology. Tell you she's forbidden fruit, you'd get interested."

"Stick to espionage. Matchmaking isn't your game."

"You walked out on her. You couldn't have hurt her worse if you raped her at gunpoint and then shot her."

"She doesn't need me."

"She doesn't *let* herself need anyone!" Ray slammed both fists down onto the counter. The cracked mug jumped and landed on its side, then rolled off the edge to shatter on the scarred wooden floor. "She's always had to take care of everybody else. Jen needs someone to sweep her off her feet and give her a chance to let go, for the first time in her life."

"Why didn't you apply for the job?" Despite himself, Blade felt a flicker of hope take root in the dark aching deep inside. "Looks to me like you belong together. You look after her, you two are so relaxed together—" The words choked him.

"You mean, do I love her? Does she love me? I care about her. I don't *need* Jen and she doesn't need me. Not the way you do. You need her so bad you're killing yourself, and you don't even know it."

"She doesn't need *me*," Blade whispered.

"To protect her and solve her problems, no. How about someone who just plain needs *her*? She needs someone who won't drain her dry, who can stand on his own two feet. Maybe she just needs someone with staying power. Maybe she just needs you to jump her bones and not walk away in the morning. Did you ever think of that? Or is it too big a wound to your ego to just be needed for sex?"

217

"Anybody who'd walk away after a night with Jen is the biggest—"
Blade wanted to punch Ray in the mouth to stop that triumphant grin.
"Why me? If you care about her so much, if you know what she needs,
why don't *you* just marry her?" he growled.

"Because it's against the law, that's why." Ray sat back and waited,
visibly eager for the torrent of questions, and just as eager to tease and
torment Blade into doing what he wanted before he would give the
answers.

Inside Blade's head, a massive, disordered jumble of information
arranged itself into proper order.

"She's your cousin," he whispered. A bark of laughter escaped him
when Ray sat up straight and that smirk fell off his face. "Shylock
cornered me. Wanted me to keep an eye on you, though he wouldn't
admit it to save his life. I swear, the two of you are..." Blade
swallowed hard, saving that observation for further consideration. "He
told me how you were trying to find your mother's sisters and all their
kids. You left the Agency because he wanted in on the fun."

"He told you that?"

"Not in so many words."

"I left the Agency because I didn't want him breathing down my
neck, demanding progress reports."

"Why should he care?"

"I don't want to know."

Silence settled into the kitchen. Each waited for the other to speak
first. Finally, Blade took a deep breath, nodded, and asked one of the
questions that didn't burn quite so strongly on his tongue.

"So, what are you going to do next? Have you told Jen?"

"Not until I'm absolutely sure. She's had too many false hopes
along the way. Speaking of which..." Ray's eyes regained that sparkle
of nasty humor. "You break my cousin's heart, I'll do more than break
your face."

"You got us into this mess. You'd better help fix it."

*   *   *

"Go crawl back under your rock," Jen enunciated as crisply and
emotionlessly as she could.

Ray just stood there, leaning against the door into her workroom at
the Bulrushes Foundation. How long he had stood there, smirking at
her, watching her fuss with the antiquated workings of a half dozen
scavenged computers, she didn't know. She didn't want to care.

"I need your help."

"You need a psychiatrist. Oh, and you might need to up your health insurance, because if you take one more step into this room, you're going to need a doctor." She turned her back on him and put the screwdriver back into the screw head. It slipped and she narrowly missed gashing her hand with the pointed tip.

"Whatever I did, I bet I'm not guilty," Ray said, and gently tugged the tool out of her hand. "How come you don't return any of my calls?"

"Busy."

"Too busy for Blade too? He's kind of worried about you."

"In a pig's eye. He's too busy gallivanting around the world, drinking champagne and sweeping some gullible twit off her feet to worry about me."

"Uh huh. What makes you think that?" He settled down on the edge of her table and tipped his head to one side to study her.

Jen yanked her screwdriver out of his hand and turned back to disassembling the computers. Ray waited several more minutes. She refused to talk to him, to let him win this little battle of silence.

"I need your help. A quick infiltration. Overnight trip." Ray waited, but Jen didn't respond. "It isn't like you to carry a grudge, Jen."

"How would you know? You're not around here that much."

"This is important."

"The country can save itself this time around. I'm tired."

"It's not national security, Jen. It's personal."

"Oh, really?" She slammed the screwdriver down on the table. "Does that mean I just go along for the ride, for old time's sake, and you don't have to tell me what's going on? That's a pretty rotten way to treat your own cousin, you know?"

Any other time, Jen would have laughed at Ray's reaction. He didn't react, except to go very still. He didn't even breathe, didn't blink, just stared into her eyes.

Funny, how she had never noticed before that they had the same big, dark, thickly-lashed eyes. The same color hair, when hers wasn't dyed for some disguise.

"Are you ever going to tell Magda she's a cousin, or were you going to play with her emotions for a few years? Why don't you drag her out of her life and make her your playmate? She'd love it. Plenty of grit for her books."

"You got further into my files, I see," Ray said on a sigh. His shoulders slumped a little. "What other files did you read?"

"Hers, and I just started to read mine before you came back. Did you ever think I could be a help? Or do you just want to know about your family, but never see them face to face?" Jen refused to blink, even though her eyes burned. She would start crying in another minute and that was the last thing she wanted.

"All I have are guesses and clues. Nothing's definite."

"Then why not ask for help?" Jen swore, startling them both. She almost could have laughed, but she suspected that would bring on the tears too. "Come on, Ray, do you know how much I'd like to have some real family? Blood needs each other."

"I didn't want to raise your hopes."

"Yeah, the Lone Ranger. Suffers all by himself. Big bad Ray has to be a hero all the time."

"Not all the time. And it's better having a partner." He waited, but Jen just gave in to the ache in her eyes and knuckled away the first traitor drops of wet. "So…help me out on this?"

"Are you going to answer my questions?"

"After." Ray rested a hand on her shoulder and squeezed. "You won't regret it."

"I'm regretting it already." Jen braced herself for that triumphant smirk Ray always wore when he beat her at something. She shivered a little when the smirk didn't come.

*   *   *

I am getting too old for this, Jen decided, as she waited for Ray to pick the lock on the cabin door.

The moon shone down soft and silvery-bright and the stars seemed close enough to touch, hanging in a black velvet sky. She wished she could just sit down on the wrap-around porch and enjoy the sweet mountain breezes and study the stars. That wouldn't happen. The cabin's owner was out for the evening, Ray assured her, but he might come back any time. They had to get in, find the journal with information about the five Sutero sisters, and get out.

The lock clicked softly. Ray looked back over his shoulder and gave her a triumphant grin. He stood, opened the door, and gestured for Jen to precede him inside.

In the shadows, it looked like the first floor of the cabin was one big room. Jen couldn't make out colors or even the shapes of the furniture, but she imagined it would be a comfortable place to live. Secure. Far away from the bustle and pain of the world. She wished she could find a place like this to hide away, just for a little while.

"Upstairs," Ray whispered, and gestured at the wide, plain plank stairs leading to what looked like a loft.

Jen nodded and left him to search the downstairs. It looked like there were a lot of bookcases lining the walls. She imagined she would be done with her search in plenty of time to come back down to help him with his.

Light came from upstairs, Jen realized before she was halfway up the steps. She glanced up and caught a glimpse of a wide skylight, letting silver moonlight spill down into the loft. She sighed, wishing even more she could find a place like this. The thought of watching the night sky while she curled up warm in bed sounded like heaven right now.

No, the light wasn't coming from the skylight. Her head got above the floorboards and Jen paused, staring at the lit candles spread out over the dresser, the headboard of a king-size bed, sitting in the windowsill, over half the floor. An ice bucket and a bottle of wine sat tucked into a corner. A bowl of strawberries sat next to it, and a basket of apples. A block of cheese and a knife sat on a cutting board.

Jen came up three more steps, slowly, without even thinking. She paused with two more steps to go and knew she had been an idiot. Ray had been wrong. The owner of the house wasn't gone. He wouldn't leave with a romantic setting waiting in his bedroom. He was—

Hard arms wrapped around Jen and lifted her off her feet, swinging her off the stairs. Before she could shake her brain back into gear, she flew across the gap and landed on the bed.

The owner of the house landed on top of her and covered her mouth with his before she could draw breath to scream for Ray. Jen tried to fight, but he pinned her down with his weight, his hands grasping her wrists and holding her arms flat and helpless.

He kissed her.

Jen wondered if she hallucinated when the warmth, the weight, the taste of his mouth struck her as…familiar.

Blade?

She went limp, knowing this had to be a dream. Any moment now, all the hungry, eager, aching feelings would rush through her body. She would wrap her arms around him, just like she had done in a dozen dreams already, and he would vanish into thin air.

"Jen?" Blade whispered. His heaving breaths rasped in her ear. "Sweetheart? Say something."

It really was Blade.

"What are you doing here?"

"This is my house," he said with a chuckle.

"Your—Ray, get your sleazy butt up here!"

"He can't hear you. The deal was for him to get you here, and then he'd take off so we could finally have some privacy."

"He's a dead man."

"That's what I told him, if he didn't help me find you." Blade rolled off her.

Jen swallowed a moan and mentally kicked herself for wasting time. She should have been appreciating the sensation of Blade's body stretched across hers, instead of plotting revenge on Ray. Now it was gone.

Blade folded his arms around her and drew her onto her side, pressed close against him.

"We need to talk."

Jen blinked hard, feeling the hot wet come back into her eyes. Talk was all she and Blade ever did, so she might as well stop hoping for more, right?

In the candlelight, pressed this close to him, Jen saw his face looked thinner and there were dark smears under his eyes. As if he hadn't slept well. She wasn't about to ask, even as her body melted from his warmth and closeness. She breathed in his warm, spicy scent and told herself to stop longing for the taste of his mouth and bruising kisses.

"So." She cleared her throat and tried to look anywhere but at him. It was hard to accomplish, when their faces were only inches apart.

"We work pretty well together, don't you think?" Blade tried to smile. "I mean, Ray, he doesn't need partners. You and me, we do our best work with partners. Someone to bounce ideas off. Someone to look out for. Makes us more alert, more careful. Maybe we don't take as many stupid risks when we're working with someone. With a partner."

"I guess." She barely managed a harsh whisper. Jen imagined her galloping pulse stole necessary blood from her brain. This was the craziest conversation to have, lying on a bed, with Blade's arms wrapped tight around her.

"Maybe you don't need me, Jen—"

"I never said that!" She swung a leg over him and flipped Blade onto his back. In half a heartbeat she was on top, her fists pressing his shoulders into the bed. She straddled his hips.

Utter silence filled the loft as she became tingling aware of their positions. From that crooked grin, Blade's rapid breaths, he was aware too. And growing more aware.

"You didn't answer my phone calls," he finally said. His breath rasped. "What was I supposed to think?"

"That I was mad at you," she whispered. Jen closed her eyes, refusing to start crying now of all times. When Blade reached up and drew her down to rest against him, she gladly gave in. It felt so right, to lie across his chest, her head tucked under his chin, with the heat of his body soothing that ache that was too tight to ever let her cry.

"I kind of guessed that. And you know what else I figured out? I got so used to working everything around you, I'm ruined. So if I'm going to be any use to anybody, we'd better be partners. Even if you don't need me. Rescue a guy, will you?"

"Who said I don't need you?" She lifted her head enough to meet his gaze. "I've been kind of useless since we worked together too." She swallowed hard, trying to clear the choking sensation that turned her voice into a rasp. "Yeah, why not? Partnership."

As the concept settled into her brain, her imagination kicked into high gear. Jen felt her head clear, even as her pulse doubled its frantic pace. It would just be a matter of time to beat some sense into him. Despite her lack of experience, Jen knew a fantastic kisser when he smothered her, and she wasn't going to let Blade Hampton get away.

"Just a couple conditions." Blade grinned and his embrace loosened a little. Jen tried not to whimper. She tried to get angry—he was using her sexual attraction for him to coerce her, wasn't he? "I want a contract to spell out what we expect. No more working on the fly, making things up as we go. I want things clear from the start."

"What kind of conditions?"

"Something along the line of lifetime commitment. Love, honor, and cherish until death. How does that sound?"

"Love?" she managed to squeeze through lips so numb she thought they had fallen off. "That sounds like—"

"Marriage vows. Yeah. What a coincidence."

"Blade, you don't have to."

"Marry you? You've got it all wrong, Jen. I love you, and I'm not taking the chance of you getting away from me again. The only reason I let Ray live is to be best man. If I ever let you leave this cabin long enough to get married."

"You're crazy." Funny, how it felt like the entire cabin had been flooded with oxygen. Everything spun around her as she let Blade slide her off him, so they lay facing each other again, tangled together. Nothing was real but the feel of his arms wrapped around her, his body pressed hard against her.

"Crazy in love with you, ever since you knocked me flat and stepped on my throat." Blade grinned when she choked on a giggle. "I know you don't need me, Jen—"

"I need you, you idiot, but you never give me a chance to tell you." Jen grabbed handfuls of his collar and dragged him closer, so their noses touched. She felt her voice vibrating in his skin. "I need you to help me feel alive. I want you so bad I'm ready to strangle somebody. I've been in love with you since you looked up my skirt and offered me wild cherry Life Savers."

"Yeah?" Blade kissed her until the feeling returned to her lips and then faded again. He laughed as they kissed, until the sound vibrated through her whole body.

"What's so funny?" she whispered as he kissed his way to her ear.

"Just wondering if you're wearing those green panties again?"

Jen squeaked and tried to slap him, but he held her too close and too tight.

"Red," she finally admitted, laughing.

"With black lace?"

"None of your business."

"Oh, yes it is. Every detail of the woman I love is my business. Don't you ever forget that."

"You'd better remind me, then. Every morning. And every night."

Jen kissed him using everything he had taught her in their short time together. There was a great deal to learn from him, and so much she knew she could teach him. That's what partnership was all about, wasn't it?

MICHELLE L. LEVIGNE

Michelle Levigne got her first taste of fantasy fiction with the *Cat in the Hat* books, and graduated to "harder stuff" with a graphic novel version of *The Lion, The Witch and The Wardrobe* in a Sunday School paper in elementary school. She has a BA in theater/English and an MA in Communications, focusing on film and writing, along with the 2-year correspondence course from the Institute for Children's Literature. She was heavily involved in fandom for several years and has more than 40 short stories to her credit in various fan magazines and universes, including *Star Trek*, *The Phoenix*, *Stingray*, *Highlander*, *Starman*, *V*, and *Beauty & the Beast* (live action TV show). Her first professional sale was in conjunction with winning first place in the quarterly Writers of the Future Contest. "Relay" was published in Volume VII. Since then, she has published ten SF/Fantasy and Contemporary romance novels through various electronic publishers, with several books pending future publication. Most of these books are in the SF universe called The Commonwealth. *The Bainevah Series* is her second foray into historical/fantasy/romantic fiction.

AMBER QUILL PRESS, LLC
THE GOLD STANDARD IN PUBLISHING

QUALITY BOOKS
IN BOTH PRINT AND ELECTRONIC FORMATS

ACTION/ADVENTURE	SUSPENSE/THRILLER
SCIENCE FICTION	PARANORMAL
MAINSTREAM	MYSTERY
FANTASY	EROTICA
ROMANCE	HORROR
HISTORICAL	WESTERN
YOUNG ADULT	NON-FICTION

AMBER QUILL PRESS, LLC
http://www.amberquill.com